Kisses and Candy Canes

WINTERBERRY HOLLOW
BOOK ONE

JENEVIEVE HERNANDEZ

AMETHYST INK PUBLISHING LLC

authorjenevievehernandez.com

Book Cover by Jillian Elyzabeth @jillianelyzstudio

ISBN ebook: 978-1-965713-08-2

ISBN paperback: 978-1-965713-09-9

For unto us a child is born,

Chapter One

24 DAYS 'TIL CHRISTMAS

It's universally known that Christmas in itself is a season. Yes, winter, spring, summer, and autumn are seasons, but Christmas is a season, too. Everyone in Winterberry Hollow acknowledges this fact, and for that, I'm eternally grateful that my parents raised me here.

The sound of skates and laughter around me fills the air, and even though it's so cold I can feel my eyelashes freezing as snowflakes float through the air, I giggle as Elisa makes a funny face across the rink at me. She's madly pointing to her best friend, Jacob, as he unstraps her laces, and I know that even if she weren't a terrible skater, he would still tie her laces.

Just last week, the town council decided it was time to fill the local soccer field with water to make our ice rink, and today, they announced that it was open to the public. More and more people slip onto the ice as the evening grows darker, and there's a sense of anticipation around us.

Tonight, since it's the first night of December, the large tree in the town square will be lit.

"Hey, Magnolia!" Lennox calls from across the rink as he shows off his terrible twirl. I almost double over from laughing at my friend's humor, but I stop as I continue to watch his performance.

Thump.

A shoulder crashes directly into mine, and I topple right on top of the person who knocked into me.

"Hey!" I yelp, pushing off the hard chest beneath the puffy jacket I'm currently lying on top of. The boy beneath me looks bewildered for a moment before he meets my gaze with some sort of question in his eyes. My movements still for a second before I remember where I am, and I quickly remove my body from his. "What gives?"

"Sorry, some of us know not to stop in the middle of the rink." The boy says with a slight accent. I can't quite place it, but the sound of it is actually quite beautiful. My cheeks flush even more as I search his face and realize that not only is his voice beautiful, but he is, too.

"Wait, what?" I say, snapping out of whatever trance he just placed me under, quickly standing from the ice. "I wasn't stopped in the middle of the rink." I huff, crossing my arms defensively.

"You most definitely were," He quips, crossing his arms the same as I am. He's much taller than I am, and when I meet his eyes, the devastating darkness of them consumes me.

"I wasn't."

"Was." He says with a smirk.

"I wasn't, and since you obviously aren't from around

here, it's apparent you don't know basic manners." His eyebrows flicker, but his smirk remains.

"You're right about me not being from around here, but you're wrong about the manners part. I definitely know not to stop in the middle of the rink. It appears as though you don't, though." He says, reaching out to brush a clump of wintery mix off my shoulder before skating off. I stand in disbelief for a moment before realizing that I'm doing exactly what I said I wasn't doing, and I move in the direction of Elisa and Jacob on one of the benches right outside of the rink.

"Magnolia, who was that?" Elisa says excitedly, giving me a wink.

"Hush. You didn't even hear what he said to me." I say, plopping down next to her. Jacob watches both of us silently as he waits for an answer from me. While Elisa is my best friend, she's also best friends with Jacob, meaning he and I cross paths pretty often when we're associating with Elisa. Same with Lennox. Since he's close with Jacob, in turn, he and I spend time together when the four of us go out.

"Well? I saw the part where you were splayed across his chest and *totally* feeling his muscles." Elisa says with a giggle, arousing a cough from me.

"Absolutely not. He bumped into me and then said it was *my* fault. Can you believe the nerve?" I say frustratedly.

"He's not from here, right?" Jacob pipes up, narrowing his eyes at the boy as he continues to skate without so much as glancing at us.

"Definitely not." Elisa and I say at the same time.

"Maybe he's here for all of the festivities? He looks like he's our age, so probably not traveling alone?" Elisa muses, looking him over one more time before turning back to me. "Either way, you should totally talk to him."

"I already talked to him!" I say, covering my mouth with a mitten before realizing just how loud I spoke.

"Talk to him as in *get his number,* talk to him." Elisa says with a nudge of her shoulder into my arm. "Who knows. Maybe that was love at first collision?" I barely keep my tongue closed and refrain from shouting no, since I'm not going to be drawing any more attention to myself.

"We'll see about that. Chances are, I won't see him ever again." I say with a shrug, standing from the bench. "I'm going to go find hot chocolate and find a spot near the tree. Tell Lennox whenever he stops acting like an idiot on ice. See you two later." Watching the tree lighting has always been one of my favorite things, and since Poppy and Charlie haven't arrived yet, I'll be watching it alone.

Poppy is the best sister ever—my *only* sibling—but with her busy schedule in New York, I can't help but feel frustrated that she's not here in Winterberry Hollow. I mean, she and Charlie are getting *married* in twenty-four days, and they're not here yet. Mom and Dad keep insisting that they'll be here on time, but the worrier in me can't help but feel like they're cutting it close.

"Thank you," I say to Mr. McKenzie as he passes me a cup of hot chocolate in exchange for a few dollar bills. The top is fluffy with whipped cream, and two candy canes peak through the mountain of sprinkles.

"It appears we meet again," The boy from earlier says near my ear as he steps in place next to me. I snatch my eyes from the dark tree in front of us and meet his teasing gaze.

He looks less like the rude stranger who knocked me over, and more like a boy just enjoying the Christmas spirit.

"It appears we met again." I echo, taking a mouthful of whipped cream in my mouth before smirking. "At least you didn't make me fall on you this time." I'm not sure why I'm teasing him, but he immediately smirks back.

"Oh, that won't be an issue. Girls always fall all over me." My jaw drops at his response, and while I can tell it's just a joke in reply to what I said, I can't help but believe him. He's insanely good-looking, even if he made me look like a fool at the ice rink.

"Excuse me," I gasp, taking a sip of cocoa before realizing that I still don't know his name.

"Carlos." He says, extending his hand out. While he's also wearing gloves, I make an effort to shake it.

"Magnolia." I reply, meeting his eyes once more before turning back to the small stand in front of the gigantic tree. It must be at least fifty feet tall.

"Thank you, lovely people of Winterberry Hollow. As your mayor, I couldn't be more excited to commemorate the one hundredth tree lighting. In just a moment, we'll all witness the hard work of our amazing volunteer team, and I hope that as we enter the season of giving, you remember to give to the community around you." Mayor Blake says, reaching down to show off both ends of the electrical cord. When the ends meet, the thousands of lights brighten the tree, and everyone cheers. Everyone except for Carlos. He glances around as though this is too much excitement for the simple lighting of a tree.

"I guess you're just too cool to clap or something?" I say,

turning to face him as Mayor Blake speaks over the microphone.

"I think I'm just astounded by the amount of cheering going on. It's nice and all, but it's a tree." He says, as though this makes perfect sense.

"It's not just a *tree*. It's the town square tree. This is a big deal here," I huff, taking a sip of my near-cold cocoa. The temperatures are practically sub-zero.

"So I gathered," Carlos responds, stuffing his hands into his jacket.

"What's that supposed to mean?"

"It means that I gathered it's a big deal here," Carlos says with a chuckle. Children rush to the base of the tree and pick up some of the candy that's being tossed out by a few of the volunteers. A candy cane drops at my feet, and I quickly reach down to pick it up and stuff it in my pocket. Carlos picks one up, too, but instead of opening it or saving it for later, he drops it in my jacket pocket.

"What are you doing?"

"It appears that you need it more than I do, Lia." He says, tapping the other candy cane in my pocket, and motioning to the two in my cup. And with that, he turns and walks through the crowd of people, leaving me both speechless and frustrated at the same time.

Chapter Two

23 DAYS 'TIL CHRISTMAS

"Why are you still in bed?" Poppy chirps over the phone. I suppress the urge to roll my eyes, and opt to roll over and glance out at the winter wonderland outside.

"Maybe because I was out late last night. Why aren't you here yet?" I put the call on speaker phone and start making my bed.

"Well, that's why I called. Charlie and I aren't going to be flying in as soon as we originally hoped." Poppy says carefully. Even though there's the muffle of hundreds of miles between us, I can still hear the slight worry in her voice.

"What? Why? We're already so close to the wedding." I respond, sitting down on the edge of my bed.

"So, you know how we're buying the shop?" Poppy questions.

"Yeah, of course. That's why you're still there, right?"

"Right," Poppy says, taking a deep breath before speaking again. "So there's been a slight change of plans with the repairs, the title, and a few other things, so we won't be flying in until the twenty-fourth."

"*The twenty-fourth?*" I practically shriek. "A *day* before your wedding? Are you insane?"

"Magnolia, I know it's a shock, but it'll be fine. Charlie and I are going to get married no matter what. We'll be there, okay?" Poppy says reassuringly. I can almost feel a pat on my head like she used to do when we were children.

"But how are you going to do any of the preparation? Shouldn't you be here to do that stuff?" My mind jumps to all of the last-minute things that still need to be done.

"Well, I was thinking that since you're there, maybe you could help out with some of that?" She asks tentatively. "If you wouldn't mind, of course."

"Poppy, I'm going to help with anything that you need, but I can actually tell that I'm having heart palpitations right now. Will you at least send me a list of the things that need to get done?"

"Yes, I'll get it all sent over. There still need to be some orders for a few things, but I'm sure you'll figure it all out easily." She says, as though it's nothing to only arrive in town a day before her wedding.

"Thanks," I say, rubbing a hand on my forehead as I imagine the things that I now have to manage.

"Oh, and one more thing. Charlie's younger brother flew in yesterday, and according to Charlie, had a taxi or something drop him off at the inn. Maybe you could include him in the planning since he's alone? Charlie feels bad about just sending his eighteen-year-old brother to winter wonderland without being there, and since you're his age, you might hit it off." Poppy quickly adds on. "I've never met him, but it would be nice if you brought him along to help, since he's going to be the best man. This will be good for you, since you're going to be the maid of honor."

"Yeah, I can do that. I'll drive down there in a little bit and invite him to lunch or something. What's his name?"

"Carlos."

"Do you mind ringing for Carlos Gonzales and asking him to come to the lobby?" I ask Maisie, Lennox's sister, as I step up to the front desk at the inn. Really, this is more of a bed and breakfast, since it was originally an old house. Normally, just asking the front desk of an inn to do something like this would be wrong, but besides the fact that Carlos and I are about to be in a wedding together, Maisie is my friend and knows that I'm not some weirdo.

"Sure thing." She says, quickly moving her eyes to the computer in front of her. "Carlos Santos, you mean." Maisie corrects as she places the call. Huh. I guess I got Charlie's last name wrong.

Glancing out the window, I shudder. The drive here was terrible, since it's not walking distance away from my house, like most of the town is. Driving in the snow is my least favorite thing, and here I am, doing it for the rude stranger I met last night.

Maisie hangs up and glances past me, her eyes narrowing in focus. "What are you..." I trail off as I realize what has Maisie's attention. A boy about our age is carrying a stack of papers into the employee area of the inn. "Who's that?"

"Be quiet!" Maisie says, reaching over to clamp a hand on my mouth. "His name is Romero, and he's new to working here."

"How convenient that you two work at the same inn," I say around her hand. "Is there a reason you don't want me talking about him?"

"Well, in a few days, the cleaners and chef are about to take their Christmas break, so we're really going to be the only people here most of the time," Maisie says, resting her hand on her elbow as she gazes into the room he disappeared into with lovestruck eyes. Oh. Now I see why she was so quick to make me be quiet. I barely stifle my giggle, and just as I'm about to say something in response, the noise of footsteps coming down the stairs stops me.

Carlos appears at the base of the steps, initially confused, but then he meets my gaze, and his eyes narrow ever so slightly. "What's up, Lia?" He asks, stuffing his hands into his jacket pocket as he walks closer.

"I need to go check on Romero. I'll be back in a few minutes." Maisie announces loudly as she rushes off to give us privacy.

"My name is *Magnolia*, by the way." I say, biting my tongue. This is supposed to be me making an effort to be nice to him. "So it appears we got off on the wrong foot, but since we're about to be spending a lot of time together, I figured I'd invite you to lunch." I offer.

"What do you mean, *spending a lot of time together?*" Carlos asks suspiciously.

"Well, it appears as though you're the best man, and I'm the maid of honor, and now we have a wedding to plan," I say as simply as possible, as though the idea of making sure everything is perfect for Poppy's wedding isn't going to give me a heart attack.

"You're joking." Carlos says, finally cracking a smile. "Where are the bride and groom in all of this?"

"I don't know if Charlie told you, but Poppy called me this morning and told me that they aren't going to be here until the twenty-fourth. We have to do all of the preparation here without them." I say, plastering a smile on my face. "Exciting, isn't it?"

"I thought that they were going to be here in a few days," Carlos says, not exactly like he doesn't believe me, but like he's confused as to why they're not arriving on time.

"So did I. You know how they're purchasing the shop, right?" I question, sympathizing just a little bit with him.

"What shop?"

"Carlos, do you even talk to your brother?" I tease. Carlos doesn't even move, and immediately, I feel bad. "Sorry, I shouldn't have-"

"No, it's fine. Go ahead, Lia." Carlos says, leaning against the large desk.

"It's *Magnolia.* Anyway, they're having to rearrange their schedule with it or something, and it's important enough to them that they finish all of that before flying in." I explain.

"Okay. So they want us," Carlos gestures between us, as though there are more people around us. "To handle all of their wedding prep?" He asks with a raised eyebrow.

"Pretty much. I know we got off on the wrong foot last night, but maybe we can move past that?" I say tentatively, meeting his dark eyes with hope.

"The wrong skate, you mean. And yes, I can agree to

move past it, as long as you keep moving on the rink and don't stop in the middle of the ice." Carlos says with a chuckle before turning to the stairs.

"Hey! Where are you going?" I yelp, chasing after Carlos.

"Do you want me to freeze? I'm not like any of you winter elves, in case you weren't aware. I believe I'm *not from around here*." Carlos says with a smirk, echoing what I said last night. Yikes.

"Wait! I'm sorry for that, by the way." I say, jogging up the stairs to catch up with Carlos.

"Don't worry about it, Lia," Carlos says, opening the door that must belong to him. I'm not sure why, but I follow him into the cozy room.

"My name is *Magnolia*." I say with emphasis on my name. Carlos glances back as he reaches into the closet.

"I heard you the first time," He says with a smile as he pulls out the fluffy jacket he was wearing last night. "What's the dress code for the place we're getting lunch from?"

"Casual?" I'm thrown off guard by his question, because I didn't give a second thought to my outfit when I put it on this morning.

"Thank you," Carlos says, picking up his mittens from the dresser. He slips on a pair of boots and pulls his jeans over them before tucking his wallet into the back pocket. Carlos' blue sweatshirt pulls tightly on his chest as he tugs his coat on, and suddenly, he stops and meets my gaze. "Have you never seen anyone put on snow gear?" He says with a twinkle in his eyes.

"What do you mean?" I respond, bewildered by the question.

"I mean," Carlos steps closer, a smirk growing on his face. "That you look fascinated by the process of me putting on my snow gear. It almost seemed like you were interested in it all. Or maybe, you were interested in-"

"What are you even talking about? It's a small room, and I was staring straight ahead. You just happened to be in my line of sight." I huff, not even trying to conceal the annoyance on my face.

"Okay, then," Carlos replies, stopping towards the door, motioning for me to exit before him. "Ladies first."

"No, no, no." I say as we walk into the bright parking lot. The sun is reflecting off the snow, temporarily blinding me.

"What's wrong?" Carlos asks, following me to my car. He glances around, as though the answer isn't obviously right in front of him.

"Don't you see? That car pulled in right next to me, and now I can't get out." I say, gesturing at the car right next to mine.

"But it's not blocking you?" Carlos asks, more confused than ever.

"I can see that, Carlos. You don't understand. I barely made it here in one piece. I can't drive in the snow. Much less pull out of a tight parking lot in snow." I respond, feeling both upset but also embarrassed by the fact that my poor driving is already apparent. I try to keep that fun fact concealed for as long as possible, because the whole *girls can't drive* stereotype annoys me, even though it might be just a little bit true for me.

"So I'll drive." Carlos says, extending his hand out,

already assuming I'm just going to hand off the keys to my car.

"Can you drive in the snow?" I question suspiciously, clutching my keys just a little bit tighter.

"Everyone can—" Carlos breaks off and clears his throat. "Of course I can." I weigh my options, and sadly, Carlos is the best one.

"Fine." I say, reaching out to drop the keys in his hand. "Just don't make me regret this."

"Wouldn't dream of it, Lia." He says, sliding into the driver's seat.

"Okay, I take it back. Give me the keys." I say, rolling my eyes at how he *still* won't use my name.

"Too late," Carlos calls out, turning the key and starting the engine. I don't know why, but a smile grows on my face as I slip into the passenger seat.

"So are you excited for the wedding?" I say as I pull on my seatbelt.

"What?" Carlos asks as he easily backs out of the spot and pulls out of the driveway.

"Are you excited for the wedding?" I ask again, lifting my eyebrows in confusion.

"I heard that part. I was wondering where it came from." Carlos says, pulling onto the road. "Before you answer that, where am I going?"

"Keep going this way for about a mile, and then the place will be on the left. It's The Berry Diner." I say, thinking about the directions for a moment, as though I suddenly forgot where to go in the town I've lived in my whole life.

"Let me guess, the logo will have a winterberry on it." Carlos guesses.

"How did you know?"

"Judging by the amount of town spirit around here, it was a well-educated guess." Carlos says with a smile as he drives without a care in the world.

"Maybe you're right about that," I agree, gripping the chair as we ease our way down the icy hill.

"What's wrong?" Carlos asks, his brows furrowed in confusion.

"I just think you're a little bit too calm for someone driving down such an icy hill." I barely make out through my clenched teeth.

"So you weren't joking about not driving in the snow," Carlos muses, as though he didn't believe me the first time.

"Now, where would you get the idea that I *like* driving in this weather?" I say incredulously.

"I mean, you made the drive to the inn in one piece, and that was with free will." Carlos says jokingly.

"That was to get you." I say as he rounds a turn.

"Still free will. You could have just let me show up to the wedding in a few weeks and walk down the aisle with the girl who was a little bit...*unwelcoming* to a stranger." Carlos teases.

"As if. I'm not rude enough to let you wander around without knowing anyone here. It's not your fault the bride and groom are so excited about their shop that they'd willingly allow us to do all of the preparation for it." I say as we slow to a stop outside the diner.

"Yeah, you're somewhat kind for doing that," Carlos says, turning off the key before stuffing it in his pocket and slipping out of the car. I reach in the back seat for my purse and after picking it up, I turn back to the door, only, there's someone *right* outside the door.

"Oh my gosh!" I gasp, realizing it's Carlos. He opens the door for me as though it's a normal habit, and I try to calm my racing pulse down. "Thank you, Carlos."

"No problem." He says with a grin. Carlos opens the door for the diner, and as the bell jingles, announcing our arrival. We're greeted with a blast of warm air, and I can feel my cheeks reddening from the temperature jump. "So what do you recommend here?" Carlos asks, glancing up and down the menu before meeting my eyes.

"Well, for breakfast I love the pancakes, but the BLTs and fries are amazing if you want something from the lunch menu." I answer, pointing at his menu to the BLT.

"Thanks," Carlos says, flipping to the drink menu.

"Hello, Magnolia. What can I get for you and your friend today?" Says our waitress, Cassie. I glance at Carlos, silently offering for him to order first.

"May I have the BLT with added avocado? For the side, I'd like the basket of fries, and a lemonade." Carlos asks, folding the menu and handing it to her.

"Of course. And for you, Magnolia?" She asks, turning to me.

"I'd actually like the exact same thing, please." I answer, passing her my menu as well.

"Perfect. I'll have your food over in a few minutes." Cassie says, giving us both a smile before leaving.

"I see your meal was inspired by mine," Carlos comments with a smile as he rubs his hands together.

"I think not," I say with a raised eyebrow. "I feel as

though I told you my order." Carlos chuckles at this, and I can't help but laugh with him. It seems as though he can't go more than a few minutes without cracking a joke.

"Maybe so," Carlos responds, his eyes moving around the diner in fascination. "What do we have to do, by the way? For the wedding."

"It's a good thing you asked, there's quite a list." I say, pulling out the notebook from my purse. "Order flowers, order the cake, pick up the dress, pick up the tuxedos, meet with the catering, and a few more things."

"That's not too much." Carlos comments, as though I didn't just list out a mountain of jobs. "When do we get started?"

"Well, some of these things are bigger items, Carlos." I warn, his nonchalant attitude is already stressing me out.

"Well, some of those things are smaller items, Lia," Carlos responds, folding his hands in his lap as he smirks.

"*Magnolia.*" I correct.

"Alright, two BLTs with fries, and two lemonades. Enjoy." Cassie says, setting down the food in front of us before I can continue my correction.

"Thank you," Carlos responds, taking a sip out of his lemonade. "You were saying?" He says as soon as Cassie leaves the table. I exaggeratedly roll my eyes, but I refuse to respond. I will *not* be baited into an argument. Carlos must just be doing this to get under my skin.

"Do you want to do some of the Christmas activities we have here?" I ask a minute later, realizing that Carlos has no grasp of how much of the festivities mean here in Winterberry Hollow.

"What do you mean?" Carlos asks in between fries.

"There's a lot of stuff to do around here, and I don't think you want to hang out at the inn all month." I say, taking a sip of lemonade.

"Sure, but I don't think this was much of a question, though." Carlos teases.

"I wasn't going to force you into anything." I insist, taking a bite of my sandwich.

"Are you sure about that?" Carlos says, eyeing the list that's stuffed into my purse.

"I'm about to revoke my offer, Carlos. Yes or no?" I huff.

"Yes."

Lunch passes by without much more conversation, and once Cassie brings over the receipt, Carlos immediately passes her his card. "Oh, I'll pay for my food." I say, caught off-guard.

Carlos looks me up and down before turning back to Cassie. "Don't listen to her."

"Hey!" I say, turning to Carlos as Cassie walks away. "I was the one who invited you to lunch. If anything, shouldn't I be paying?"

"As if." Carlos says with a skeptical side eye. I meet his eyes with annoyance, but maybe just a little bit of amusement, too. "Where are we off to after this?"

"The Christmas tree farm is having its visitor day today. We could drop by and look at the trees and drink some hot chocolate." I offer.

"Eat some candy canes?" Carlos offers with a quick raise of his eyebrows.

"Hey," I begin, his comment from last night flashing through my mind. "I happen to just appreciate candy canes more than the average person."

"Which is why I added the candy canes part." Carlos says easily, as though he's forgotten about how he basically insulted my love for them last night.

"Yeah, sure." I huff. Cassie brings back Carlos' card, and we walk out to my car. Carlos immediately slides into the driver's seat, and I realize that he still has my keys.

"You're going to drive again?" I question as I climb into the passenger seat.

"I'll be the designated driver from now on. We have a wedding to prep, and I don't think we'll be of much help six feet under." My jaw drops, but I have to agree with him. The snow and I have never gotten along when it comes to driving, and this might just be for the best.

"Okay, then." I agree, buckling my seat belt as Carlos easily pulls onto the road. "So have you met Poppy before?"

"No."

"Really?" I find it hard to believe that he's never met her before, but I've only ever met Charlie once, so who am I to judge?

"Have you met Charlie?"

"Once. He and Poppy visited a few months ago, but other than that, I haven't spent any time with him." I respond truthfully. "Poppy was ten when I was born, so there's always been a distance between us, meaning I don't know a lot about her personal life."

"So you're seventeen?" Carlos asks. "Charlie is about the same for me."

"Yep. I turn eighteen in January. What about you? When did you turn eighteen?"

"November twenty-second." Carlos responds.

"Oh, so you're not much older than me," I comment. "Did you do anything fun for your birthday?"

"My parents and I went out to dinner, and some friends and I spent the afternoon together."

"That sounds fun. Speaking of your parents, when are they arriving in town? They're coming to the wedding, right?" I question, realizing that I have no idea about anything concerning his parents.

"Yeah, they'll be here. I think they're flying in a day before the wedding." Carlos says. "Take a left here?" He asks, gesturing to the *Get your Christmas trees here!* Sign on the side of the road.

"Yes, take a left." I confirm. "So why did you fly in so far in advance?" I can't help myself from asking these questions, but Carlos doesn't seem to mind them. He's still wearing the easy expression he had this morning.

"Charlie was supposed to be here sooner, and he said that he would spend some time with me. Obviously, that's not going to happen now, but that was the original plan."

"Oh, I guess I can see that. I was excited to spend time with Poppy, too." I lament, knowing how he feels. "Hopefully you won't be too tired of my face by the time Charlie and Poppy get here." I tease.

"I doubt I will." Carlos jokes back as he parks in the tree farm lot.

"Thanks. I'll try not to get tired of yours, too." I respond with a laugh as I step out of the car. "I think that some of my friends are working here today. You can meet some of the people our age."

"That's cool. I guess you're friends with everyone here?" Carlos asks as he slips on his gloves. We fall into step as we walk to the first booth in the clearing. The trees are all to the right of us in well-organized rows, and in the distance, the laughter and squeals of children running around them fill the air. I catch sight of Anastasiya as she passes out hot chocolate a few booths down, and I give her a quick wave.

"Thank you," Carlos says next to me, snapping me away from Anastasiya and back to the vendor in front of us. The man behind the cart passes Carlos a bag of candy canes, and he immediately pulls one out and carefully breaks the seal before passing it to me.

"Oh, thank you, Carlos." I say, taking the peppermint candy.

"Don't worry about it, Lia." Carlos says with a smirk as he strides next to me. The snow crunches under our shoes as we walk around the booths, and even though the sun is out and blinding as ever, my body still feels chilled.

"What do you think of Winterberry Hollow so far? Is it the winter wonderland you expected?" I ask a few moments later when we start weaving through the rows of Christmas trees.

"It's definitely a winter wonderland. I keep expecting some elves or something to jump out of a tree." Carlos jokes.

"We still have time for that." I tease, brushing his shoulder with mine. "I was thinking I should introduce you to the reindeer before that, though."

"Do you actually have reindeer here?" Carlos asks.

"Yeah, there's a farm a little bit down the road that has them. This farm, however, has the big draft horses for the sleigh rides and everything. Do you want to see them?"

"You're the tour guide." Carlos answers with a shrug. While I would find this rude from anyone else, in just the few hours I've known him, I don't think he's rude at all. Just...nonchalant? Chill? I don't know the right word to use, but he just seems calm. Easy. Unbothered.

"I'll take that as a yes, then," I say, turning to guide him away from the trees and to the barn. "Lennox should be working in the barn right now."

"Who's Lennox, again?" Carlos asks as we stride down the path.

"He's one of my friends. We all go to school here, but he's siblings with the girl who works at the inn you're staying at. Maisie." I respond, as though he should just know Maisie from the few hours he's been in Winterberry Hollow.

"Oh, that redhead girl at the front desk?" Carlos asks. "The one from this morning who called me down?"

"Yeah, that's her. This is her brother, Lennox." I say as we enter the barn. Lennox is helping a family feed one of the horses a treat, but gives me a wave as he enters.

"Can I tell you something funny?" Carlos asks when we stop in front of one of the stalls. The horse inside—Bell, judging by the nameplate on the stall—lowers her head for me to pet.

"Yeah, go ahead," I say, my pulse quickening. What is he going to say?

"When she called me down, I was worried for a minute that I'd done something wrong, and I was about to be scolded or something. Then, when I saw you, I was even more confused." Carlos says with a chuckle as he rubs his gloved hand against Bell's forehead. "Had I known that coming down would mean that I had to prep a wedding, I might not have answered."

"Really? You don't want to be here?" I say, feeling slightly dejected.

"What? No. That was a joke." Carlos says, still smiling. His eyebrows furrow as though he's surprised by my reaction. "You need to lighten up a little, Lia. I was just teasing you." Carlos' arm drops from Bell, and he gently pats my back, as though he's not exactly sure how to comfort me.

"Yeah, but you just said that you wouldn't have come down, so how did you think I was going to react?" I say, frustrated at how Carlos is just so *chill* when it comes to his jokes. "How was I supposed to know that you were joking? And my name is *Magnolia*."

"Do you think I would willingly spend the day with someone I didn't like?" Carlos asks exasperatedly, as though he didn't realize his joke would land this poorly.

"Well, I don't know. I don't know *you*." I huff, turning and marching out of the barn. "I was just trying to be a *nice* person and invite you along, but clearly you don't care about that." Of course he doesn't want to spend time with me. I was a complete jerk last night, and any sane person wouldn't want to be with me after our ice incident.

"Lia, wait," Carlos says from behind me. "I didn't know you would take so much offense to that. I really just meant it as a joke."

"Yeah, well, maybe you should keep your jokes to yourself," I say, finally making it back to my car. Apparently, it's been lightly snowing the whole time we've been here, because there's fresh snow on the windshield, and it's even deeper now. I tug on the passenger door, but of course, it's locked. "Can you please unlock my car?" I huff. The *click* of the lock sounds, and I quickly slip into my seat.

Carlos slides into the driver's seat, but doesn't make a move to start the car. "Lia-"

"Carlos, please at least get the heat on." I interrupt, shivering from the cold air. "And my name is *Magnolia*." Carlos obliges and twists the key, and I reach out to turn on the heat at the same moment he does, and our bare fingers brush, sending little bolts of lightning up my arm. Stupid cold.

"I didn't mean to hurt your feelings. I was just joking. I promise." Carlos says after a moment of silence. At this point, I'm less frustrated with him for teasing me, but more angry at myself for reacting the way I did. Why do I always do the wrong thing?

"I've heard that, Carlos. It just hurt my feelings, since I'm already going out of my comfort zone to include you. I accept your apology, though." I finally say, knowing that I'm overreacting. I can't stop myself from feeling so stressed out, and then when Carlos said he wouldn't have agreed to be around me, it sent me into a spiral or something. Talk about embarrassing.

"Thank you," Carlos says, placing his hands on the wheel before turning to me. "Where to next, boss?"

After Carlos and I left the Christmas tree farm, I told him to just drop me off at my house and to take my car back to the inn. The weatherman predicted snow, and I told him that I wouldn't be able to pick him up with even more snow on the ground. Carlos seemed slightly confused by this request, but I reminded him that since he's going to be the best man, it's not like he can just jump ship and drive off with my car.

Now, I'm just waiting for him to pick me up so we can drive down to one of the local flower shops to see if they can fulfill the order that Poppy listed out for me. She wants fifty amaryllis bouquets, and while this is rather last-minute, it doesn't hurt that she gave me Charlie's bank information to pay for everything.

"Poppy called to let us know that you and Carlos are going to be doing a lot of the wedding prep," Mamma says as I gear up for a day out and about. She and Pappa are still finishing their coffee and crispbread, but they'll be leaving for work in a few minutes.

"Yeah, we are. I'm about to go with him to the floral shops to try and find the flowers that Poppy wants."

"Did you loan him your car?" Pappa asks a moment later as he looks out the front window and into the driveway, where Carlos is currently pulling in.

"Yeah, I did. He's a little bit better at driving in the snow, and I was too scared to drive back down the hill last night if I were to drop him off at the inn." I say sheepishly. I know that neither of my parents care, since I bought the car myself; rather, they're just curious.

"Well, have fun, Magnolia." Mamma says as she brushes past me to climb the stairs to her and Pappa's room. He follows, and just as I'm reaching for the door, a soft knock sounds on the other side.

Carlos.

I open the door and allow Carlos to step inside as I reach for my boots under the bench. "Good morning," I say, sitting down to slide on my boots. "How was the drive over here?"

"Morning," Carlos says, glancing around the winter wonderland that is my house. "It wasn't bad. It snowed even more last night."

"I noticed," I reply, tightening the laces on my left boot. I glance up for a moment, and Carlos is still looking around the room as though he's never seen this many Christmas decorations in his life. "Is it a bit too festive for you?"

"No, not at all. If the inn bedrooms are any indication of how much this town celebrates Christmas, then I have a pretty good idea of what every home here looks like on the inside." Carlos teases, stuffing his hands in his jacket pocket as he rocks on his heels.

"It's a serious event here," I reply, standing and brushing my hands on my pants. "Ready to go, driver." Carlos chuckles as he opens the door and allows me through.

"Do you need to lock it or something?" He asks in confusion as I don't spare the door a second thought.

"What? No. Besides that one break-in or whatever a few weeks ago, it's pretty much crime-free here." I respond easily. "Also, my parents are home, so they might lock it when they leave."

"If you're sure," Carlos says, following me down the steps.

"I am," I say with a giggle, pulling open the passenger door.

"So where are we going today?" Carlos asks as he starts the engine.

"Well, we need to find somewhere to supply fifty bouquets of amaryllises." I begin, glancing down at the notebook in my purse. "And then after that, we can go to The North Pole to make some decorations."

"The North Pole?" Carlos scoffs. "That might be just out of my chauffeur job description." He says with a laugh.

"The community center here is nicknamed The North Pole during Christmas, because so many events are held there. So now, there's a sign outside of it that says *The North Pole* that will stay up until January." I explain. Carlos nods his head as I speak, and a small smile grows on his face as he listens.

"I see. Please forgive me for not offering to take you to The North Pole." Carlos jokes. "Where am I going, by the way? I don't know where any of the flower shops here are."

"Oh, right." I picture a town map in my head for a moment before speaking again. "You need to turn left in a minute, then it will be on the right. *Francine's Flowers* is the name."

Carlos barely manages to hold in his laughter, but I can see the amusement on his face.

"What's so funny?" I ask, raising an eyebrow.

"Well, let's just say that I've heard about The North Pole and Francine's Flowers this morning, and it's a lot for a non-wonderland resident to take in." Carlos says with a chuckle.

"I suppose that there are a few...*unique* names here," I admit, understanding his point. "But that doesn't mean that they won't grow on you. You have another month here, right?"

"Something like that. I'm staying until a few days after the new year, and then I'll be flying back with my parents. Charlie and Poppy are going to Hawaii for their honeymoon, right?" Carlos responds as he stops in front of the flower shop.

"Yeah, they are. Apparently, since Poppy chose to have the wedding here in the middle of winter, Charlie insisted on somewhere warm for the vacation." I say, thinking back to what Poppy told me when she was explaining all of their plans.

"Understandable." Carlos says with a chuckle as he slips on his gloves. "We weren't made for this cold weather." He teases.

"Oh really, now?" I joke as we exit the car. "And we Larsens are?"

"It's in your name, Lia." Carlos jokes as he reaches ahead to open the flower shop doors. "It's Norwegian, right?"

"Yeah, it is. Hey, my na-"

"Good morning, Magnolia. How are you doing?" Francine asks from her chair behind the front counter. Her gray hair is piled on her head in loose curls that are somewhat pinned with little clips, and her large glasses perch on her nose as she looks over them to meet my eyes. "And who is this lovely man you've brought along with you?"

"Good morning, Francine. I'm doing well," I answer, gesturing for Carlos to stand next to me so I can introduce him. "This is Carlos. He's going to be the best man at the wedding."

"Hello, ma'am." Carlos says with a smile, reaching out to shake her hand.

"How nice to meet you, Carlos." She says with a grin, giving me an anything but sly wink. I press my lips together to stifle a giggle, but I ignore her old-lady tendencies.

"Which, speaking of the wedding," I say, stepping closer. "We're here to ask you about flowers for it."

"Oh really? What are you looking for, honey?" Francine asks, scooting her chair forward. "I have a lot of options, but I'm sure that Poppy has everything already picked out."

"So, she wants fifty bouquets of amaryllises," I say, realizing just how much of a tall order that is. "Do you happen to carry them?"

"Oh, well, that's quite the order. I don't happen to carry amaryllises, because they're grown in warmer temperatures, and need all of the fancy greenhouses to grow somewhere this north." Francine says with an apologetic smile. "I have other bouquets if she's interested in other options?"

"Thank you so much, but I think she's pretty set on this, so I have to find these amaryllises." I apologize, biting my lip. How will I find these crazy amaryllises here in the middle of a mountain hollow?

"Thank you, Francine. We're going to try a few more shops, but if we change our minds, then you'll be our first call." Carlos says, turning to wrap his arm around my shoulder. "We'll figure this out, Lia." He says quietly as we walk out of the door. It's soft enough that no one else will hear him, but he's close enough that I hear him clearly.

"I know, but it's just that I want to make this perfect for Poppy and Charlie, but this just feels like a bad start to everything." I admit as he opens the passenger door for me. Why does everything go wrong?

"We'll find these amaryllises, and then we can move on to the next thing on our list. And if this takes more than a day or so, we can start on our next thing." Carlos says as he slides into the driver's seat. He turns on the car and taps away at his phone screen for a moment before pulling onto the road. I gaze out the windshield for a moment, but I'm startled from my pity party as Carlos' hand taps my jacket. He's offering me a candy cane while still keeping his eyes on the road.

"Thanks, Carlos," I say, taking the candy cane that has the tree farm wrapping on it. He must still have the bag he bought yesterday in here. "You're kind of good at pep talks, you know?"

"If that was a good pep talk, I think you might need to invest in a real pep talk and be amazed by how much more motivating they are than what I just did." Carlos says with a chuckle. I'm not sure why he's selling himself short, but I already feel better, so something he said worked.

"You were still pretty good, though," I say. "Where are we going, by the way?"

"My phone map says that there's another flower shop around here, so I figured we'd get a second opinion before we decided to drive to a city around here." Carlos says as he pulls in front of a larger shop. *Rose's Roses* reads from the sign hanging in the window.

"That's a good idea, Carlos," I say as we step out of the car. "The nearest large city—May—is about an hour away."

"I saw that. It's not a terrible drive, and we can do it if we need to." Carlos says as he opens the glass door.

"Hello, hello! What can I do for you two today?" Rose says from the edge of the room. She's tending a bouquet of Winterberries, and is wearing a floral apron, with her long brown hair falling down well past her shoulders.

"Hi, Rose. We were wondering if you carry amaryllises." I say, stepping closer to her as I speak.

"Oh, that's a hard one. I think I might have a few in the back. How many do you need?" She asks, brushing her hands on the apron.

"Fifty bouquets," I say tentatively, already expecting her reaction.

"Well, that's a large order. Let me guess, they're for Poppy's wedding?" Rose says gently.

"Yeah, they're for the wedding. How many bouquets do you have here?" I venture, already knowing that she won't have enough.

"I have two, but they're not going to make it to the wedding and still look nice. You'll need to find somewhere else to get them. There's a shop in May that will definitely have them, though." Rose says apologetically.

"Thank you," Carlos says, and then we're back in the car, at square one again. "So, I guess we're going to May."

"Yeah, we'll need to drive out there to order them." I say as I hold my hands in front of the heater.

"Then let's do that," Carlos says, checking the clock on the car. "Can we grab lunch, though?"

"There are a lot of options in May, so can you hold off until then?" I offer.

"Yep." Carlos hums as he pulls onto the street. All around us people are walking up and down the streets with shopping bags and desserts, and for a moment, I wish that Poppy didn't decide to have her wedding on Christmas Day. Christmas is my favorite season, and now I'm spending all of my time preparing for her wedding instead of on my favorite holiday traditions.

Stop. I'm her sister, and it's my job to be there for her no matter what. Especially for her *wedding* of all things.

"So when do we have to be at The North Pole?" Carlos asks a few minutes later, once he's on the main road that will lead us over the mountain and to May.

"The decorating starts at six, I think, so sometime around then," I say, checking the text Elisa sent me this morning. She's one of the volunteers for a lot of the North Pole events, so she texts me about the events going on each day.

"So we'll have plenty of time, then. It's only eleven right now." Carlos comments.

"Hopefully."

"Hopefully it's actually eleven, or hopefully we'll have plenty of time?" Carlos teases.

"Hopefully, we'll have plenty of time. This mountain is no joke, and it's rather..." I glance out the window at the mountains of snow around us. "Snowy."

"It's nothing I can't handle." Carlos says easily. He fiddles with the radio as he turns it on and increases the volume. Immediately, I start humming to the Christmas song that plays over the speakers. "Do you like this song?"

"I like all Christmas music." I tease.

"I see," Carlos says as he taps his fingers along to the beat of the music. The mountains around us fade into a flurry of snow and wilderness, but I almost don't notice it over the music and easy expression Carlos wears.

"Hello, what can I do for you two today?" The florist behind the counter asks as we enter his shop.

"Hello," I say with a cheery wave. "We're looking for fifty bouquets of amaryllises for a wedding later this month. Would you be able to supply that order?"

"Why, absolutely!" The man says excitedly. "I would love to supply your wedding bouquets. Now what day is your wedding?"

"Oh, it's not our wedding," I say hurriedly, a blush creeping up my neck as I speak. "We're the maid of honor and the best man." I gesture between Carlos and I, as if to point out even more that we are *not* the bride and groom.

"Please forgive me for assuming." The man apologizes.

"Now, how can I assist you with the wedding you're *planning*?"

"The wedding is on Christmas Day, so what day should we have them delivered or picked up?"

"You'll want them two to three days before the big day, so the twenty-second or twenty-third." He answers politely as he checks his calendar. "We do offer delivery, which is a small extra fee, but most prefer to have them delivered."

"Delivery works just fine." I give the man the payment information and delivery instructions.

"Thank you for your business, ma'am. Have a lovely day." He calls out as Carlos opens the door. The blast of cold air on my cheeks is sharp, but I almost don't mind it.

"I see a cafe over there. Do you want to get lunch?" I ask Carlos as he falls into step next to me. He's been quiet since we entered the flower shop, and barely spoke a few words the whole time.

"Yeah, that sounds good." He says as he rubs his gloved hands together. "Why is it so cold here?"

"It's not too bad," I tease, bumping my shoulder against his as we walk down the bustling sidewalk.

"Oh, it's definitely that bad." Carlos teases back as he opens the cafe door. We're greeted with the aroma of baked treats, soups, and coffee. Apparently it's a popular spot in town, because there are only two booths left, and after Carlos and I choose one, just minutes pass by before the last one is claimed.

"Hello, sweetie. What can I get for you today? Do you want to start off with a drink and study the menu for a few more minutes?" Our waitress asks as she pulls out a notepad from her apron pocket. Her dark hair is pulled back into a bun, with a few stray curls framing her face.

"I'm ready to order right now," I say, turning to Carlos as he gives me a nod.

"Perfect, what can I get for you?"

"I'd like the grilled cheese with tomato soup, and a lemonade, please." I say, folding the menu and passing it to her.

"I'd like the same thing, but with added pickles, please." Carlos says, meeting my eyes with a twinkle in his.

"So who is copying my order now?" I tease, shrugging off my coat and setting it on the fabric of the bench next to me.

"Contrary to what you believe, I already chose that before you said anything." Carlos says, accepting the lemonade that our waitress brings back. I take a sip of mine after opening a straw and dropping it in.

"Whatever," I tease, reaching into my purse for my notebook. "At least we can cross off the flowers from our list."

"Good job, Lia." Carlos says, leaning across the table to glance at the list. "What's next?" I bite my lip instead of telling him *again* that my name is Magnolia, because I don't want to ruin the moment by correcting him.

"So for the main things, we still need to order the cake, pick up the dress, pick up the tuxedos, and meet with the catering." I say, reading off the list.

"That's not too much. We should be able to get that done with plenty of time to spare between the wedding." Carlos says. "We should probably leave here after lunch and get back to Winterberry Hollow if we want to make it to the decoration making." Just as he says this, our waitress brings our food to the table, and the scent of grilled cheese sandwiches and tomato soup is overwhelming.

"So how long have you lived here?" Carlos asks a few moments later.

"In Winterberry Hollow?"

"Yeah,"

"We moved when I was one or two. I wasn't born there, but I don't remember living anywhere else but there." I answer, thinking back to all of the magical years I've spent there. "Poppy was eleven or twelve, so while she still loves it there, she's not as attached as I am, since she remembers life before we moved there."

"Do you want to live there forever?" Carlos asks a moment later.

"Probably. My parents aren't going to move, and I really love it. There's so much tradition and community, and I don't think I'd be able to trade that for anything else." I answer truthfully. "What about you? Where do you live?"

"Right now, I live with my parents in New York, but I don't want to live there forever. Charlie was made for city life, but I don't think it's for me." Carlos says thoughtfully. "I'm his adoptive brother, you know?"

I furrow my eyebrows in confusion at the statement. "I didn't know that, actually. If I'm being honest, I don't know that much about Charlie. I've only met him once."

"Yeah, we've always tried to be close, but I think that our lives are too different, and we want different things. He's always dreamed of the big city life, and I've always wanted someplace that felt like home."

"I can understand that. Poppy was excited when she

moved to New York for college, and we all assumed that she'd move back at some point, but I don't think she will. At least she and Charlie found someone who shares their dream." I reply, unsure of what else to say.

"I agree with that. Charlie used to always say that he would never get married, but here he is." Carlos says with a chuckle.

"Oh, really? Poppy always dreamed of getting married. It's crazy how two people can be so similar yet so different." I muse, taking another bite of my sandwich.

The rest of lunch is spent with almost no conversation between us, but it's comfortable. I like knowing more about Carlos, which is something I didn't expect. Sure, I don't even know a lot about him now, but learning more about his relationship with Charlie and how he grew up is interesting. You know, since I need to know him because we both play key roles in the wedding, of course.

"You weren't lying," Carlos says as we pull into the parking lot for The North Pole.

"About what?"

"It's actually called The North Pole," He says with amusement as he reaches into the back seat for his jacket.

"Of course I wouldn't lie about something as important as that." I huff, reaching back at the same time he does. Our heads bump together with a painful *thump* just as I do so.

"Ow!" We both yelp at the same time. Carlos leans towards me and immediately reaches out to move the hair away from the spot where we collided. Everything around me blurs as he gently uses his fingers to move the hair covering the injured spot.

"Does this hurt?" Carlos asks softly as he brushes his fingers over it. My mouth opens slightly as I try to speak, but nothing comes out. Electricity sparks around the car, filling the space with enough crackling tension to light the town square Christmas tree. Have Carlos' eyes always been so beautifully dark? Has his nose always been so adorably wide at the bottom? "Lia? Are you okay?"

"What?" Why am I so breathless? What has Carlos been saying? Has he been talking? Why can't I seem to remember how to form a sentence?

"I think you might have hit your head a little bit harder than I did," Carlos says with a chuckle, his hand still firmly in place on the side of my head. "Can you count to three for me?" He says this as a joke, but there's just enough tension in his voice to tell me he's actually worried.

"Of course I can count to three, Carlos. I was just shocked when our heads knocked into each other, and I was spaced out for a minute." I huff, pulling my head back. "One, two, three." Carlos' eyebrows furrow at my sudden rudeness, and truthfully, I don't even know why I'm doing this.

"If you're sure you're okay, then let's go decorate some ornaments." Carlos says, reaching back to pass me my jacket.

"Thank you," I say, stepping out into the cool air. It's a stark difference from the warmth of the car, but I almost feel as though I need it. I need to clear my head after whatever just happened. I mean, one second I was reaching back to get my coat, and the next, I couldn't even remember what happened, and Carlos' hand was on my cheek!

"Hey, Lia," Carlos says as he opens the door of The North Pole. I turn to face him, and he's passing me a candy cane.

"What's this for?" I say softly, still unsure of what to make of the whole...*incident* in the car a few moments ago.

"Do you not want it?" Carlos asks with a smirk, retracting his hand as though he's about to slip the candy into his pocket.

"I never said that!" I exclaim, quickly wrapping my hands around it and pulling it back. However, there must be static electricity on him, because there's a shock as my hand brushes his.

I try not to dwell on it as I unwrap the peppermint candy, but the shock felt more electric than I've ever felt in my entire life.

"Everyone, let's all pick an ornament or two, and find a chair to work at," Elisa calls out from the front of the room. Jacob is next to her, pointing at the ornament boxes, and I give him a wave as I catch his eye. He does the same, but frowns when he sees Carlos. Remembering my little rant that I gave him and Elisa the other night, I quickly shake my head, in an I'll-tell-you-more-later gesture. I feel bad now about judging Carlos so much, but in the heat of the moment, I was frustrated that he bumped into me and was blaming me.

"Who is that guy?" Carlos asks, lowering his head so that his mouth is right next to my ear. His breath sends goosebumps down my neck, and on instinct, I lean even closer to him.

"That's my friend, Jacob," I reply, keeping my voice as even as possible.

"Why doesn't he like me?" Carlos asks. I wince, realizing he probably just saw the whole exchange between us.

"What do you mean?" I reply, trying to play it cool.

"When he saw you, he waved. When he saw me, he frowned." Carlos answers simply. Yikes.

"Maybe he just didn't know who you are."

"So the people here really aren't as friendly as they advertise," Carlos comments, reaching out to take an ornament from the box a few feet away. He waited until most of the younger kids got them, and now it's the teenagers and adults reaching in.

"What do you mean?" I ask, picking up an ornament for myself.

"I mean that when we met, you made sure to comment that I'm not from around here, and now you're saying that your friend must not like me because he's never met me," Carlos says with a chuckle as I follow him to a nearby table. "It sounds like you Winterberry people have a real hospitality issue."

"That's not true." I say, somewhat defensively. Yes, Carlos has a solid point here, but that doesn't mean he's entirely correct, either.

"Okay," Carlos says easily as he reaches for a paintbrush. What's that supposed to mean? How does he have the capability to make me feel breathless and give me goosebumps one second, but the next, have me irritated?

"Hey, Magnolia, come here for a moment," Jacob says, leaning down to our table. Carlos lifts his eyes for a moment to meet mine, but instead of saying anything, he just lowers them back to the ornament he's currently decorating.

"Why?" I ask. Jacob doesn't say anything; rather, he just shrugs his shoulders and starts walking away. "I'll be right back, Carlos," I say, standing to follow Jacob.

"Don't worry about me." He hums, not even looking up from his work.

Jacob walks through the doorway and to one of the back staff rooms, where Elisa is leaning over a paper. "I brought her for you," Jacob announces as we enter the room.

"Magnolia! Who is that boy?" Elisa practically shouts as soon as she turns around. "Make it quick, because technically, Jacob and I are getting the stuff for the next group of people ready, and we can't leave everyone out there for too long.

"Nice to see you, too," I say, crossing my arms.

"Right, right. Now, who is he?" Elisa demands. "He is the same guy from the other night, right?"

"Yeah, he is," I say, chewing my lip before continuing. "His name is Carlos, and he's going to be the best man at my sister's wedding. We're working together to do the last-minute prep."

"Oh really? Because that's not what I saw." Elisa says with a raised eyebrow.

"What did you see?" I ask defensively.

"I saw you two in the car a few minutes ago. When he had his hand on your cheek." Elisa answers.

"This feels like an interrogation," Jacob comments as he shuffles through the boxes of undecorated ornaments.

"That's exactly what this is." I huff, agreeing with him. "That wasn't what it looked like, Elisa. I need to go back to my ornament, but you can tell Jacob that he did a good job delivering your hostage." With that, I turn to leave. I don't know why I feel so defensive about Carlos, but Elisa's demand to know more about him rubs me the wrong way.

Maybe it's because I was so rude when I was talking about him the other day, and I'm not quite ready to admit that I was so wrong, or maybe it's because her sudden interest in him is making me protective. As I sit back down in my chair, Carlos doesn't even lift his gaze from the ornament, and for some reason, that hurts.

"How is your ornament coming along?" I ask, picking up a paintbrush to carefully trace over the pencil lines I made before I left.

"It's coming," Carlos says easily, still not lifting his gaze. I can't even see his ornament from the way his hands are holding it, and for some reason, I'm still intrigued.

"That's good," I comment, unsure of what else to say at this point. Maybe he's just really focused on his ornament and isn't into small talk while he's working.

"Are you ready to go?" Carlos asks as I pick up my now-dried ornament. We worked in complete silence for the whole hour, and while I wouldn't classify myself as someone who's rather talkative, the urge to say *something* to Carlos has been eating me alive.

"Yeah, are you?" I pick up my jacket from the floor next to my chair and drape it over my arm as we walk towards the exit.

"Yep," He says, reaching out to open the door. Carlos' voice isn't cold, but it's not exactly warm and inviting, either.

The drive back to my house is quiet, and just before I climb out, Carlos speaks. "Hey, Lia, will you keep this for me? I don't have space in any of my bags." He says, reaching out to drop the ornament he made in my hand.

"What? Are you sure you don't want to keep it?" I ask, completely confused. There isn't *any* room in his bags?

"Positive." Carlos says with a shrug of his shoulders as he pulls his arm back and places his hand on the wheel.

"Hey, do you want to build snowmen?" I blurt out just before closing the door.

"Right now?" Carlos asks, looking out at the near dark sky.

"No, sorry, I meant tomorrow. There's always a town snowman making competition in the park, and maybe you want to participate?" I ask tentatively, realizing how stupid I sound.

"Yeah, I'll come. What time do I need to pick you up?" Carlos asks, his expression softening ever so slightly.

"Maybe ten?"

"I'll see you at ten, Lia." Carlos calls out just as I close the door, and as I step into the headlights of the car, I meet his eyes through the windshield.

"It's *Magnolia*!" I shout. Even though I'm sure he can't hear me, Carlos chuckles as he backs out of the driveway.

Chapter Four

21 DAYS 'TIL CHRISTMAS

"So, how much of a competition is this?" Carlos asks as we walk down the candy-cane marked path towards the people gathered around the barrels of supplies for snowman making. There are barrels of coal, carrots, twigs, and even hats.

"There's always a winner, but it's usually a child who gets chosen. It's more of a community event to get the people together." I say, reaching into a barrel for a carrot. Carlos pulls out a handful of coal and sets it in the pail he's carrying, and then places two twigs on top.

"Interesting," Carlos muses as we pass by children who have already thrown themselves into the snow to make angels, as their parents do most of the heavy lifting for the snowmen. "Have you ever won?"

"My parents say I did when I was five, but I don't remember it," I answer, sifting through the many years of snowman competitions I've attended.

"Oh really?" Carlos says with a chuckle. "And there's no award or something to look back on?"

"No, it's more of a, *if you were there, you remember it* kind of thing," I say, realizing just how silly this tradition must seem. "What about you? What Christmas traditions does your family have?" Carlos sets the pail on the ground as we find a spot, and after a moment of thinking, he finally answers.

"We have Christmas dinner, and buy gifts for each other. We're not really into the traditions, I don't think." He says, furrowing his eyebrows before talking again. "I was nine when I was adopted, so by then, Charlie wasn't really around. We kind of just try to spend Christmas together, and if we're all at the house on Christmas Day, that's a win." Carlos says with a chuckle.

"Oh, I see," I say, the idea of not having set traditions more than strange.

"We're not all as Christmas-crazed as some people." Carlos teases with a pointed look. "That's not to say I dislike it at all, but we've just never made such a big deal out of it. Of course, it's still the day our Savior was born, but the actual festivities aren't something we spend a lot of time on."

"So is this a lot for you?" I ask, motioning around us. "Have you ever seen this much Christmas cheer in your life?"

"Never." Carlos replies, a smile growing on his face. "But it's definitely interesting to observe."

"By the wedding, you'll be just as obsessed with Christmas as I am." I promise, patting Carlos' arm as I step by him.

"I don't think that's possible," Carlos teases. "But you're welcome to try."

"I won't even need to try, because this town and the magic of Christmas will do that all for you," I say, dropping to my knees to start forming a ball of snow. "Have you ever made a snowman before?"

Carlos glances down at me, the sun just behind him, haloing him in light. "No."

"You're about to," I say just before grabbing his coat sleeve and pulling him onto the snow with me.

"Hey! What was that for?" Carlos gasps out as he sits up next to me. His hat fell off when he hit the ground, and now there are tufts of snow throughout his jet-black hair.

"You needed to get in the snow," I say simply, tossing a small snowball in his direction. "You know, get acclimated to your environment and all."

"You're crazy, Lia." Carlos says with a teasing roll of his eyes.

"My name is-" I don't get a chance to finish my sentence, because a snowball slams into my back. "Hey!" I call out, spinning to see Elisa about twenty feet away.

"Oops!" She calls out, not the least bit ashamed of her attack.

"I thought she was your friend." Carlos teases, passing me a snowball he just formed.

"She's not about to be," I say, throwing the ball at Elisa. Unfortunately, I miss her, but only because she tugs Jacob in front of her. Fortunately, it lands squarely on Jacob's chest.

"Hey, when did I volunteer to be a human shield?" Jacob calls out, throwing a snowball right back at me.

"When you let her surprise attack me!" I shout playfully,

standing as I throw another ball at Elisa. "Carlos, are you going to help me?" I tease, looking down at him as he watches me square off with my friends. Instead of saying anything, he just passes me a ball as he stands, a smile growing on his face.

Just as a full fight is starting to break out between Elisa, Jacob, Carlos, and I, a voice calls out from near me. "Hey, cousin, do you want some help?"

"Julia?" I ask, whirling to face her, and a boy following close behind her. She works at the bakery in town, and usually doesn't have mornings off. Julia grins as she scoops up snow for herself, and the boy she has in tow does the same.

"No fair! Four against two is wrong!" Elisa calls out as she and Jacob throw more balls at us.

"Jacob, how did you get in this mess!" Lennox calls out as he and Anastasiya run over to their side. Is everyone here right now? Lennox and Jacob have been best friends since they were children, and it's no surprise that he chose their side.

"Elisa dragged me into this all!" Jacob teases.

"Oh, come on," Anastasiya barely makes out through laughter. I'm surprised she's here with Lennox, and Maisie isn't with her. She and Maisie have always been best friends, but I guess since she's working with Lennox, they're hanging out together.

"A snowball fight without us?" Maisie screams, running up the hill towards us, with...the boy Julia just had with her? I turn, and sure enough, Julia's boy is still with her, but I now recognize that the boy with Maisie is from the inn a few days ago. Twins? I vaguely remember a new family moving in town last month, but that was right before school let out, so I don't think I ever met them.

"Do you know all of these people?" Carlos asks, lowering his head to whisper in my ear. Ouch. He knows no one here.

"Yes," I say immediately. "Well, no. I've never met those twins, but everyone else? Yes." I answer. Carlos throws a ball with such aim that it lands directly on Jacob, and because I was foolishly watching him and not defending myself, Anastasiya's ball smacks right into me.

We laugh as more and more snowballs fly at us, but with the advantage of two more people, we quickly close in on Elisa's team. "We surrender!" Lennox shouts.

"Yes, we surrender!" Elisa echoes as she realizes the odds aren't looking too good in her favor. "Let's all be friends again."

After a few minutes, we start introductions with everyone, and the twin with Maisie introduces himself as Romero, while the twin with Julia introduces himself as Leo.

"I'm Carlos," Carlos says, after we all greet the twins, and he extends his hand to everyone. Julia eyes me suspiciously, but doesn't say anything as he continues. "I don't live here, but I think you all figured that out." He says with a chuckle.

"You're really not related to them?" Lennox asks, eyeing both Carlos and the twins. I've seen Carlos' face enough these past few days to notice the obvious differences, but if I were to just take a glance at him and the twins, their skin is the same exact dark mocha with red undertones, and while the twins both have curly hair and Carlos has loose waves, it's the same jet-black color. Even their noses and jawlines are similar.

"We've never met him before," Leo—I think—says with a laugh. "Although, he could pass as our brother, now that I'm looking at him." Carlos laughs at this.

"Yeah, I've never met them either, but I feel like with the right theatrical effects, I could be a triplet." Carlos says. I smile at how comfortable he's already becoming with my friends, and I don't know why, but it means a lot that he's a part of the group.

"You're too tall, man." Romero jokes, stepping closer to Carlos to measure their heights. Carlos is a good three inches taller than both twins. "You'd pass as an older brother, but the height would throw people off."

"True, true." Carlos answers, stepping back so that he's next to me.

"So, where are you from, Carlos? Are you going to be staying for Christmas?" Anastasiya asks as she fixes her hat.

"Mexico," Carlos says with a chuckle. So that's where his accent is from. He must have been adopted from somewhere in Mexico. Interesting. Just as I'm about to open my mouth and ask him more, he continues speaking, obviously realizing that no one here gets his joke. "I'm here for the wedding. I'm the best man, and since I'm here early, Lia is showing me around town." Everyone nods, but too many sets of eyes shoot to mine as he says *Lia.*

"We need to all hang out together more before Christmas," Elisa says pointedly at me. I avoid direct eye contact with her, because I know she's giving me that look friends do.

"Yeah, we definitely all should," Julia says, bumping her

arm into mine. It's not hard, but I'm not prepared, and I bump right into Carlos. Lennox and Jacob start talking about something, and the twins and Carlos begin a conversation. It sounds like they're speaking Spanish, but I can't be sure, because all of a sudden, all four girls are surrounding me in a group huddle similar to the one you'd find at the playground.

"You three have some serious explaining to do." Anastasiya practically shouts, looking over Maisie, Julia, and I. "You three just show up with these boys like it's the most normal thing in the world, while Elisa and I haven't even met them!"

"I agree," Elisa says, nodding her head vigorously.

"Well, I didn't just show up with a random guy," I begin. "I don't know what excuses these two have, but he's the best man for Poppy's wedding. She asked me to spend time with him and have him help out with the wedding preparations."

"That's valid, but you could have mentioned to us all that you're spending so time with a good-looking boy our age," Elisa says pointedly.

"Hold on, now," I say, raising a hand. "We're friends. Co-workers, practically. You saw me with him at The North Pole."

"If Magnolia gets that excuse, we do too." Julia says immediately. "I work at the bakery with Leo, and I know that his brother, Romero, works with Maisie."

"Thank you, Julia," Maisie says, nodding her head in agreement. "We're all friends with these guys."

"Right," Anastasiya says, sounding suddenly less sure of herself.

"Didn't you see me and Leo at the decorations

yesterday? I think I saw Maisie and Romero there, too." Julia asks. I definitely didn't see them, but then again, there was the second group later on that evening.

"Were you in the second group?" Elisa asks.

"We were," Maisie answers.

"Us, too," Julia says.

"Jacob and I had to leave early because one of the kids had a little accident, and we needed to take him to the hospital. The other elves were still there with the other kids, though." Elisa says with a shudder.

"Elves?" Anastasiya asks.

"Oh, since we're working at The North Pole, it only makes sense to call ourselves elves," Elisa explains sheepishly.

"Okay, we're getting off track," Maisie announces. "We need to be discussing the important things, which-"

"Which is?" Romero asks, striding up to Maisie. Her cheeks flush, but she doesn't do anything else besides glance over to her older brother, Lennox. I know he's super protective of her, but really, it's not like she's dating Romero. He's just someone she works with, who happens to be her age.

"Which is when we're going to start building snowmen." Maisie stutters, glancing over at Anastasiya for help.

"Right, right. We're all about to start building." Anastasiya says, turning to the rest of the guys who are slowly starting to mingle with us girls. "Is everyone ready?"

"Carlos and I are!" I say, reaching out to tug his arm and pull him out of the group. "Come on, let's finish ours first!"

"No fair!" Julia screams, running to a spot not too far

away from us, Leo in tow. Everyone else disperses, and within a minute, there's a boy and a girl on each team.

"Now, how did I get roped into this mega competition with the elves of winter wonderland?" Carlos teases as he begins rolling the base of our snowman.

"Elves is a stretch," I say, making a medium-sized ball of snow for the middle. "But how you got here is thanks to a Christmas wedding."

"Who would've known that a wedding would have this much of an impact on my life?" Carlos muses as he makes the head of our snowman.

"What do you mean?" I ask, dropping to the ground as I begin carefully placing the coals along the middle of the snowman.

"I mean that one minute my brother is telling me he's getting married, and the next, I'm in a tiny town called Winterberry Hollow building a snowman."

<h1 style="text-align:center">Chapter Five</h1>

20 DAYS 'TIL CHRISTMAS

"Remind me, what are we looking for right now?" Carlos asks, lowering his head so that I catch his words over the loud chatter of people strolling through the carts and booths set up. Snow crunches underfoot as we breathe in the aroma of desserts, soaps, flowers, and everything else that could be included in a town market. Every year, just before Christmas, the streets are shut down to allow vendors of all types to set up and promote their products. Women with crocheted, knitted, and embroidered items boast the perfect Christmas presents, and my eyes catch on a light pink scarf. The color is exquisite, and I stop in my tracks. "Earth to Lia." Carlos teases at my sudden halt.

"What? Sorry," I say sheepishly, realizing I didn't even respond to his question.

"I asked if we were looking for anything in particular for the wedding." Carlos asks as we begin walking again.

"Poppy asked me last night if I would taste test the

bakeries that are set up today, and then find the one with the best chocolate cake or cupcakes," I say, narrowly avoiding a small child chasing after his sibling, his face covered in chocolate. "And judging by that kid, there has got to be someone close."

"What about me? Do I get to have input on the tastiest chocolate here?" Carlos teases, as we stop in front of a booth with a sign that reads, *Chocolate here!*

"I guess you can offer your input occasionally." I tease, striding up to the woman behind the table. "Hello, Darlene."

"Magnolia, it's been too long since I've seen you. How are you doing?" Darlene asks as she reaches out to take my hand.

"I'm doing well, how are you?"

"Just amazing, dear. What can I get for you today?" She asks with a wide smile. Her cheeks are rosy red from the crisp air, and I can't help but mirror her smile.

"We're looking to taste the chocolate cakes and cupcakes you have, since we're in charge of finding the perfect cake for Poppy's wedding." I explain, gesturing to Carlos while I speak.

"Isn't that just lovely. Here are a few of the samples I have." She offers, placing the sample tray of desserts on the table. I take one of the plates that has a piece of chocolate cake, and use the fork to take a bite.

"Wow, this one is amazing. What do you think, Carlos?" I ask, offering him the plate. On most occasions, I wouldn't share my food with anyone, but we shouldn't take two pieces of cake when we're already going to be trying a cupcake, too.

Carlos eyes the fork for a moment before taking it and

scooping up a bite of his own. He nods his head approvingly as he swallows, his Adam's apple bobbing. "This one is the best so far." I try not to linger on the fact that he's offering me the cake back, and now I'm going to be eating after him. Not that I find it gross, but for some reason, it feels intimate.

I almost giggle at his words, since we haven't even tried any other ones yet, but this brings the biggest smile to Darlene's face, and I know that was his intention. "Thank you, honey. Do you two want to try the cupcake? Those are a different recipe, but I also use it in some of the cakes, too." She extends a chocolate cupcake with perfectly whipped icing on top.

"You can try it first, Carlos," I say, allowing him to have the first bite of the cupcake while I finish the slice of cake.

"This is really good, ma'am." Carlos says after swallowing his half of the cupcake.

"Thank you, dear," Darlene says as she turns to fix one of her displays.

"Here," He offers the cupcake to me, but between my hands that are in mittens, my purse, and the plate and fork in my hands, I don't have enough space for it. "Open your mouth." Carlos says, reaching out as though he's about to set it in my mouth.

"Wai-" Carlos must have taken my open mouth as accepting his offering and not as me trying to speak, because suddenly, I have half of a chocolate cupcake in my mouth. My cheeks flush, and butterflies stir in my stomach as I slowly chew the cupcake. Carlos' eyes never leave mine, and all of the chatter of people fades into the distance.

"Well, what do you think?" Darlene's voice slices like a knife through whatever is happening between Carlos and I.

"Oh, um, it's really good," I answer enthusiastically. "I love it."

"Thank you," Darlene says with a smile. "I understand if you're not ready to make a final decision about the cake yet, so why don't you do more testing before committing?"

"Thank you, we'll do that," Carlos says with a smile as he reaches into my purse to pull out the notebook and pen. I pass Darlene the plate and fork and fall into step with Carlos as we continue walking down the street.

"What are you doing?" I ask, trying to get a glimpse of whatever he's writing in my notebook.

"I'm writing down my ranking of the cake and cupcake, and then you can do yours. By the end, we can compare which ones rank the highest." Carlos explains, offering me the pen and paper. In neat cursive, he wrote down his ranking of the cake and cupcake, and there's a spot for me to do the same. He wrote *Lia* instead of Magnolia, and I consider adding the beginning of my name just to correct him, but just this once, I'll let him get away with it.

"Thanks," I say, adding my own ranking. We stop by a few more tables, but by far, the best ones were Darlene's.

"Do you want to find lunch?" Carlos asks as we stroll through the throngs of people.

"Definitely." I agree, following Carlos as he weaves through the people to a table that's selling croissant sandwiches and small bags of popcorn.

"How about this?" Carlos offers, stepping in line behind the two people ahead of us. I nod in agreement, and soon enough, we have our food. We find a bench on one of the sidewalks, but we have to squeeze in to fit next to an older man on the other end of the bench. One of my legs is pressed against the arm of the bench, and the other is against Carlos' leg.

I try not to notice how warm he is against me, or how comfortable I feel, but it's hard to ignore. It's hard to ignore how much I'm enjoying spending time with Carlos.

"So are we in agreement that the best option is the chocolate cake from Darlene's bakery?" Carlos asks a moment later. I glance down at the list just to clarify that was my top choice, even though I already know it is.

"Yeah, we are." I agree.

"You don't have to consult your list all of the time, you know?" Carlos says teasingly. "Trust your instinct every now and then."

"What's that supposed to mean?" I question, slightly defensive. Carlos has now told me something along those lines every single day now.

"I mean that..." Carlos trails off as though he wants to be careful with what he says. "You're very dependent on your lists and schedules, and you might be a little bit happier if you lightened up every now and then."

"I'm happy," I argue back. Sure, I consult my list every other moment and stress about anything and everything going wrong, but that doesn't mean I'm not happy.

"Okay, Lia." Carlos says, dropping the topic for now.

"Magnolia." I say quietly. The older man next to Carlos glances over as though he's trying to subtly listen to our conversation, but I try to ignore him.

"Can we come to a truce?" Carlos asks as we climb into the car. We've been less talkative since our little dispute during lunch, and it seems to be gnawing at Carlos as much as it has for me. I glance up to see that Carlos is extending a candy cane as a peace offering. The wrapping has already been peeled back, as though he's already opened it for me, and I can't help but accept it.

"Yeah, we can." I agree, placing the end of the peppermint candy in my mouth.

"Thanks," Carlos says with a grin. He starts the car, but just before pulling out, he turns towards me. "Do you mind waiting here, actually? I just remembered something I wanted to buy when I was back there."

"I don't mind," I say, leaning my head back on the seat. "What are you going to get?" Instead of answering, since he's already halfway out of the car, Carlos just closes the door and briskly walks back into the center of the market.

Carlos returns fifteen minutes later with a gift bag, and he quickly places it in the back seat before climbing back into the driver's seat. After he weaves through both the foot and vehicle traffic, Carlos pulls onto the road.

"Alright, thank you so much for placing an order. I'll have the cake ready for pickup on the twenty-third, if that works for you?" Darlene says. On the drive home, we agreed to place our order in the morning.

"Will it still be perfect on Christmas?" I ask, unsure of what the proper timeline is for wedding cakes.

"Yes, it'll still be perfect. You'll just want to keep it chilled, of course." Darlene confirms as she types up our order on her computer.

"That sounds great. Thank you," I say, reciting all of the payment information to her.

"Thank you, Magnolia." She says, giving us a wave as we exit the bakery.

"Yay, we get to cross off cakes, now," I say, pulling out my pen and paper.

"What's next?" Carlos asks as we climb into the car.

"We need to meet with catering," I say, buckling my

seatbelt. "Poppy already has the restaurant picked out, but we need to place the order and work out all of the details."

"Do you want to do that today?" Carlos asks, glancing over at the clock that reads eleven-thirty.

"It's a Saturday, so they don't have all of their staff in today for that," I say, remembering what their website said last night. "But, there's an arts and crafts at The North Pole, if you want to do that for a little bit." I offer.

"Arts and crafts?" Carlos asks.

"Yeah, it'll be fun," I say, dropping my purse into the back seat.

"Let's do some arts and crafts." Carlos agrees. And with that, we're back on the road.

"So did you have fun?" I ask as we walk out of The North Pole. We made little snowflakes, cards, and a few other things.

"Tons," Carlos teases as we climb into the car. "You need to keep these, though. I don't have space for Christmas crafts in my bags."

"Again?" I tease, accepting the little crafts. Our fingers brush as he passes them, and for a minuscule second, neither of us move.

"At least I'm agreeing to these things," Carlos finally says as I move my hand away from his with the crafts.

"Fine," I admit. "Hey, by the way, will you come to church with me tomorrow? I kind of need a driver, but you're also just invited anyway."

Carlos smiles at this, but doesn't take his eyes off the snowy road. "Sure. What time do you need me to pick you up?"

"Eight."

"I'll see you at eight tomorrow." Carlos says, and for the rest of the drive, there's comfortable silence between us.

"Thank you for these," I say as I step out of the car. I flash the crafts Carlos gave me, and he smirks ever so slightly before responding.

"My pleasure."

Chapter Seven

18 DAYS 'TILL CHRISTMAS

"So this is where they're going to get married, right?" Carlos asks as we step through the large wooden doors of the church.

"Yeah, this is the place," I respond. We walk through the aisles of pews to the spot where my family usually sits, and Mamma and Pappa are already waiting for us.

"Carlos, how lovely of you to join us," Pappa says, extending his hand for Carlos to shake.

"I'm glad to be here," Carlos replies, shaking his hand. Service starts a few minutes later, and we all fall into a hushed silence as our pastor begins the sermon.

"I think the wedding will look really pretty here," Carlos says as we exit the church two hours later.

"I think so, too. Poppy was very adamant that she

wanted to be married there," I say, falling into step beside him as we near my car. "Hey, do you want to go on a sleigh ride?"

"An actual sleigh ride?" Carlos asks as he reaches out to open the passenger door for me.

"Yeah, the Christmas tree farm has sleigh rides all throughout December, but today is their main day," I say as he slides into the driver's seat.

"Don't you think we should change first?" Carlos asks, eyeing my dress.

"It's long-sleeved." I huff. "And even though these aren't technically snow boots, they're still warm.

"Warm isn't practical." Carlos teases.

"If you don't want to go, just tell me now," I say a moment later as Carlos moves the car in line to leave the parking lot.

"No, we're going on a sleigh ride, Lia."

Practical isn't exactly what I would classify these boots as, but Carlos' teasing glint in his eyes is enough for me to keep my mouth shut. So what? Maybe he was right about needing to change first.

"Magnolia, Carlos!" Anastasiya says as we approach her. She's near the barn, managing the table with waivers, guides, and everything else the farm needs to inform guests of before they move on to the sleigh rides.

"Hey," I answer as we step closer.

"Did you two come straight from church?" Anastasiya

asks as she studies our clothing. "Even I had time to change before I started work."

"It wasn't a timing issue," Carlos says teasingly. I turn to give him a glare, but he's conveniently not even looking at me. Of course.

"I see," Anastasiya says, pulling out two papers for us. "Sign here, and then you're welcome to walk over to the edge of that field, where one of the sleighs will be arriving in a few minutes.

"Walk?" Carlos and I say at the same time.

"Did you expect your driver to pull up right here?" Anastasiya teases.

"I guess not," I say, taking the paper and signing it before passing Carlos the pen to sign his.

"Perfect, thank you," Anastasiya says, tucking the paper into her binder.

Carlos and I begin our walk, but the edge of the field that Anastasiya told us to walk to must be at least a mile away. Carlos' shoes are much better suited for the walk, as are his pants. Sure, I have leggings on under my dress, but they don't really do anything when you're in the middle of a field with snow that's at least two feet deep.

"Hop on." Carlos says as I trip for the fourth time.

"What?" I ask as I steady myself. These shoes *really* aren't practical.

"Hop on." Carlos repeats, dropping to his knee as though I'm about to climb on his back.

"No, that's not fair at all," I say immediately. "Besides, you can't walk the rest of the way carrying me as well."

"Lia, I'd rather carry you now before I'm carrying you with a broken ankle." Carlos argues back.

"It's *Magnolia.*" I huff, climbing onto his back. Carlos easily stands and starts walking, as though I weigh nothing. I don't think I'm very heavy, but when a guy offers to carry you, you start to worry about something like that.

"Hey, there's our ride," Carlos says as the sleigh pulls to a stop about twenty feet away from us. A small family climbs out, and the driver gives us a nod as he sees us approach.

"Honey, you should be more like her boyfriend and carry me more often." The woman comments to her husband teasingly as they stride past us.

My cheeks flush, but before I can respond, they're already out of earshot. Carlos doesn't say anything, either, but surely he must have heard her, right?

Carlos lowers to his knee again as he stops at the edge of the sleigh, and I quickly slide off. My face is still flushed, both from the woman's comment and from the whole situation. He offers me his hand as I step up into the carriage, and just after I let it go, he flexes it before sliding it into his coat pocket.

"There are a few blankets on your seats, and I ask that you stay seated the entire ride." The driver says politely as we settle in. A blanket sounds amazing right now, considering my whole body feels like a popsicle.

Carlos lifts the blankets and layers them over us, and they must be at least ten pounds, because I feel immediately warm.

"See, wasn't this worth it?" I ask, turning to Carlos as the horses begin pulling the sleigh. We're sitting so close that our bodies are touching, and there's a smile on Carlos' face as he answers.

"Yes, it was worth it."

For a moment, I allow all thoughts of the wedding to slip away as I bask in the glory of right now.

Right now, there's nothing but the gentle trot of horses, the sleigh bells tinkling as they rock, and Carlos next to me. And right now, that's enough.

"Now remind me where we'll be eating at the wedding," Carlos says as I climb into the car. Since it's Monday, we're stopping by the restaurant Poppy wants us to talk to about catering.

"The reception will be held at our house, so that's where we'll be eating. I say, passing Carlos my phone with the directions for the restaurant.

"Interesting." Carlos hums as he follows the map.

"Yeah, it'll be a little party of sorts, with only the close friends, and both families." I say, going over the guest list in my head. "Most of the town will be at the ceremony, but then afterwards, the reception people will meet at our house a few hours later."

"So we'll all have a few hours to get changed and rest?" Carlos asks.

"Exactly."

"I'm sorry, but our catering chef has this Christmas off. We aren't accepting catering bookings from the fifteenth until January first." The restaurant manager explains politely. "Maybe you'd be interested in booking then?"

"This is for a wedding on Christmas Day, so those other dates don't work." I say, feeling my pulse quicken. This can't be happening right now.

"I'm very sorry, but I do hope you work something out." She says, stacking a few of the papers on her desk. "Please do think of us if you're in need of other catering during our available dates, though."

"We will," I say softly. Carlos and I stand and leave the room, and by the time we reach the car, I'm a nervous wreck. "What are we going to do now?"

"Lia, this isn't the end of the world. I'm sure we'll find another option." Carlos says gently as he starts the car.

"Carlos, there aren't any other restaurants here that serve the options she wants. We're back to square one right now, and we only have seventeen days to figure this out." I say, my words coming out quicker and quicker as the gravity of the situation sinks even deeper.

"We still have all day to find something that will work. Why don't we search for restaurants that will cater on Christmas Day?" Carlos says, pulling out his phone to do an internet search. I do a search of my own, but before I can find any options, Carlos is passing me his phone. "Why don't we check this place out? It says it's in a smaller town about forty-five minutes away."

"I've never been to that restaurant, but I know where the town is. We can try it out." I agree glumly.

"Lia, we're going to figure this out. Don't be so down." Carlos says lightly.

"Don't be so down? I'm *stressed,* Carlos. I have a wedding to be responsible for, and it seems like everything is going wrong."

"How has it all gone wrong?" Carlos counters as he begins driving.

"Well, the flowers weren't here," I start.

"But we already ordered those. That's done." Carlos says.

"It took us hours to sample the cakes, but we decided to go with the very first one." I stutter, surprised by how quickly he deflated that worry.

"So? We got it done and had some great chocolate along the way." Carlos replies.

"And now there's this. We don't have catering." I say exasperatedly.

"And now we're going to figure it out. This won't be too hard to work around. There are a hundred other restaurants in a hundred-mile radius, Lia. We're going to figure it out." Carlos says easily, reaching down near his feet. He lifts a candy cane and carefully breaks the seal before extending it towards me.

"It's *Magnolia.*" I say, accepting the candy. A smile that I have no control over rises on my face as I bring the peppermint candy to my lips. "You're rather good with your peppermint timing, though, Carlos."

"I know, Lia." Carlos says with a smile of his own.

"So the menu is glazed salmon, asparagus, steak, potatoes, and a variety of other vegetables and sides?" The manager of the restaurant we drove to asks. Her office is filled with Christmas decorations, and she has a bright smile as she goes over her notes.

"Yes," I answer, glancing over to find Carlos wearing a smirk. So what? Maybe he found the restaurant and saved the day even though he knows nothing about the area, but that doesn't give him the right to smirk like that. For some reason, the longer I stare at his smirk, the warmer my neck and cheeks become.

"Excuse me?" The woman asks, and I blink furiously, realizing she's been talking to me, and I've been ignoring her in favor of Carlos' smirk. Perfect. Just perfect.

"Sorry, what did you say?" I apologize, the flush on my neck turning to embarrassment.

"No worries," She says politely, offering me her folder. "This has all of the agreement details, and the form you'll need to fill out with all of the details. After that, I'll need your payment information, and then you're all ready to go."

"Thank you," I say, accepting the folder and pen she offers me. "Do you want to fill some of this out?" I offer Carlos. It seems like the right thing to do, since he's the one who found the place, but he just silently shakes his head.

I get to work filling out all of the order information, and after twenty minutes, I finally pass her back the paperwork. During the time I was filling it out, my eyes would drift upward, where I would find Carlos watching me intently. I'm not sure if his gaze ever left me the whole time. I'm also not sure why a flush would rise on my cheeks each time, or why my stomach would swoop with butterflies.

"Alright, just input your payment information here, and then you're all set." She says, turning the computer to me. I add all of the information for Charlie's banking, and with that, Carlos and I are on our way.

"See, we have that all fixed now. Not so bad." Carlos teases as he pulls onto the road.

"Be quiet." I huff.

"I'll be quiet if we can stop and grab food somewhere before we hit the main road," Carlos says, and I can almost hear his stomach grumbling.

"Okay, fine. There are probably some fast food restaurants around here." I agree. After a moment of cruising down the street, we find a cute burger joint that has a drive-through.

"Are you okay with this?" Carlos asks before pulling in behind the one other car.

"Yeah, hamburgers and fries sound really good, actually." I say, just as he pulls forward to order.

"Hi, what can I get for you today?" A boy's voice calls over the speaker.

"I'd like two hamburger meals with fries and ketchup. For the drinks, I'd like two milkshakes. One peppermint, and one chocolate, please."

"Your order will be at the window." The boy calls back before the microphone cuts off.

"How do you know I want a peppermint milkshake?" I ask suspiciously as he pulls forward.

"I like to call it intuition," Carlos says with a wink as he passes his card to the cashier.

"Okay, Mr. Intuition, maybe you were right." I tease as he passes me my milkshake. "This is actually really good."

"Good," Carlos hums as he takes the other food from the staff working at the window.

"Do you want to try it?" I offer. Maybe it's the fact that we shared the chocolate the other day, or the fact that he carried me across a snow-covered field, but the idea of allowing him to sip from my straw is almost natural and doesn't gross me out like it usually would.

"No thanks. I don't want to take your peppermint from you." Carlos says lightly, a teasing glint in his eyes.

"I wouldn't mind," I answer honestly.

"Really, I have my chocolate and I'm good." Carlos says lightly as he takes a sip of his own milkshake.

Does it offend me slightly that he doesn't want to try my drink when I'm offering it to him? Yes.

Should it offend me? No.

"Do you like scavenger hunts?" I ask as we near the *Welcome to Winterberry Hollow* sign thirty minutes later.

"I haven't done one in years, but I don't mind them. Why?" Carlos answers.

"There's a town scavenger hunt today, and if you have time, we could look for a few of the items." I offer, glancing over expectantly. I'm not sure why I'm even offering, because I've never really cared about the scavenger hunt.

Because you want to spend more time with Carlos.

Something in my brain screams this, and I push the

thought away, because there's no way that's the truth. Maybe I just want a friend to hang out with today, because all of my friends are working. Maybe I'm just doing what Poppy wanted me to do, and I'm showing Carlos around Winterberry Hollow.

"That sounds fun," Carlos says, glancing over at me before speaking again. "I'll do the scavenger hunt with you."

$$\mathcal{C}hapter\ \mathcal{N}ine$$

16 DAYS 'TIL CHRISTMAS

"**I**'d love to." I agree over the phone. "What time do you want to pick me up?"

"Well, Elisa agreed to pick up Anastasiya and Maisie at ten, so I'll pick you up right around then, too," Julia says, her voice muffled as she moves the phone. "Anastasiya spent the night with Maisie, so they're already together."

"Okay, that sounds fun. I'll call Carlos and let him know that we're going to take the day off from wedding preparations." I say, feeling slightly bad that he'll have to spend the day alone at the inn.

"Oh really?" Julia asks, suddenly perking up.

"Yes, Julia. We've been spending every day prepping the wedding." I say, hearing the sly tone that slipped into her voice.

"Just wedding preparations?" Julia says with a giggle. "You two seemed pretty close at the park."

"We're friends," I say firmly. "He's the best man and I'm the maid of honor."

"Whatever you say, Magnolia."

After a few more minutes on the phone, we hang up and agree to meet in an hour at my house, since Carlos still has my car. I suck in a deep breath before dialing Carlos' number, since we haven't really texted or called at all.

"Hello?" Carlos answers. His voice is deep, and for a moment, I forget that I'm supposed to speak. "Lia?"

"Hey, sorry for calling so early," I say, trying to remember why I even called in the first place.

"You're good." He answers, waiting for me to talk again.

"Do you want to take a day off from wedding preparations?" I blurt out. Is my tongue tied or something? Why can't I form basic sentences right now?

"I'm not opposed to it. Is there a specific reason why you want a break?" Carlos asks, sounding confused.

"I'm going to spend the day with some friends, and we're going Christmas shopping, so I won't have time." I say, realizing how it sounds like I'm excluding him. "It's a girl thing."

"Oh," Carlos says. "Yeah, I wouldn't mind a day off. Have fun." Really? Have fun? He doesn't sound upset, but is he?

"Will you be okay on your own?" I fret.

"Why would I not be?" Carlos asks with a chuckle. A rustling on the other end of the line catches my attention, and I realize that it sounds like he's still in bed. Did I wake him up?

"I don't know. Will you be bored? Lonely? Hungry?" I say, listing off the first things that come to mind.

"Lia, I'm an adult. You can spend a day not worrying about me." Carlos says, pausing as though he's thinking for a moment. "If I were bored, I would read a book. If I were lonely, I would go to the parlor and talk it up with the old people down there. If I were hungry, I would go to the dining room."

"You have this all figured out," I comment, his answers all valid.

"I flew here by myself, Lia. I'll be okay today." Carlos says with a chuckle. "Go shopping and let me go back to sleep."

"How rude," I tease, reaching into one of my drawers for my lip gloss. "Here I was, trying to check on you, and you're practically telling me to leave."

"I'm not practically telling you to leave," Carlos says, pausing for a moment. "I'm *telling* you to leave."

"Bye, Carlos." I barely make out through laughter. If I was worried about him before, I'm not anymore.

"Bye, Lia."

"I think there's more to you and Carlos than what you're letting on," Julia comments a few minutes into our drive. We're going to the area of town with the most shops and boutiques to find last-minute gifts.

"I think you're wrong." I counter, glancing over to meet her gaze.

"I think not. You were looking at him like you've never seen the male species before." Julia teases.

"That's not true."

"Oh, yes, it is. Let's ask the girls what they think." Julia says as she parks her car behind Elisa's. All three of them are already waiting outside of the car in their hats and gloves.

"Let's not-"

"Do we think Magnolia likes Carlos?" Julia calls out before we can even greet the other girls.

"Is that even a question?" Elisa asks.

"Did you see her face whenever she looked at him?" Maisie says with a giggle.

"Absolutely." Anastasiya agrees.

"Oh, come on, guys. This one isn't different from any other guy just because we're working together to prepare the wedding." I say, trying to sound as cool as possible. He *is* different from every other guy, but I don't want to admit that to any of them, because they'll take that as me admitting to liking him.

"You guys will never believe what I saw the other day," Anastasiya says as we walk into our first shop of the day.

"Tell us!" Maisie squeals, grabbing onto Anastasiya's arm.

"Well, we all know that I work at the tree farm, and there happened to be a certain couple that came by on Sunday." She says, glancing over at me for a dramatic effect. Oh no. I know exactly what she's going to say. "Their names were Carlos and Magnolia."

"You went on a sleigh ride together?" Elisa gasps, turning to face me. "And he's just your friend?"

"It's not exactly what it sounds like," I say, trying to protest against all of their curious gazes. My cheeks flush as I try to find a way to describe our relationship.

"Well, that's not all." Anastasiya continues. "Magnolia wasn't wearing the most *practical* clothes, so Carlos carried her across the field to the spot where their sleigh picked them up."

Everyone gasps, and then all of them are giggling. "Magnolia, he's *so* into you!" Julia exclaims. "You need to go get your man and stop pretending that you don't like him."

"He's not my man, and I'm sure he just sees me as a friend, too." I protest, knowing that it's pointless to even try to stop them at this point.

"Yeah, I'm sure that's what he thought when he was being all manly and carrying you across a snowy field to your magical sleigh ride." Elisa teases, giving me a pointed look.

"Guys, this is going too far." I huff, moving through the dresses in the rack in front of me. Why is everyone so invested in what's going on with us?

Julia sighs, but doesn't say anything else. Since she's my cousin, she's always teased me more than anyone else, but she seems to be realizing that I don't want to talk about this right now, and she's actually going to stop for a while.

Within a few minutes, we're chattering about what they're all going to wear to the Christmas ball on Christmas Eve, and that's when panic begins to race through me. I don't have a dress to wear, and I haven't even begun thinking about it. I guess that with Poppy's wedding, I've been too distracted to even remember that the ball is the night before.

Pulling out my notebook, just under the wedding list, I write *find dress for Christmas ball.*

"Tell us about Leo, Julia," I say as we squish into the booth at the diner.

"Wha- what about him?" Julia stutters, surprised by my sudden question. "What do you want to know?"

"What do you know?" I tease, noticing how her cheeks flush.

"He's just my coworker at the bakery. I guess he and his twin brother Romero," She glances over to get Maisie's agreement. "Just moved here with their parents."

"Yeah, I think Romero said they moved into their house on the fifteenth of last month." Maisie agrees.

"And?" Anastasiya prods, obviously curious about the twins, too.

"Well, he's an excellent baker, is kind of funny, and also really annoying." Julia finishes.

"That blush really shows how annoying he is." Elisa teases.

"Yeah, it really does." I agree, looking back at Julia.

"Okay, maybe he's a little bit cute, but he really is annoying sometimes. He's always teasing me, and almost gets us in trouble a lot." Julia persists, a small smile growing while she speaks.

"How?" Maisie asks, her eyebrows furrowing. "Romero isn't like that."

"He just... I don't know. He makes me laugh while I'm taking an order, or baits me into throwing flour at him." Julia says, as though this is the worst thing in the world.

"Wow, how terrible." Anastasiya laments. "I'm sure you get really *annoyed* by that."

"I do!" Julia pleads, but the flush on her neck and cheeks is enough to let us know that she's not being completely honest.

"Maisie, tell us about your twin," Elisa says, turning to Maisie.

"He's not *my* twin." Maisie quickly says, her voice turning squeaky as she hurries to shut down the idea of anything happening between her and Romero. "We both work at the inn, and we're really just coworkers."

"Yeah, of course." I tease.

"Yeah, of course." She echoes. Our food is delivered a moment later, and for a moment, there's peace again.

Chapter Ten

"Poppy called me earlier and said that the dress is ready for pickup in May," I say after I close the passenger door behind me.

"Hey, that's great. What time do we need to pick it up?" Carlos asks.

"Anytime today. She wants it dropped off at the seamstress here, because she wants the pearls on the back secured a little bit tighter, so we'll just need to do that before they close for the evening." I say, offering Carlos my phone so he can look at the directions.

"Okay, we can leave now, then." He says, putting the car into reverse. "How did your shopping go yesterday?" I blush thinking about how much I was hounded about him.

"It went well. We got a lot of Christmas gifts, and then went to lunch. Do you remember the girls from the park?"

"I don't remember their names, but I do remember them," Carlos says. "Were they who you went with?"

"Yeah, they are. We've all been friends for a few years,

and one of them is even my cousin." I say, suddenly feeling the urge to tell him everything about them. Why do I want him to know all of this about me? I never want to open up to people I haven't known for a while.

"Oh really? Which one?" Carlos asks, humoring me.

"She's the one who came with Leo, one of the twins," I say, hoping that it will jog his memory.

"I remember both sets of them coming, but I'm going to be honest and say that I couldn't tell the twins apart." Carlos says nervously with a chuckle.

"Neither could I," I reply with a giggle. "I hadn't met them before, since they're new to town. Julia—my cousin—isn't the one who works at the inn. That girl is Maisie, and the twin she works with is Romero."

"Oh, that's right. I guess since I didn't see her yesterday, I forgot that there was that connection there." Carlos says.

"Yeah, she was also with us yesterday. Her older brother is Lennox, and he works at the Christmas tree farm. You saw him, I think." I say, trying to remember that day when we went to the farm.

"Yeah, I think I remember him. Who was the guy who worked at the ornament decorating thing?" Carlos asks.

"Oh, that's Jacob. He's best friends with Lennox and Elisa—the girl who works there with him—and since Elisa and I are super close, us four hang out together a lot."

"That's cool." Carlos says, glancing out of his window. I follow his gaze to realize he's looking right at the edge of the mountain. My eyes widen as I realize that we're on the worst stretch of road. "Who was the girl we saw at the Christmas tree farm?"

"What?" I barely gasp out, my eyes never leaving the window.

"I asked who that girl was. She was at the park, right?" Carlos asks easily, as though we're not on the side of a mountain on a road that's covered in slush.

"Well, yeah, she is," I say, my mind scrambling. "She's best friends with Maisie, so they hang out a lot even without the rest of us. She's really nice, though."

"What's her name?" Carlos asks with a chuckle.

"Oh, right, that's Anastasiya. She works with Lennox, too. So she sees those siblings a lot." I say, remembering how Maisie had grumbled when she found out her best friend and brother would be working together. "Maisie felt left out for a while, but then she quickly got over it when she didn't have to work outside all of the time. She's much more of an indoors person."

"I haven't talked to her much while I've been at the inn, but she seems to enjoy her job," Carlos comments. "The guy working there—Romero, I think—doesn't seem to mind it either. I actually think that he works in the kitchen, sometimes."

"Really? I mean, it makes sense, since their chef always takes December off." I say, remembering what Maisie told me a few weeks ago.

"Why December?" Carlos asks, oddly intrigued.

"Maybe they have family elsewhere? I don't know, actually." I reply.

"Makes sense." Carlos comments, tapping his fingers on the steering wheel. "Where do you work?"

"I work at the library during the summer, but I'm not allowed to work during the semester or Christmas break," I say, smiling at the memories of organizing the shelves and reading to children. "What about you? Where do you work?"

"I work at a museum," Carlos says slowly, and before I can decipher why he's suddenly not as engaged in the conversation, he picks back up. "I give the tours."

"Do you enjoy it? What kind of museum is it?" I ask. For some reason, I *need* to know more about what he does. I need to know more about *him*.

"Yeah, I love it, actually. Sometimes the people make it less enjoyable, but other than that, it's still fun." Carlos says with a smile. "It's a Native American history museum."

"That's really cool, Carlos," I say, turning in my seat to watch him closer. "How do they make it less enjoyable?"

"Sometimes the guests are rude, or I have to tell them not to touch something a thousand times." Carlos says with a small laugh.

"Oh, interesting. How long have you worked there?"

"Two years, but I'll be quitting in a few months." Carlos says.

"Why? Don't you enjoy it?" I ask, confused.

"This is my last semester in high school, so I need to focus and work on my next steps in life." Carlos says easily, as though this is an obvious answer. "I do enjoy it, though. It's just something that won't last forever."

"I guess I can see where you're coming from there," I say, thinking about my next question for a moment before speaking. "What are your next steps in life? College? Moving?"

"College," Carlos answers. "And I'll move afterwards, but I don't know where, yet."

"Interesting," I hum as we pull into the dress store parking lot.

"Carlos, I don't want to seem like a backseat driver, but we need to hurry up if we're going to get it to the seamstress by five," I say, worry creeping in as I realize just how close we're cutting it.

"I'm driving as fast as the speed limit will allow," Carlos says calmly. "We're going to make it in time to drop it off."

"It's already four-fifteen, though." I counter. How are we ever going to make it in time?

"Lia, I can't drive any faster. We have until five, and we're only twenty minutes away." Carlos says evenly.

"My name is *Magnolia*." I say with a huff. Logically, I know that Carlos can't do anything other than keep driving. Illogically, I want him to come up with some sort of way to get us there faster.

"Tell me about your job at the library," Carlos says a minute later, breaking the silence that's filled with tension just as I begin looking out of the window at our current icy-road surroundings.

"What do you want to know?"

"What do you do? Do you enjoy it? Why aren't you allowed to work during the semester?"

"I fix the books when they're out of order, read the books out loud whenever there are events, and order new books, mostly." I say.

"So you're into books?" Carlos says with a chuckle.

"Pretty much. I love to read, so working at the library seemed like the best choice for me." I say with a smile. "Do you like to read?"

"Yeah, I enjoy it. I like a lot of non-fiction, though." Carlos says. "History, mostly."

"Ah, like the museum, right?" I say, connecting the dots.

"Yeah, exactly." Carlos agrees with a nod. "So what do you read?" I blush slightly at the question, because my answer usually opens me up to teasing.

"Well, I like to read romantic fantasy, but mostly contemporary books that have a lot of romance," I say, beating around the bush.

"So romance, really?" Carlos finishes.

"Well, yeah," I say sheepishly.

"Why don't you just like saying you read romance?" Carlos asks, genuinely curious.

"You like reading history and non-fiction, and I like reading romance. It makes me sound...uneducated or something, I don't know." I say, pressing my lips together as I try to find a better word to describe it. "People always tease me for reading romance books, so I try to avoid the topic as much as possible."

"Why do people tease you?" Carlos questions.

"I don't know. People are just rude, I guess."

"I guess," Carlos says, glancing over at the clock before speaking again. "So why don't you work during the school semester?"

"My parents don't want me to be distracted from my studies, so that's why I only work summers."

"And why don't you work during breaks?" He presses, as

though he's just dying to know why I don't work all of the time.

"Because usually during Christmas, when I'm not preparing for a wedding, then I'm hanging out with my family or being around the community." I begin. "My friends and I do a lot together during Christmas, and it's important to my family for us to be present together and with our friends."

"Interesting," Carlos says as he makes the final turn before Winterberry Hollow. "What in the..." He trails off as a line of cars in front of us slows us to a near stop.

"What's today?" I say quickly, glancing around for the date.

"The tenth," Carlos says. "Why?"

"This isn't happening." I breathe, reaching up to run my hand through my hair. "We're never going to make it to the seamstress on time tonight."

"Why not? What's going on?" Carlos asks, confused, but also concerned. "What's wrong, Lia?"

"This is the town light show. There's a guide car a few miles ahead of us, and they're going to lead everyone down a path that has Christmas lights." I say, trying to find the right way to explain it. "It's like little stories and scenes that are made out of the lights, and basically the whole town piles into their cars and goes through all of the scenes."

"But can't we just...*not* go with them?" Carlos asks, as though this is the obvious answer.

"Well, besides the fact that we're already in line and that we're going to be here for a while before we even need to turn," I say, taking a breath. "All of the other streets are closed. There is literally no other way to get out of this besides getting to the end."

"Oh," Carlos says, glancing over at the clock that now reads four-fifty. "So we're not going to make it to the seamstress tonight."

"Yeah, we're not going to make it to the seamstress tonight." I echo, feeling both frustrated and worried.

"So we'll just take it in tomorrow. Really, it can't take them that long to alter it, right?" Carlos says, as though this will make everything better.

"Well, I don't know, because I can't ask the seamstress, since we're not there." I huff.

"Well, I know that fixing a few things on the back of a dress can't take more than an hour." Carlos counters. He doesn't sound frustrated, but he does sound a little bit tired. "I guess we need to sit back and enjoy the show."

"How are we supposed to enjoy it when there's a wedding dress in the seat behind us that isn't ready for my sister to wear for her wedding?" I say, my voice coming out an octave higher than usual.

"Lia, there will always be hiccups, but I'm sure this is all a part of a bigger plan." Carlos says reassuringly.

"My name is *Magnolia*, and like I said, *everything* is going wrong." I feel tears prickling at the corners of my eyes and furiously blink them away. Why can't I ever make things go right?

"It's going to be okay," Carlos says softly. He reaches out to run his finger right below my eye, as though he's wiping away the tears before they can appear. I don't even pull away from his touch. It's soft and gentle in a way that I've never experienced before, and the second his finger moves away, I feel the burning heat of right where he touched me.

"But how do you know that? How do you know that I'm not going to ruin Poppy's wedding?" I say, quieter now. My voice is less full of frustration and more of worry.

"Because I know that we're going to handle it, and everything will be as perfect as we can get it." Carlos says firmly.

"But what if it's going to take weeks for the seamstress to alter it?" I question. "What if we don't even get all of the other stuff on the list done?"

"We will." Carlos says, full of conviction and earnestness. "Look, everyone is starting to move." I glance up to watch as lights all around us turn on. I can't help but smile at the bright lights, even though it's the last thing I feel like doing right now.

"They are rather pretty," I admit. "I think that Jacob might have helped with setting up some of them around The North Pole. We should be going around the whole town, so I guess we'll see."

"Really?" Carlos asks as he slowly accelerates the car. "Have you ever helped set up any of the lights?"

"Last year I went with Julia and we helped with some in the park. That's where most of the show will be, but you kind of have to look around everywhere for little lights here and there." I say, glancing out to see the first set of snowmen that are illuminated by red and green lights.

Carlos reaches out and switches on the local radio, which is playing Christmas music that should match most of the scenes. The main ones, at least. "Pay attention to the songs and the scenes around us," I say softly, unable to keep from explaining some of the tradition.

"Why?" Carlos asks with a smile. "Are they going to have a theme or something to match the scenes outside?"

"You just took the fun out of it." I tease, a smile rising on my cheeks, too."

"Oh really?" Carlos teases back. "You're the one who told me to pay attention."

"Yeah, but anyone can say that," I argue back. "You're being too smart right now, but what should I have expected from someone who reads history books for fun?"

"I was just trying to keep up with all of the crazy traditions that winter wonderland has to offer." Carlos teases back. "I don't know what to expect at this point. If you told me Santa Claus was going to fly overhead with his reindeer, I might believe you."

"I don't want to spoil that surprise for you, so I guess I won't say anything," I joke back.

"That sounds rather cryptic," Carlos says, sounding intrigued before turning his eyes back to the windows. "Do they do the same scenes every year?"

"What do you think this is? Of course not," I tease, rolling my eyes in mock-horror. "There is very careful thought put into what scenes are going to go where. We never do the same scenes over and over again. Especially not in order."

"Oh really now?" Carlos says lightly. "I guess I should have known better from someplace called Winterberry Hollow."

"You absolutely should have known better." I teasingly agree.

As the scenes roll by, my eyes keep drifting to Carlos. Which is weird, since all of the flashing lights are outside. Why can't I keep my eyes where they should be?

Carlos is watching out the window with the attention of someone who hasn't seen this much dedication to a Christmas light show in his entire life. I can understand how it might seem a little bit crazy, but it feels normal to me. It feels normal to celebrate the most wonderful time of the year with all the enthusiasm possible.

"Do you want a candy cane?" Carlos asks a moment later as we drive by the dancing candy cane scene. The peppermint candies are lined up to appear as though they're at a dance, and the flashing white and red is enough to mesmerize me for a moment.

"Why not?" I tease, taking the candy cane he's offering me in his outstretched arm. My fingers brush against his, feather soft, but it feels as though I've been shocked by the touch. After a moment, I notice that Carlos isn't eating a candy cane with me. "Why aren't you eating one, too?"

"I'm still full from lunch," Carlos says easily, as though the food is still enough to fill him up so much that a candy cane multiple hours later would destroy him.

"And you're seriously so full you can't have a candy cane?" I tease, placing the end of the peppermint candy in my mouth as I wait for his answer.

"I guess so." Carlos teases back.

"I guess you can just miss out then," I say, as though this will tempt him to have a candy cane with me.

"I guess I'll just miss out," Carlos agrees. We continue down the road, and soon enough, we're by the reindeer display. The Christmas light reindeer are obvious, but I hold my breath as I wait for Carlos to realize what else is outside.

"Are those..." Carlos trails off as his eyes focus on the animals within the reindeer display. "Real reindeer?" I giggle as his eyes widen in amazement.

"Yes, they are," I say with a smile.

"So you weren't actually joking about having a reindeer farm here?" Carlos asks, as though he didn't think I was telling him the truth that day.

"Of course I wasn't joking," I say, mock-indignantly. "Like you said, it's a winter wonderland here."

"Yeah, I guess it really is," Carlos says, but instead of facing the bright lights around us, he's only looking at me. Heat floods my body from my toes to the tips of my ears, but I can't figure out why. Why is my body having such a reaction to Carlos? Why am I looking right into his eyes instead of out the window and at the Christmas magic all around us?

As the light show goes on, my smile becomes easier, and the deep sense of worry in my chest loosens. The church is covered in light-angels, and on the large back wall, there's even a nativity scene, which has been done in such detail that it's breathtaking.

"That's really beautiful." Carlos comments as we pass it. "Are you sure you don't have actual elves out here putting these things together? They're all basically flawless."

"I know, right? I used to think that elves would come do them, because you almost never see them being put up." I admit. "They're done periodically throughout December, and since it's basically only lights, you don't notice them until they're lit. I remember being in awe every time we would drive through them for the light show every year."

"How come you're not with your parents driving through it?" Carlos asks a moment later.

"Well, besides the fact that I'm with you," I tease, gesturing between us. "My parents still love Christmas, but they really wanted *us* to love Christmas. They enjoy the Christmas service and decorating each year, but they're not as into the other things like driving through Christmas lights anymore."

"It's nice that even though they're not as into it, they still made an effort to bring as much joy to the season as possible." Carlos responds, sounding genuine.

"Yeah, it was." I agree, leaning back in my seat as we reach the end of the light show. "I'm so tired, and it's only six."

"You're tired?" Carlos teases. "I've never been any place that gets this dark so early. I'm constantly around lights in the city, even when it's night. It feels like bedtime for me as soon as it gets dark here."

"Really?" I ask, turning in my seat to face him. "You've been tired all of these days that you've been here?" Carlos smiles and nods his head.

"I'm seriously not used to it getting dark so early. My internal clock still hasn't gotten the message that just because it's pitch black outside, it's not time to sleep." Carlos says somewhat sheepishly.

"Oh wow. Here I am complaining about being tired, and I'm not even the driver." I say with a small laugh.

"No, it's fine." Carlos says quickly. "I don't mind being the driver."

"What, you just enjoy driving because you know that we're going to get to our destination in one piece?" I tease.

"I mean…" Carlos trails off jokingly. "Besides that, I just don't mind driving, either. It doesn't bother me."

"You'd be bothered if you were in the car with me driving." I tease, thinking back to all of the times I've accidentally hit a curb or taken a turn too sharply.

"Why's that?" Carlos asks. We're still technically in line, since it's going to take a while for all of the cars ahead of us to break off in the directions that they need to go.

"Well, this sounds bad, but it feels like the curbs jump out at me or something," I say, fighting back giggles. "And sometimes I don't know when to turn until the very last minute, so I end up swerving." Carlos raises his eyebrows at this.

"What are the odds that one of those things happens if you're driving around town?" He asks curiously.

"One hundred percent," I answer, covering my face with my hands in embarrassment. "I promise I passed my driver's test."

"So the curbs just come for you specifically?" Carlos teases as he finally eases out of the line.

"Exactly." I agree, nodding my head enthusiastically.

"I'll be sure to have a talk with the curbs here, then."

Chapter Eleven

14 DAYS 'TIL CHRISTMAS

"We're definitely going to make it to the seamstress on time today," Carlos says as we pull up in front of the building. The sign that reads, *Caroline's Thread,* is lit up with little Christmas decorations, and inside the large glass windows, I can see rows of cloth patterns and small pillows that are on display.

"Yeah," I agree as we step out of the car. Carlos opens the back door and pulls out the wedding dress box, carefully gripping it so that there's not a chance of it falling into the snowy slush around us.

"Do you mind opening the door?" Carlos asks as we walk to the front entrance. After I let him pass through, I follow along.

"Magnolia, how nice to see you. I just got a call from your sister a few weeks ago, and she told me that she would be bringing in the dress for a few alterations." Caroline says from behind the counter. Her jet-black hair has a few gray streaks within it, but they blend beautifully in the long braid that travels down her back.

"Oh, I'm sorry to disappoint you, but she's not in town yet. We're dropping off the dress for her," I say with all of the cheeriness I can muster.

"Well, isn't that nice of you," Caroline says, reaching out to take the box from Carlos. "She already gave me all of the instructions and the payment information, so all I need you to do is sign this paper that says you're the person who dropped it off."

"Okay, thank you," I say, stepping forward to sign my name on the dotted line.

"You're good to go, honey. I should have the dress ready for pickup by the seventeenth." My eyes widen at this, since that's just eight days before the wedding, but since Poppy already called in to give Caroline the instructions, she must know the timeline.

"Thank you, Caroline," I say as we leave the building. Once we're back in the car, I reach into my purse for our checklist. I cross off wedding dress, and just as I'm about to put my notebook back in the bag, Carlos speaks.

"Can I see the list?" He asks, glancing over at the things we still have to do.

"Sure," I say, passing it to him as I drop my pen back in the bag.

"What's the Christmas ball?" Carlos asks a moment later. I furrow my eyebrows and glance over, before realizing where he saw that. The other day, when I was shopping with the girls, I wrote down that I needed a dress for the ball on the same sheet of paper as the rest of the wedding checklist.

"Oh, there's like a Christmas ball here on Christmas Eve,

and I completely forgot about it until the other day when the girls and I went shopping." I say.

"Are you going to the ball?" Carlos asks, his voice curious.

"Yeah, probably. My friends and I always go." I say, chewing my lip as a wild idea comes to mind. "Do you want to come?"

"To the ball?" Carlos asks, turning even more to face me.

"Well...yeah?" I say, feeling self-conscious now. "If you don't want to go then-"

"I want to go with you, Lia." Carlos interrupts before I can continue spiraling. My pulse quickens, and I blink a few times before responding.

"You want to go with me?" I verify, needing to hear him say it again. Why does this mean so much to me?

"Yes." Carlos says, not missing a beat.

Chapter Twelve

13 DAYS 'TIL CHRISTMAS

"Do you want to do something different today?" I ask over the phone.

"Like what?" Carlos asks. He sounds more awake than he did the other day when I called him, but he still sounds somewhat asleep.

"So there's this white elephant thing going on at The North Pole for all of the local teenagers, and I still haven't bought a gift to bring. You could come along with me, and if you're interested, you could also participate with us." I explain.

"That sounds interesting," Carlos answers. "What time do you want me to be there?"

"Forty-five minutes?" I ask tentatively.

"I'll be there in forty-five minutes."

"So is it just going to be teenagers at the white elephant tomorrow?" Carlos asks as we stride through the shop doors. I chose one of the local boutiques to start with, and my eyes immediately catch on a mug that has a candy cane handle.

"Yes, it should be," I say, taking the cup off the shelf. "I think that I just found the first part of my gift."

"Already?" Carlos teases.

"Well, I need a few small things to add, but this is definitely going to be the base of the gift." I say confidently.

After a moment of walking around together, we both stroll our separate ways, and I pick up a few pens, candy canes, and a Christmas-themed notebook.

I glance over to see Carlos picking up a few items here and there, and after a few more minutes, he walks over to where I'm flipping through the stacks of classic books.

"Did you find all of your items?" Carlos asks, glancing down at the items I have in my arms. I picked out a small basket to go with it, and it appears as though Carlos did, too.

"Yep," I say, stepping towards the checkout register. "Did you?"

"Yeah, I think I found a few things that go together." Carlos says, setting his items in front of the woman behind the register.

"So what did you get?" I ask as I set my things on the counter, too.

"It wouldn't be much of a surprise, then." Carlos says as the woman places his things into a bag. He takes it and pays for them, and then I do the same with my stuff.

"It doesn't have to be a surprise." I comment as we walk out to the car. "Who's to say that I'll get your basket?"

"Who's to say you won't?" Carlos counters as he reaches out to open the passenger door for me.

"Fine, but it's not fair that you saw the mug in mine." I say as Carlos starts the car.

"What mug?" Carlos asks with a smile. His hair flops slightly as he turns to me, and for a moment, even if I wanted to speak, I wouldn't be able to. The twinkle in his dark eyes is more present than ever, and it's almost blinding.

Chapter Thirteen

12 DAYS 'TIL CHRISTMAS

"The white elephant is at seven, so that will give us plenty of time to go get the tuxedos and get back before we need to be at The North Pole," I say as we begin the drive to May. The tuxedos arrived at the store in May, and Poppy called last night right before bed to let me know that they're ready.

"Will there be any light shows tonight?" Carlos teases. I roll my eyes before responding.

"I should hope not." I tease. "But really, the lights will turn on every night when it gets dark, but there won't be another guided one like the other night."

"So we could just drive by the lights anytime we want now?" Carlos asks as he reaches over to turn on the radio.

"Yeah, we could," I answer, starting to hum to the Christmas tune. "Do you want to?"

"It might be nice to drive by them every now and then," Carlos says, his voice almost far away as his eyebrows furrow in thought.

"Why?" I ask, intrigue filling my voice.

"Do I need a reason to want to immerse myself in winter wonderland?" Carlos asks, mock-accusatory. "I would think that an elf of Winterberry Hollow should know that sometimes you just want to feel the magic of Christmas."

"Fine, fine, you're right." I agree. "But there's no other reason besides just wanting to drive by the lights?"

"What else would I want to do?" Carlos asks, as though I should have an answer.

"I don't know, you tell me." I tease, reaching down to pick up my water and take a sip.

"Maybe I just want to drive by the lights and feel like I'm in winter wonderland."

"Thank you so much, ma'am," I say as Carlos picks up the two tuxedos in their pressed bags.

"Of course," She says as she passes me the receipt. "Is there anything else I can help you with today?"

"No, I think we're good." I say, adding the receipt to my purse.

"Alright, then. Have a lovely day." She says as we walk out the door. Carlos carefully rests the tuxedos in the back seat, and within a few minutes, we're back in the car.

"Do you need to do anything else here today?" Carlos asks before he turns the car on.

"Like what?"

"I don't know," Carlos says with a chuckle. "We're already in the city, so if there's something you want to do before we leave, since we still have time, I don't mind not driving back to the hollow yet."

I consider his offer for a minute, and the first thing that comes to mind is finding a dress for the ball. Would that be weird to ask Carlos to come with me? Would he mind?

"Okay, where are we going?" Carlos asks with a smile.

"I never said I had to go anywhere," I quickly protest. Carlos is going with me to the ball, and up until this very minute, it hasn't sunk in.

I'm going to the ball with Carlos.

"Yeah, but your face said that you want to go somewhere." Carlos counters, turning in his seat to face me. How did he know that?

"Well, I need to get a dress for the ball, and there is a big mall right around here that would probably have some good options." I say slowly, a blush heating my cheeks as Carlos' expression changes slightly. I can't figure out exactly what he's thinking, but the expression on his face is adorable.

"So let's get you a dress for the ball," Carlos says as he starts the engine. "Where to?" I pass Carlos my phone with the directions, and he studies it for a minute before pulling out onto the road.

We step out of the car and into the bright parking lot a few minutes later, and the sun reflecting on the snow is blinding. "It's crazy to me that this is your view from the mall." Carlos comments as we start walking to the main entrance. I look down to watch my footing as I almost bump right into a car, because I'm on the side closest to the vehicles. It's so bright outside that I'm fighting my eyes to stay open and not shy away from the light.

"It's pretty cool, isn't it?" I say, glancing up to catch his reaction to the mountains around us.

"Yeah, it is." Carlos agrees.

The squealing of brakes jolts my attention to the car right in front of us as it begins sliding right towards us on the slushy lot. Just as my brain tells me to move to my left and go through the parked cars next to us, Carlos grabs my hand and pulls me to the right, all the way across the aisle. Our bodies slide into each other on the slippery slush, and just as we're stopped, the car lands with a *thump* against the cars that we were standing right next to, bumping them together.

"Are you okay, Lia?" Carlos asks, looking over my face carefully as though he's not still holding my hand. I blink furiously, completely still in shock from the whole event. "Lia?"

"Oh, yeah," I say, finally finding my voice. "I think I'm okay. I wouldn't have been if you hadn't pulled me this way, because I was completely going to move between those two cars."

Carlos barely smiles at this before glancing behind me at the man getting out of the car. "Are you two okay? I'm so sorry. I hit a patch of slush and completely lost control." He explains. His voice is deeply apologetic as he walks across the aisle to us. A few people start to gather around us to asses the damage, and while I'm aware of them, I'm more aware of the way Carlos' hand is still firmly gripping mine.

"We're okay," Carlos answers calmly. His voice is much slower and more cautious than it usually is.

"I need to go find the owners of these vehicles, if you're

sure that you're okay." The man says, glancing us both up and down as if to scan us for injuries that aren't visible to us.

"We're okay," Carlos agrees, squeezing my hand tightly before nodding his head. Once the man leaves and all of the people around us go in their separate directions, Carlos looks down and meets my eyes. "Are you still up for finding your dress?" Now that the initial shock has worn off, I feel pretty much like normal. My heart rate might be a little bit elevated, but it feels like it has more to do with the fact that Carlos' hand is still firmly wrapped around mine.

"Yeah, I am." I say with a nod. "Are you?"

"Never been better," Carlos says lightly, as though we just weren't almost crushed by a car.

"Dress shopping it is." I say.

"Have you ever assisted in dress shopping for a Christmas ball?" I ask Carlos as we stride through the doorway of the dress shop. He glances around before shaking his head profusely.

"Not at all." Carlos answers with a laugh.

"Look at you, gaining all of these new experiences on what was supposed to be a wedding vacation." I tease before stepping towards the first row of dresses. Carlos follows right along, and even if our hands weren't still firmly wrapped around each other, I still feel as though he would follow along.

"Life is funny like that," Carlos agrees.

"This is really pretty," I comment as my fingers run along the fabric of a red dress.

"If you want, I'll hold the dresses you want to try on." Carlos offers as I pull it off the rack. I pass the dress to him, and unfortunately, he drops my hand to take the dress.

"Thanks," I say as I pass him another dress. Carlos smiles as I continue to pass him dresses, and once I've picked out six to try on, we walk to the dressing rooms.

"I'll put these in the room for you, and then I'll wait out here." Carlos says as he steps into the room to place the dresses on the racks. After he leaves the room, I try on the first dress.

While I love the red sparkles, it feels too close to the dress I'm wearing at the wedding. I slip out of it and try on the green mermaid-style dress, and even though I think the straps are gorgeous, it's not the right style for the ball. I'm beginning to lose hope as I reach the last dress I chose, because the last five dresses haven't been what I wanted.

It's a dark ocean blue, with colors varying from dark blue to near-ivory, and off-the-shoulder sleeves. The sweetheart neckline lands just where I'm comfortable, and the gold detailing on the corset finishes the look.

This is the dress.

Should I show Carlos? Would it be weird to show him? Does he want to see?

"Are you doing okay?" Carlos calls through the closed door, as though I just mentally summoned him.

"I'm good!" I call back, slightly panicked because I didn't get a chance to decide whether or not to show him. "I found the dress I'm going to buy." I finally say, deciding that it's the easiest thing to do.

"That's good," Carlos says, sounding as though he's thinking. "Can I see?"

"Um, yeah. Give me a second." I call back through the door. Where did I put my hair tie? I took it off when I started trying on dresses so that I could tell how they looked with my hair.

Giving up after a minute, I push open the door and step into the room where Carlos is waiting. He's seated on one of the couches, leaning against the back with his legs sprawled out in front of him. Carlos dips his head slightly as I step in front of him, and his Adam's apple bobs as he nods.

"Wow," Carlos breathes. He swallows loud enough that I can hear him, and as he sits up straighter, his eyes never leave me.

"What do you think?" I ask somewhat shyly. His reaction has my toes tingling and my heart racing, but he hasn't said anything about what he thinks.

"I think you look...irresistible." Carlos says breathlessly. His eyes widen right after he finishes speaking as though he didn't mean to say that out loud. "The dress is perfect."

"You think so?"

Carlos nods quickly. "I know so."

"You made it!" Elisa squeals as we walk through the doors of The North Pole. "And you brought Carlos, too." She says, excitedly.

"Yep," I respond easily, as though showing up with the

boy I've been saying I don't like is the most normal thing ever.

"Well, come on, then. Everyone is just getting set up." Elisa says, tugging my hand as she leads me to the room where everyone else is. I glance back and meet Carlos' eyes as he follows us, carrying both of our baskets.

We all take seats around the room as Elisa explains the rules and shows us an example of how the game will work. "If everyone is ready, then let's begin." She finishes, reaching for the table to grab one of the baskets. Elisa draws a name from the bowl and calls out. "Julia."

After Julia opens the gift and shows everyone, Elisa moves on to the next person, and so on. Things start moving quickly as we progress, because we aren't exactly following the rules, and people are swapping left and right. Elisa doesn't seem to mind, neither does anyone else, and within a few minutes, the chorus of calls around the circle are so loud that I can't even tell what's happening.

"I'm setting a timer for one minute! By the end of that minute, the game is over, and whatever you have is your final gift!" Elisa calls out as she makes a show of setting a timer on her phone.

The shouting only intensifies as people move with a new rush to get the gift that caught their eye. I spy a set of classic books, and immediately start working towards it, but the game ends just as I get a basket that's not the books. Even though it was something that I wanted, I'm not sour about it, of course.

"Okay, everyone, show us what you have." Elisa calls out, her eyes bright with excitement.

Ahead of me in the circle, people start showing off their

gifts, and I notice that Maisie got my basket. Once it's my turn, I lift the basket that has a leather notebook, gel pens, wool socks, chocolate, and a Christmas bookmark that reads, *Joy to the world.*

Beside me, Carlos shows off his basket, and when I glance over, it's the classic books.

"The person who put together my basket did a good job," I comment as Carlos drives me home. We hung out with everyone else at The North Pole for a while, but when Carlos suggested that we leave, I agreed, since he still has to drive to the inn.

"You think so?" Carlos asks curiously.

"Absolutely. It has literally everything you could want." I say, nodding my head enthusiastically.

"That was the one I made." Carlos says with a smile.

"Really?"

"It has the notebook, socks, and chocolate, right?" He verifies.

"It does." I agree, suddenly giddy at the thought of getting the basket Carlos made. "You did a good job with it."

"Thank you," Carlos says, his voice almost bashful. After he pulls into my driveway, I don't get out immediately.

"Do you want to leave the tuxedos here with me? I'm going to take my dress, but I know that your tuxedo is in there, too." I ask, meeting Carlos' eyes.

"I'll take mine with me, but leave Charlie's here." Carlos says, glancing back at the back seat, which has accumulated more than a few things today. "I'll carry them in for you."

I pick up my dress as Carlos grabs the tuxedos, but I decide to make a second trip for my gift basket, just to be safe with my dress. "Where do you want these?" Carlos asks as he follows me into the entryway. My parents texted me to let me know that they would be out at dinner, so the only lights on are coming from the Christmas tree in the corner of the living room.

"Let's hang them up in the spare bedroom," I say, leading him into the downstairs guest bedroom. "The closet is empty, so you can hang them up there." Carlos follows my lead and hangs them there, and once he steps back, I hang my dress, too. It'll stay the safest here, since my closet upstairs is a little full at the moment.

"Do you want me to grab your gifts from the car? I'll get your purse, too." Carlos offers as we exit the bedroom.

"Yeah, that would be nice." I agree as I stop at the front door and take off my shoes. I'm hanging my jacket up as he walks back in the door, and he's carrying both of the gift baskets. "That one is yours."

"I'm not really into the classic romances, so you should have them." Carlos says easily as he extends it to me. I smile at his explanation, but hesitate to take it.

"Do you want the basket you made, then?" I offer, glancing at the gifts in his other hand.

"Lia, you're taking both of these baskets," Carlos says with a laugh as he presses the handles into my hands.

"If you're sure," I say, feeling slightly bad about him not having a gift anymore.

"I'm more than sure." Carlos says lightly. "I like how

your house looks like this, by the way. It really sells the winter wonderland package."

I glance around as though I'm taking it in for the first time at night, and it *is* pretty magical. "Thank you," I say softly.

I lift my eyes to Carlos' face, not expecting him to already be watching me. My breath quickens as the toy trains on the coffee table that run every hour start to twinkle, but I don't move my eyes from Carlos'. He doesn't even blink at the sudden interruption, and the room around us starts to crackle with electricity. The overwhelming urge to reach up and touch his face takes over my hand, and my fingers twitch with anticipation. What would happen if I brushed back the hair that's flopped on his forehead? What would Carlos do if I wrapped it around my fingers?

Wait, what? What am I doing? Why am I thinking this?

Carlos suddenly clears his throat and steps backwards, bumping into the door and tripping on the shoe I took off a few minutes ago. "I should probably get going." He says almost breathlessly. "Good night, Lia." And with that, he walks out the door, closing it carefully behind him.

What just happened between us? Carlos must have felt that, right? There's no way he didn't.

I rush upstairs and watch out of my window as Carlos backs out of the driveway. Something in my heart pulls for him to come back and retry whatever that was. What would have happened if I stepped closer and ran my hand through his hair?

Chapter Fourteen

"So, The North Pole is the place to be during December," Carlos concludes as I fill him in on today's agenda. We're going to volunteer as elves for The North Pole, because today is the day when hundreds of feet of popcorn get strung for the local community establishments. Families come by and drop their kids off for free entertainment, and in turn, there are plenty of extra hands to make the decorations.

"Absolutely." I agree as we get out of the car. "I usually volunteer a few times during December, but this year, with all of the wedding preparations, I haven't been able to. It's really fun."

"How hard can wrangling a hundred kids be?" Carlos teases as he reaches out to open the door.

"I know, right?" I joke back. "It's not like we're giving them a sharp needle and gigantic bowls of popcorn or anything." Carlos swallows loudly but doesn't say anything as we walk through the hall to the large room where Elisa, Jacob, and Anastasiya are finishing setting up.

The tables and chairs each have bowls of popcorn, needles and thread, and snacks.

"This is quite the setup," Carlos comments as he glances around at the tables.

"You can thank me for that," Anastasiya calls out. "These two had nothing ready when I got here an hour ago."

"Not true!" Jacob calls back. "We were busy all morning, and working as fast as possible."

"Jacob is telling the truth." Elisa agrees with crossed arms. "Being an elf is a busy job."

"Uh-huh." I tease as we walk closer to them. "We'll see just how true that proves to be today."

"Oh, you and Carlos will be thanking us for the many hours spent here, and will regret doubting our dedication to work." Elisa teases. "This year especially has been so busy. It's too bad that Julia won't be here."

"I was texting her this morning, and she told me that since it's the cookie decorating here tomorrow, she and Leo are working on all of the cookies today. Apparently, the board ordered about a million cookies." I offer. Since The North Pole is run by the city, they decide all of the events that will take place over Christmas. Every December, they change up which local businesses they're going to purchase the activities from, and this year, it's the bakery that Julia just started working at.

"Yeah, there are supposed to be a lot of people this year, after it was such a big hit last year." Jacob agrees.

"At least Maisie and Lennox will be able to come," Anastasiya says, trying to brighten the mood.

"They're coming?" Elisa asks, turning to Anastasiya. She nods quickly.

"Yeah, they're coming. Yesterday, Lennox told me that since they both have the day off, they were going to come by and be unofficial elves." She explains.

"Unofficial or not, more elves are always welcome when needles are involved." Jacob jokes. "Hopefully, everyone who drops off their kids reads the warning sign."

"Magnolia, can you help me with this popcorn? I can't get it through." A little boy to my left asks. He's staring up at me brightly as I thread the piece for him. "Thank you."

I glance over to see Carlos crouched beside a group of little girls as he strings the first few pieces of popcorn. They're all giggling around him as he works, but he's completely focused on the popcorn. It almost looks as though he's chewing his lip in deep concentration.

He passes off the string to the girl closest to him, and her braids bounce excitedly as she takes the popcorn. Carlos immediately stands and steps back as they all begin on their own strings. I glance down to make sure everyone at the table I'm monitoring is doing okay, and walk over to Carlos.

"It seems like you're quite the teacher," I comment as I stop next to him. Our bodies are so close that I could move just a few inches and then be touching him. The Christmas music playing over the speakers changes, and the gentle piano of one of my favorite songs begins playing.

"Something like that." Carlos agrees. He's watching all

of the children at his table carefully, and doesn't look over when he speaks.

"Are you having fun?" The question pops out of my mouth before I even realize what I'm saying, and I cringe.

"Why wouldn't I be?" Carlos asks, his voice completely surprised.

"I don't know," I answer truthfully. "You just seem kind of quiet."

"I'm having a great time, Lia." Carlos says lightly, as though he doesn't know what else to say.

"You keep having fun, then. I have to get back over to my group." I say with a smile before turning back to my table.

"How did you have enough time to watch all of your kids *and* make a whole popcorn string?" I ask Carlos as we drive back to my house.

"I don't know," Carlos says with a smile. "I just wanted to do something with my hands, so I guess I just made it in between helping them all."

"It's really pretty," I say, noticing how he methodically added in a few of the cranberries throughout the chain.

"You can keep it." Carlos says easily. "I don't have anywhere to put it."

"You can't keep doing this, Carlos." I say exasperatedly.

"Doing what?" Carlos asks immediately. His eyebrows furrow as he tries to puzzle out what I'm referring to.

"Giving me gifts because you don't have space." I huff.

"I haven't given you any gifts, and here you are, giving me something almost every time we go out."

"I don't think of it that way, Lia." Carlos says quickly. "I don't expect anything in return from you, and I really don't mind giving you these things that I don't have space for." I glance over to meet his gaze, which is earnest and kind.

"We're going to need to buy you another suitcase or something so you can take your memories of Winterberry Hollow with you, so that you don't forget about it." I say, not realizing just how soft my voice is. Carlos presses his lips together before speaking.

"I'm never going to forget this month, Lia."

Chapter Fifteen

10 DAYS 'TIL CHRISTMAS

"Do you want to get lunch before we decorate cookies?" Carlos asks over the phone. I glance over to the clock that reads nine forty-five, and run through the things that I have to do before I can agree to going anywhere.

"I'd love to," I answer, leaning back on the chair before speaking again. "I need to do a few things around the house before I can leave, but I should be done by about eleven. Does that work for you?"

"Eleven is fine." Carlos says quickly. "What are you doing around the house?" His voice is curious as he asks, and I can almost picture the face he's making.

"I need to tidy a few things and plan dinner. I'm going to be making dinner tonight, so I need to make sure I have it all ready, that way, I can have my parents stop by the grocery store after work."

"That sounds nice," Carlos says, and I hear the rustling

of something on the other side of the line before he speaks again. "What are you making?"

"Fish, potatoes, and vegetables," I answer, taking a sip of my hot chocolate as fuel. "Do you want to eat dinner with us?"

There's silence on the other end of the line, and I almost hang up right then and there. Of course Carlos doesn't want to eat dinner with us. Why would I even ask that?

"I'd love to."

"You know, we could go by the grocery store after we decorate cookies, if you want to." Carlos offers as we study the lunch menu. "If you don't want to have your parents go after work."

"That would be amazing, actually." I agree, glancing up to meet his eyes. "Thank you."

"Don't worry about it," Carlos says with a smile. "I'll be receiving the real Winterberry Hollow grocery shopping experience."

We order a few moments later, and a text buzzes through on my phone. It's from Julia, asking if I'm going to be at the bonfire tomorrow night. A wild thought pops into my head, and I act on it without thinking of the repercussions.

"Do you want to go to a bonfire with me tomorrow night? It's something a lot of teenagers put together each year, and a few of my friends will be there." I ask, looking at Carlos expectantly. Say yes, please.

"That sounds fun," Carlos answers with a smile. "Will I freeze out there, though?" He asks with a laugh.

"I mean, it's pretty cold here in general, and even colder at night, but the fire kind of balances it out." I offer.

"Then it's a date." Carlos says. Before I can ask him what he means by that, our food is being delivered, interrupting us.

"I know everyone can see the lovely cookies over there, and I know that they smell absolutely delicious, but please refrain from only eating the cookies today. We're here to decorate." Elisa calls out from the front of the room. Jacob is standing next to her, but he allows her to do all of the speaking. "Of course, you can munch on a few cookies, but let's remember to decorate before we eat." She gestures for Jacob to finish.

"With that amazing speech from Elisa, everyone is welcome to start decorating." Jacob finishes, gesturing to the platters of cookies on the tables that line the walls. There must be at least a thousand cookies.

Julia and Leo are nowhere in sight, and I wonder if they decided to take a break from cookies for the day, since they're both off after hours and hours of baking and packing these last few days.

"Ladies, first," Carlos says as he lowers his head to speak softly in my ear. Goosebumps flood my skin as his breath warms my neck, and for a moment, I don't even register what he's saying.

"Oh, right," I say, stepping forward as the children who

swarmed the platters rush to tables and start picking up bags of icing and sprinkles. Julia and Leo made all of the icing and decorations, and my head starts to spin as I imagine making all of this.

I pick a few different cookies to decorate, and Carlos is behind me, choosing a few of his own. He carefully looks over the cookie names and ingredients, as though the titles are the most important thing in the world.

For a moment, I glance around for an empty table, and I finally spot one last empty table at the corner of the room. Carlos is close behind me as I walk towards it, and instead of sitting at one of the other chairs at the table, he sits down in the chair right next to mine.

"So, what are we making?" Carlos asks as I reach for a green icing bag.

"What?" I ask, not even considering the question.

"What are we making?" Carlos questions again with a grin. I can't even help a grin from growing on my cheeks as I turn to him, our faces inches apart.

"I'm making a wreath on this one," I say, lifting the cookie currently in my hand. Carlos nods and allows me to use the green on my cookie before using it to make a wreath on his own cookie. "Are you going to copy me?" I tease.

"Let's call it taking inspiration," Carlos teases back.

"I'll allow it, I guess." I say, leaning over to bump my shoulder against his.

"Hey, now you're sabotaging me?" Carlos asks, mock-horrified. "I'm surprised with you, Lia."

"Sabotage, now? What an accusation, Carlos." I tease back. "I would *never*."

"Yeah, I believe you." Carlos says with a roll of his eyes.

"Thank you," I say, turning to look up with a smile. "I appreciate your agreement."

"Whatever you say, Lia." Carlos says with a smile equally as wide.

"Now, tell me what we're going to be getting today," Carlos says as he grabs a shopping cart. A nice blast of warm air and Christmas carols greets us as we stride into the supermarket, and I shrug off my purse to set it in the basket up front.

"I need some vegetables, a dessert, spices, bread, and milk," I say, going over the mental list.

"Lead the way," Carlos says with a dramatic gesture of his hand. We start in the produce section, and I allow Carlos to choose the mushrooms and bell peppers while I find the potatoes.

After we gather everything but the dessert, we walk to the in-store bakery, which has the delicious aroma of baked goods floating around the store.

"What should we get for after dinner?" I ask, turning to Carlos. He's been dutifully following me with the shopping cart, occasionally offering his opinions as I pick up things.

"What do you want?" Carlos asks as he steps up next to me. The assortment of cakes, pies, cupcakes, and cookies is wide, and if it were up to me, I'd probably buy one of everything here.

"I asked you." I tease, stepping over to bump my arm against his. "Give me your opinion first."

"I really like lemons, so maybe something with that?" Carlos offers vaguely.

"I can get on board with that," I agree, glancing over the desserts with lemon. "What about that lemon meringue pie? Do you enjoy those?"

"I do," Carlos says slowly. "Do you?"

"Of course I do." I tease, reaching into the fridge for the pie. "Do we agree on the pie?"

"Yes," Carlos says with a smile as I set it in the cart before starting the short walk to the checkout line.

"Do you want to try one of my cookies?" I ask Carlos as he parks in my driveway. We've been sitting here for a few minutes without much conversation, but it hasn't been uncomfortable. Rather, I'm *too* comfortable.

"What kinds do you have?" Carlos asks curiously.

"All of mine are peppermint chocolate. The icing is different, though." I answer, lifting them so he can see them.

"No thanks, then. I don't want a lot of chocolate right before dinner." Carlos says apologetically.

"Are you sure? You can't just say no to my offering." I say a little bit defensively. "It's not like they're poisoned or something." Carlos chuckles at this, and a small smile cracks on his face. Of course he doesn't want to eat one of my cookies. Why would he want to?

"Lia, I'm not even going to eat one of my cookies before dinner. Thank you for the offering, though." Carlos says easily. "It's not like I can stay in shape by only eating cookies instead of dinner." I instinctively glance over at his arm. Sure, he's wearing a sweater, but there is obvious muscle definition beneath it.

"Okay, okay," I say, my cheeks heating as I become flustered with the turn in direction my mind went. "Do you want to just hang out here while I make dinner? That way you don't have to drive to the inn and then come back in about an hour and a half?"

Carlos smiles and nods, and I can't help but smile back at him. His teeth are pearly white and so perfectly straight that it's illegal. "I'd like that."

Carlos follows me in the door, and after taking my boots off and hanging my jacket up on the hook, I turn to him. "I'm going to run to my room and then I'll be right back," I say, gesturing to the staircase. "You can hang your jacket there, and put your boots under the bench."

I take the stairs two at a time, and after making my way into my closet, I pull out an older sweater to exchange for the top I'm currently wearing.

"You can come into the kitchen and sit at the stools," I offer Carlos as I walk past him. "Do you want anything to drink?"

"A water would be nice," Carlos says as he follows me into the kitchen. "I don't mind helping, too. I don't want to just sit here and do nothing."

"You're the guest, though." I counter as I pull my apron out of the pantry and reach for a cup.

"And?" Carlos asks as he steps forward to take the cup and use the water filter to fill it. He takes a sip before glancing down at me. "I'm a good chef."

"Okay, well, you're also a guest." I say, at a loss for words for a moment. "You should take a rest from all of the driving and just relax."

"Cooking is relaxing." Carlos says with a raised eyebrow. "I'll even do the boring jobs like peeling potatoes." I press my lips together in defeat because there's no way I can keep telling Carlos no.

"Fine, you can help," I say as I loop the apron around my middle. "There's another apron in the pantry, if you'd like to wear one." Carlos reaches into the pantry and pulls out my backup apron, and instead of putting it back like a normal person would, he laughs before putting it on.

It may or may not be the epitome of Christmas cheer, but all Carlos does is laugh again as he ties the middle. The stitched depictions of Santa, reindeer, candy canes, cookies, hot chocolate, and a few other things cover the apron, and I have to say that it looks *really* good on Carlos. Why does he have such a defined waist?

"So do you want to start peeling some potatoes?" I offer Carlos as I pull out everything he'll need. "I'm going to start on the vegetables."

"Yep." He says as he takes a potato and a knife to peel it.

A few minutes pass by, and I can't help but fill the silence. "Do you do a lot of cooking at home?" I ask, glancing up from the vegetables I'm cleaning.

"I think so," Carlos says with a smile. "I don't cook all of the meals or anything, but I do cook here and there."

"Same." I agree, nodding my head. "I try to cook dinner once or twice a week, because I see meal ideas on the internet or something, and then I want to try them out."

"So is this something you're making for the first time?" Carlos asks as he gestures to the fish, vegetables, and potatoes. "Obviously, you've made these things separate before, but all together?"

"This combination is actually pretty common in Norwegian households," I say sheepishly. "So I've made it more than a few times."

"Oh, I see," Carlos says as he nods in acknowledgment.

"So what do you usually make? New recipes or ones that you've perfected?" I ask.

"Both. I mostly stick to learning traditional Mexican dishes, but then I like to try out whatever is popular at the moment."

"That's really cool," I say, meaning it. "I bet you're a pretty good chef."

"Thank you," Carlos says as he looks up from the potatoes he's cutting. He doesn't say anything, but his whole face is concentrated on mine, and it seems as though everything around us stills when our eyes meet.

My fingers flex at my side as I imagine running my hand through his dark hair. It must be *so* soft. The way Carlos' soft waves flow down his head and cover his ears is both adorable and extremely hot.

As if acting on their own accord, my eyes lower to his puffy lips, and I don't miss the way his tongue quickly slips out of his mouth and moisturizes them, making them even more noticeable.

The front entry door clicks shut, and I blink rapidly as I turn and glance around the wall to the hallway. "Hi, Mamma," I call out. "Hi, Pappa."

"Hello to you, too," Pappa says as he strides into the kitchen. "Hello, Carlos. Are you going to be joining us for dinner?"

"Yes, sir." Carlos says with a smile.

"How lovely!" Mamma calls out as she joins us. "Why didn't you tell us that we'd be having a guest? We would have brought some dessert home or something. Here, why don't I run up to the bakery and grab a cake?"

"We already went to the grocery store, and we picked up a dessert, too," I say quickly before she can reach for her car keys. She removes her hand from her purse and lets out a quick exhale.

"Oh, thank you, Magnolia and Carlos. I was worried there for a moment." Mamma says with a light laugh. "Sorry, Carlos, hosting is a very big deal for me."

"No worries, ma'am," Carlos says easily, as though this whole interaction hasn't surprised him. Once my parents leave to change out of their office clothes, Carlos looks up with a grin. "I can tell which of your parents you resemble more."

"I know, right? People always say that Pappa and I have the same eyes." I say, nodding my head.

"No, I meant that you and your mother have the same personality." Carlos says with a laugh. "It was like you were talking to yourself right there."

"What do you mean?" I ask quizzically, narrowing my eyes in confusion.

"I mean that everything from her mannerisms to how she speaks is like you. Well, I guess you're like her, but you get the point." Carlos says as though this is obvious.

"You think so?" I ask, mulling over my interaction with Mamma. Nothing interesting or out of the ordinary happened.

"One hundred percent."

"So, Carlos, tell us a little bit about yourself. Poppy said that you're eighteen, right?" Mamma asks over dinner.

"Yes, I just turned eighteen last month," Carlos confirms. "Well, I live with my parents in New York, I'm a senior in high school, and that's pretty much it for interesting facts." Carlos says sheepishly.

That's it? What about how he works at a history museum? Or how he doesn't want to live in the city forever?

I'm pretty quiet through the rest of dinner, since Mamma and Carlos are keeping up a rapid conversation, and frankly, I don't trust myself not to say something I'll regret later. Like everything I know about Carlos, when Mamma asks something about him.

Every so often, Carlos will glance over and meet my eyes as he's speaking, as though he's wondering why I'm not contributing to the conversation.

Chapter Sixteen

9 DAYS 'TIL CHRISTMAS

"I know that this isn't your job, but if you wanted to help me moderate the hot chocolate and movie tonight at The North Pole, I'd be forever grateful." Elisa says over the phone. "One of the other elves called in sick, so it's going to be just me and Jacob tonight."

"Yeah, I don't mind helping. If I ask Carlos and he says yes, do you want his help, too?" I ask, knowing that he'll say yes.

"A million times over." Elisa agrees immediately. "And, it might be fun for you two to hang out together."

"Elisa," I say carefully. "We're just friends."

"Just friends? That's literally my *least* favorite saying in the entire world." Elisa says, frustratedly. "Can't people just communicate or something? I don't know."

"Are you going to the bonfire tonight?" I ask, changing the topic.

"Yeah, I think I will. I'm going to be there later than everyone, since I'll be on cleanup and everything for The

North Pole." Elisa says. "You're not on cleanup or anything, by the way."

"Carlos and I will be there at about seven, if that's okay," I say, leaning against the doorframe to study my ball dress. It really is gorgeous, and I can't wait to wear it.

"That works just fine. The movie starts at about seven forty-five." Elisa agrees. "Thank you again. I don't know how *only* Jacob and I got scheduled for tonight. This is a task for a minimum of four people."

"Don't worry about it. See you in a few hours."

"Hot chocolate and a movie sounds like a fun way to prepare for a freezing cold bonfire." Carlos chuckles as we walk up the street. He called and asked me this morning if I'd like to go on a walk around town, since he hasn't really explored the downtown areas.

"I know, right? We'll be all set to freeze for a few hours." I tease, looking up at him with a grin. There must be something infectious about Carlos' laugh, or maybe just him in general, because every time I'm around him, I end up laughing.

"Freezing with you doesn't sound too terrible, though," Carlos says a moment later. What? Did he just say that in general, or does he really mean that he doesn't mind the conditions if he's with me? He probably didn't mean to add that part.

"You think so?" I ask curiously a moment later.

"I think so." Carlos says, glancing down with a smile that sends my stomach into somersaults.

Why does his smile make me feel so happy and excited? Why does my heart flutter every time he looks at me like there's no one else around us?

"Are you excited for the ball?" I ask as we pass a dress shop.

"I have no idea of what to expect, but yeah, I am. I think it's going to be really fun." Carlos says with a nod of his head. "How many times have you been to it?"

"Five times," I say, trying to remember each and every ball.

"So everyone will know exactly what they're doing except for me." Carlos says lightly. I can tell that it's meant as a joke, but it might carry some weight behind it.

"There's no right or wrong thing to do," I say quickly. "You can dance, right?" Carlos nods.

"Yeah, I took ballroom dancing lessons from the time I was ten to fifteen. My mom was very serious about being able to impress a girl with dancing abilities." Carlos says with a small laugh. "Hopefully it'll work."

Does that mean he's trying to impress me with his dancing? Or just in general? Is there someone else he's going to try to impress at the ball?

"It's cool that you've taken so many dancing lessons. I'm sure you'll be more prepared than most of the people there." I say quickly, still flustered from his comment about trying to impress someone. "There will be food, dancing, and all of that fun stuff, so nothing too crazy."

"That sounds simple enough. I'll try not to embarrass

you with my lack of Winterberry Hollow tradition knowledge." Carlos teases.

"Nonsense," I say hurriedly. Carlos smiles at this, and I desperately want to know what he's thinking about. I want to know all of his thoughts. I want to know everything about him.

"And what would you like in your hot chocolate, honey?" I ask the tiny girl in front of me. She must be six or seven, and her big, dark eyes are the cutest things I've ever seen.

"Peppermint, whipped cream, sprinkles, and cinnamon, please." She says excitedly, wrapping her arms around her middle as she anticipates her hot chocolate.

I turn to Carlos, who is doing the actual making of the cups, and he nods before quickly preparing her drink.

The hot chocolate is far from hot since we don't want any burned mouths around here, and Carlos works quickly to mix everything. He first adds whipped cream to the bottom of the cup, then adds the cinnamon, then the hot chocolate, more whipped cream, and he finally takes careful caution to unwrap the candy cane and place it inside the drink, all without touching it. Of course, we've been told to be sanitary, but you would think the Health Department is a call away by how careful he is not to touch anything.

"Here you go, kiddo," Carlos says as he passes her the cup. I tell her which spot to sit down at and begin taking the next kid's order.

Thirty minutes go by before we get everyone with their drink, and Elisa finally clicks play on the movie. The children all calm down, and the loud chatter becomes hushed whispers. Carlos and I make our way to the back of the room, where we lean against the wall. Elisa and Jacob are on the other side of the room, and they seem to be having a hushed conversation.

"This is pretty fun," Carlos comments a moment later. His mouth is dangerously close to my ear, and while the sparks of electricity in the air flit around us, goosebumps flood my skin.

"The movie?" I ask, moving even closer to him. Our bodies are so close, but it doesn't feel like enough. The pull to him is so strong, and right now, in the darkened room with his deep voice by my ear, I feel as though anything could set my body on fire.

"Being here with you." Carlos answers. I still for a moment before turning to face Carlos.

"Do you mean that?" I ask, glancing up through my eyelashes as I speak. I await breathlessly for his response.

Carlos' Adam's apple bobs when he nods. "Yes."

"It's going to be a cold walk." I comment as we walk to the car. All of the children have been picked up, and Carlos and I are officially clocked out of our 'job.'

"How far will we have to walk?" Carlos asks as he opens the passenger door for me.

"Probably about a half-mile," I say. "The path isn't super rough or anything, but it will be snowy."

"Just tell me where to park," Carlos says as he pulls into the town park a few minutes later. The path through the trees starts near the parking lot, so at least there's a real spot to park.

"Right about here is probably good," I say as he slows near a car I recognize. "This is Julia's car, so she's probably already there."

"She's your cousin, right?" Carlos asks as he puts the car in park.

"Yep," I say with a nod. "Look at you, remembering everyone here in Winterberry Hollow."

"I wouldn't go that far, but thank you." Carlos teases as we get out. "I need to get my jacket out of the backseat."

I walk behind the car and wait for Carlos as he rummages around the car, and just as I'm about to check on him, he finally walks over to me.

"Ready to go?" I ask, looking up at him through my eyelashes.

"Yes." He agrees, reaching down to pick up my hand with his. Sure, it's rather hard to hold hands while wearing mittens, but I don't mind.

I really should have packed a scarf or something. The wind isn't too terrible, but my neck feels frozen. My free hand lifts to my hood again as I try to tighten it around my head, but it doesn't do any good.

"Are you cold?" Carlos asks. We must be about halfway down the trail, and the faint smell of smoke drifts toward us. We're entirely alone, and the only sounds around us are the branches rustling together in the wind and the crunch of snow underfoot.

"Just a little bit." I say sheepishly. "I'm fine, though. Once we get there, I can sit facing away from the wind."

Carlos smiles softly, and I wouldn't be able to catch it without the bright moonlight above us.

"I've been meaning to give you this, and right now seems like the right time to do so." Carlos says, reaching into the small satchel he grabbed from the car. I squint for a moment as I realize what he has in his hand. It's a scarf.

Not just any scarf, but the one I was admiring at the Farmer's Market a few weeks ago. When did he get it? How did he know I wanted it?

"Oh my gosh, when did you get it?" I ask, a small smile growing on my face. "This is the one that I really loved."

"I know," Carlos says with a small laugh. "That's why I got it."

"How did you know?" I question, turning to face him better.

"I saw you looking at it like you thought it was the prettiest thing ever, and it seemed like a good gift." Carlos says softly. "I hope you like it, Lia."

"I love it, Carlos." I say, stepping even closer so he can wrap it around me. Carlos carefully unwraps it and begins gently tying it. "Thank you so much."

"You're welcome," Carlos says softly as his hands move over the scarf. I still entirely as his fingers brush my neck. My heart pounds in my chest, and I can feel it all the way down to the tips of my fingers.

"I'm sorry I haven't gotten you anything like this. I've been a terrible-"

One second, I'm speaking, and the next, Carlos is using

the ends of the scarf to tug me even closer to him, and then his lips are on mine.

Carlos' lips should be cold and firm from the freezing temperature around us, but they're warm a soft as he gently kisses me.

They're *so* soft.

My hands are only at my side for a moment as I try and figure out what to do with them before I bring them to the sides of Carlos' face and draw him even closer.

My lips finally begin moving against Carlos' with gentle coaxing from his lips, and this is decidedly the best kiss I've ever experienced.

This is the best kiss in existence.

Maybe my knowledge is very limited, and I haven't kissed every person in the world, but there's no doubt in my mind that anyone has ever felt this from a kiss before.

The sound of my heartbeat must be audible to the whole forest, because it's all I can hear in my ears, and every vessel in my body is pounding with the racing thrum of it.

Carlos' fingers drift up from my scarf and to my cheeks as he moves his lips even more intensely on mine.

I'm not even sure if I'm breathing at this point, and it could be seconds or hours that we're kissing. However long it is, it's not enough. I wrap my hands around the back of his neck and pull him in even closer, deepening the kiss.

Carlos finally pulls away, and it looks like he's gasping for breath. I'm not entirely sure, though, since I can't hear anything over the pounding of my own heartbeat and the rasp of my lungs as they scream for air. Is it normal to feel so breathless over a kiss?

My knees still feel weak, but when I glance up at Carlos,

he's smiling at me with the face of a boy who can't believe what he just did.

"Why did you kiss me?" I ask a moment later once we're walking down the path again. The chatter of people is becoming louder and louder, and I can see the glowing orange and red of the fire through the trees.

"Besides the fact that I've wanted to kiss you since the first time we met?" Carlos asks with a chuckle. My jaw drops at this, because there's no way he has wanted to kiss me for this long.

"Is there another reason?" I barely get out.

"You just started apologizing for not getting me a gift when you were never expected to, and then you started going down this stressed-out spiral, so I don't know," Carlos says nervously. "It just seemed like now or never, I guess."

"Well, what a reason," I say with a laugh as we walk into the clearing. So was it really just because he wanted me to be quiet?

The fire is huge, and I can already feel the heat radiating off it. I glance around for any of my friends, but with everyone seated on the logs or in their chairs, bundled up in jackets and blankets, it's hard to tell who is who.

Maisie is sitting with Anastasiya in a large camp chair a small distance away, and Julia is sitting with Leo on the other side of the fire. I don't see anyone else I'm close with, but I do know everyone else here.

"So do we just sit wherever we'd like?" Carlos asks a moment later as I watch people make s'mores and hot chocolate from the table a few feet away.

"Yeah, we can." I agree, nodding my head quickly. "But do you want to make me a s'more first?" I ask, looking up with my best pleading eyes possible. Carlos nods immediately.

"Yeah, I can do that. How browned do you like your marshmallows?" Carlos agrees.

"Not very," I say, thinking for a moment. "You know right when it's starting to get brown and looks like it's about to start melting on the skewer?" I ask with a tilt of my head.

"Yeah, I can do that." Carlos says easily. "I'll be back in a minute with your s'mores."

I move to a nearby log that has space for one more person, and watch Carlos as he browns the marshmallows and walks to the guy who's helping with the crackers and chocolate. Carlos says something to him, which makes him laugh, and he places my s'mores on a plate before handing them to Carlos.

"Two s'mores for Lia." Carlos announces as he sits down next to me. He offers the plate to me, which only has two s'mores on it.

"You don't want one?" I ask as I bite into the s'more. The chocolate has little peppermint chunks, which are *so* good, and the crackers are honey-flavored.

"No, I had so much popcorn at The North Pole that I don't think I could eat anything else without exploding." Carlos says with a laugh. He did have some popcorn, but not enough to be this full, right?

"Really?"

"Yeah," Carlos says with a small nod of his head. "They smell good, though."

"You did a good a job." I say, looking up with a smile as I bite into the s'more.

"I put my best effort into it." Carlos teases. "It felt very important to nail it."

"Oh, it's *very* important." I tease. "I might have had to sit with someone else if you weren't able to make me a perfect s'more."

"Then I'm glad I put so much care into it." Carlos replies, looking down with a smile of his own. His nose and eyes are scrunched slightly as he smiles. "I wouldn't want you sitting with someone else."

"Hey! Stop!" Someone across the fire screams. Carlos and I both stand, but around whatever is happening, people are crowded. Some people are screaming stop, some are shouting to keep going, and there's the unmistakable sound of people fighting.

"Lennox! Stop!" Maisie screams, and I see her pushing past the throngs of people to reach the boys who are fighting. I immediately start pushing through the crowd, and I can feel Carlos at my heels.

"Jacob! What are you doing!" Elisa screams, running after Maisie.

"You're going to hurt him!" Anastasiya screams, right behind the two of them. Although I'm not even sure who she's talking about, because Jacob, Lennox, Leo, and Romero are all fighting each other. Well, it seems like the twins are against Lennox and Jacob.

"Hey! Stop!" I scream, running to where the girls are trying to push in between the boys.

"Lia! Stop!" Carlos shouts from behind me. Suddenly, I'm not moving anymore, and my feet aren't on the ground. Carlos has his arms wrapped around my middle, and I can no longer move. "You can't get in between them, Lia. You're going to get hurt."

"They're going to hurt each other!" I protest. It's almost humorous how I can't shake off Carlos' grasp, but also maddening. "Those are my friends, and while I don't know the twins very much, I don't want them getting hurt, either."

"I know, Lia." Carlos says near my ear as he lowers me back to the ground. "If you stay here, I'll try to get them apart. You can't get in between them, though." I press my lips together, weighing my options. I can agree, and then at least Carlos will help. If I disagree, neither of us will be helping.

"Fine." I bite out. Carlos places me on the ground before running right into the middle of them.

People are still shouting, recording, and screaming, and just as Lennox is swinging his arm to hit Romero—I think—Maisie runs in between them, barely missing Lennox's fist.

"Stop!" She screams, stopping right in front of him and meeting his gaze with more determination than I've ever seen her have. She's always been the quietest and shy out of us, but right now she looks as though she's ready to do whatever it takes to stop the fighting. I start jogging forward, but the snow is making me slow.

Elisa reaches Jacob just as Carlos does, and he grabs him from behind as Julia jumps forward and grips Leo's arm. Surprisingly, that's enough to completely shift his focus from Jacob. He stops and meets her gaze somewhat apologetically.

Jacob tries to shrug off Carlos, but Carlos doesn't let go before Jacob turns to face Elisa.

"Maisie, you need to get out of the way right now." Lennox says darkly.

"You're going to drop this right now, Lennox." She hisses, stepping closer to him.

Romero is still a few feet away from Maisie and Lennox, and while his face is still angry, he's softened just a little bit. I'm not scared of him, but after seeing him and Lennox dueling it out a few moments ago, I approach him tentatively.

"Are you okay?" I ask, stepping closer. He turns in surprise, but just nods.

"I'm fine," Romero says quickly.

"Lennox, you're going to stop this stupid-"

"Maisie, you need to leave." Lennox says, interrupting her and looking right past her at Romero, who I'm right next to.

"Treat your sister with some respect!" Romero shouts, meeting Lennox's gaze with a tilt of his head. "Maybe you could get through to her if you didn't treat her like some child you have ward over."

"Maybe you could stay out of it!" Lennox shouts back, taking a step forward. Maisie steps even closer to him and doesn't look back.

"Lennox, I'm telling you right now that you need to *stop*! Go do whatever you want, but stay out of my life!" She screams in his face before whirling around and marching right past me. Romero turns to jog after her, and just as Lennox tries to follow both of them, Carlos steps right next to me and blocks him for a second.

"Man, I don't know what all of this is about, but you

need to stop right now. People are recording, and I'm not really sure how small-town police operate, but this is going to be the next big thing for them in about five minutes once all of the videos are on social media." Carlos says quickly as he grabs Lennox's arm. "Get out of here and get home."

Lennox glares at both of us but doesn't say anything as he storms off in the direction of the path back.

Jacob, Leo, Julia, Elisa, and Anastasiya are standing near each other, and as Carlos and I approach them, there's a range of emotions surrounding each person. Elisa looks more than angry, Julia is concerned, Leo looks angry, Anastasiya looks worried, and Jacob is somewhere between angry and concerned.

"I'm going to suggest that you all get out of here quickly," Carlos says, taking charge of the whole situation. "I can guarantee you that at least five videos of whatever that was are on social media, or at least sent to the police. Things are about to get bad regardless, but getting home and cleaned up will help your cases."

"And you're Mr. Knowledgeable?" Jacob says rudely.

"Actually, I am." Carlos bites back. "I have a special interest in law, and I happen to know that this little fight between all of you *adults* looks rather poor. I'm not saying anyone here has consumed a drop of alcohol, but that's not going to be apparent when the police are here in five minutes. At least it's dark out here, and only Lennox and Maisie were called out by name."

"He has a point." Julia agrees. "You boys are all so stupid." Leo looks over but doesn't say anything.

"Go home before there's any more trouble, and

hopefully this will blow over." Carlos says before he takes my arm and starts pulling me towards the path. "I'm for sure in those videos, and you probably are, too. Neither of us were fighting, but we don't want to be here when things go even more south."

"What's your special interest in law?" I ask once we're in the car. Carlos quickly pulls out of the parking lot, but is careful to abide by the driving laws.

"I'm going to law school when I graduate," Carlos says easily.

"You're joking." I say, turning to him with my mouth agape.

"Nope." Carlos says nonchalantly. "Law has always interested me, and I think that I might be somewhat good at it one day."

"Wow, that's so cool." I say, turning to him with complete awe.

"Thanks," Carlos says somewhat shyly.

"So what are the chances we're going to get in trouble for being there at the scene of the fight?" I ask a minute later when a car that looks suspiciously like a police car passes us. It's late enough in the night that pretty much no one is on the road, and it's heading right in the direction of where we came from.

"I mean," Carlos scratches the back of his head in uncertainty. "I don't really know how a town this small handles issues like this, because I'm sure at least someone there has a parent or family member in politics or in the police."

"So you're saying that it will probably be cleared up

within a few days?" I ask hopefully. "And we're not going to jail for something we didn't do?"

"Well, to start, I can't promise anything, but jail is very much a stretch. If anything, it's going to be Lennox." Carlos answers.

"Why Lennox?" I ask curiously.

"I asked Jacob and Leo what happened, and they said that he's the one who threw the first swing at Romero." Carlos replies. "From what I've gathered from the five minutes I had to ask everyone what happened, Lennox said something to Romero, they went back in forth, and then Lennox attacked him."

"Why?"

"I don't know that part," Carlos answers with a shake of his head. "But then Romero's twin, Leo, jumped in to get Lennox off, and that's when Jacob got there, and apparently he and Lennox are best friends, so he started helping Lennox or something, since it was two against one."

"Oh," I say, pressing my lips together as I try to picture the outcome had no one intervened. "So were they just going to kill each other or something? They seemed really angry."

"I don't think they would *kill* each other, but whatever Lennox is angry about is enough for him to attack Romero, and then not stop when Leo jumped in." Carlos says with a frustrated shake of his head. "I thought you guys were all best friends or something."

"Well, yeah, but there is a new dynamic with the twins here, and with everyone's new jobs." I say, leaning back in my seat as I think. "You know what? Lennox and Maisie's dad is the police chief. Do you think that will play into whatever happened?"

"Oh, that's definitely going to carry some weight." Carlos says with a nod of his head as he pulls into my driveway. "I'll call you when I get back to the inn."

With the car parked and Carlos looking at me the way he is, it almost makes me forget how terribly everything went earlier, and how, before everything got crazy, we kissed.

Carlos kissed me.

I kissed Carlos.

We kissed.

Carlos bites down on his lower lip as though he's considering something, and furrows his eyebrows.

How easy would it be to lean across the space between us and press my lips to his? Would he kiss me back? Surely, he would.

"Have you had any water recently?" Carlos asks suddenly.

"What?" I ask, blinking furiously as the thoughts racing through my head crash and burn.

"Have you had water recently?" Carlos asks again, as though this is normal. "You look a little bit dehydrated or something."

"I haven't had water since we were at The North Pole," I say slowly. "What do you mean by, 'you look dehydrated?'"

"I mean, your face just looked dehydrated or something." Carlos says nervously.

He thinks that I, while I'm imagining leaning over to kiss him, look *dehydrated?* Of all the things, *dehydrated?* Mortification washes over me, and I scoot back in my seat.

Of course Carlos doesn't want to kiss me again. Why would he?

"I'll be sure to have a glass of water when I'm inside." I say quickly as a blush heats my cheek. "Good night, Carlos."

"Good night, Lia!" Carlos calls out as I step out of the door. His voice doesn't sound normal, but then again, apparently, my face doesn't look normal, either.

"It's *Magnolia.*"

Chapter Seventeen

8 DAYS 'TIL CHRISTMAS

I'm still irritated when I wake up, and I know that Carlos' comment shouldn't have this much of a hold on me, but it does. Does he think that I'm not pretty? Does he think that whatever face I was making is gross? Was I even making a face?

Ugh. Why do I care so much about what Carlos thinks of me? Why do I care at all?

My phone starts ringing as I'm making my bed, and I glance over to see that it's a call from Carlos. Impulsively, I reach over and answer it.

"Hello?"

"Lia, I'm sorry about offending you last night. I really didn't mean it that way, and I shouldn't have said anything at all." Carlos says quickly. "I've thought about it a lot and I feel terrible about it."

My heart softens a little bit at his apology, but hurt still lingers as I think back to how embarrassed I was.

"I accept your apology, Carlos."

"Apology candy cane?" I ask as Carlos passes me a candy cane from his pocket while he opens the car door for me.

"Maybe," Carlos says with a grin. "Can it be a 'just because' candy cane?" I chew my lip as I look at him from the seat. Our eyes meet, and instantly, I'm taken back to last night when he kissed me.

"I like 'just because' candy canes." I reply as he closes the door. "They taste better when you're not thinking about anything that upsets you."

"Then it's a 'just because' candy cane." Carlos says simply.

"Do you want one, too?" I ask as I spot the bag of candy canes near his floorboard.

"Nah, I just had a cookie before I left, so I'm a little bit full." Carlos says easily. "I'll pass you another one if you want it, though."

"No, I just figured you might want one." I say. The end of the candy cane is in my mouth for a minute, and the peppermint candy tastes *so* good.

"Thanks," Carlos says with a nod. We drive in silence for a moment before Carlos clears his throat. "So did anything happen with the whole fight?"

"Like the police showing up at my door?"

"Yeah, or your friends saying something about it." Carlos replies.

"No, I haven't heard anything from them today. I planned on texting Julia or Elisa about it, but I forgot." I admit sheepishly. "I'm surprised they haven't said anything about it to me, though. I'm definitely not going to ask Lennox about it."

"Why wouldn't you ask Macy about it?" Carlos asks a moment later. "Isn't she Lennox's sister?"

"*Maisie.*" I correct lightly. "And yeah, she's Lennox's sister, but I don't really want to ask her, because it's obviously something a lot deeper than she wants to share. Elisa or Julia might know the reason for the fight itself."

"I see." Carlos says with a nod of his head. "*Maisie*, not Macy."

"Yeah, but sometimes I say it so quickly that it's hard to differentiate." I say easily.

"No, I just forgot." Carlos says easily. "It's not your fault."

"How come you're willing to say her name right but not mine?" I tease, looking over with genuine interest.

Carlos grins and glances over for a second. "Can I not call you Lia?"

"Well, it's not that you *can't*, but *why* do you do it?" I press, lifting the peppermint candy to my lips.

"I just do," Carlos says with a chuckle. "I like calling you a name that no one else does."

What is that supposed to mean?

"Why?"

"I just do," Carlos says again as he pulls into the open spot in front of the seamstress's shop.

"Be all mysterious then, Carlos." I tease as I slip out of the car.

"Hello, again!" Caroline calls as we step through the shop doors. "I presume you're here to pick up the dress?"

"Yes," I answer with a smile. "Thank you so much."

"Don't worry about it, dear. I'm just doing my job." She says with a kind smile. "I'm very excited to see it on the bride, though. Poppy is going to look just beautiful."

"I can't wait, either." I agree.

"If you'll give me just a moment, I need to grab it from a rack in the back." Caroline says. She quickly strides down the hall, and I turn to Carlos with a smile.

"I'm so glad the dress is done." I say.

"Me too." Carlos agrees with a nod. "This is one of the most important parts, so I'm glad it's safe."

"Here it is, honey," Caroline says as she passes the dress to Carlos so he can carry it. "Be careful." She teases.

"I will be." Carlos says with a smile. "I'll go put this in the car."

"Thank you, Caroline." I say, turning to give her a hug. "I'm sure you did an amazing job."

"You're welcome, Magnolia. Have a lovely day." Caroline replies, squeezing my shoulders lightly before returning to her chair behind the counter.

Carlos is waiting in the car for me, and he's already started the engine with the heat on.

"Do you want to take it to your house and then call Poppy to show her everything?" Carlos asks as I close the door behind me.

"Yeah, we can. She might be at work, but I'm sure she'd like to see the alterations, since she hasn't seen it since it left New York." I agree. "I'll text her and let her know that I'm going to video chat her in about ten minutes."

"So, what do you think?" I ask Poppy as Carlos unzips the dress. We hung it in the guest bedroom, and Poppy's bright face is on the screen as she awaits the grand reveal.

Her face falls slightly, but she squints her eyes as though she can't see very well. "Can you move a little bit closer so I can see it better?" Poppy asks.

"Yeah," I say, stepping close enough that she can see the neckline and sleeves of the dress. "How about here?"

"Magnolia, I'm trying not to freak out right now, but that's not my dress. Did Caroline give you the wrong one?" Poppy asks quickly. My stomach falls to the floor, and I feel my throat go dry.

"No, this is the dress we brought her from the place in May." I say, lightheadedness sinking in. "The people there gave us the dress and confirmed that it was yours."

"Clearly they were wrong, Magnolia," Poppy says quickly. She's never been the one to worry about pretty much anything, but I can see stress lines forming in her forehead. "Is there a way to go back to that other place and get the right dress?"

"I mean, we can go there and try to sort it all out, but this is freaking me out, Poppy." I say through gritted teeth. Why does everything always go wrong? Why couldn't I have picked up the right dress a few weeks ago? Carlos watches as I talk to Poppy, and his eyebrows furrow as he listens.

"Hey, don't get freaked out, Magnolia. I'm sure this can all be sorted out, and everything will go to plan. Just drive back to the shop and then explain to them the issue." Poppy says, her earlier worry already evaporating. "I'm sure that the other bride has either figured out that there's an issue, or she will soon."

"So what are you going to do if your dress isn't there?" I ask breathlessly. My heart is pounding so loud in my ears that I can hardly hear myself.

"We'll buy a new dress." Poppy says simply. "Hopefully, it all gets sorted out, but if it doesn't, then you'll help me get a new dress there."

"*I'll* help you get one?" I squeak out.

"Well, yes. There aren't any dress shops in the city that don't have at least six months of wait time. I'll need something off the rack from somewhere in May." Poppy says easily. "You and Carlos can do that, right?"

"We can," Carlos pipes up from next to the dress. For a moment, I almost forgot that he's here.

"Thank you, Carlos. You've been a good partner for Magnolia this month." Poppy calls from the phone. Carlos grins, but instead of looking at the camera when he responds, he only looks at me.

"I've been enjoying it."

"Let's just start driving up to May, and then once we get there, we can explain everything." Carlos says once we're in the car. "I think calling ahead will be too confusing, and we just need to get there and lay it all out in person."

"Whatever you think is best." I say in a defeated slump

in the passenger seat. "I've never just *loved* my car before, but I've seen the interior of this thing way too many times this month, and many of those times have been with bad news." I huff.

"Hey, we've had some fun in here, though. We've seen the Christmas lights, had great food, and listened to way too many Christmas carols." Carlos argues back with a chuckle.

"Yeah, you're right, but what about all of the bad times, though?" I ask as he moves onto the main road that will lead us around the mountain and into May.

"You only see the bad in stuff, sometimes." Carlos comments. "You just hone in on what's going wrong instead of living in the moment or just fixing it as best as you can and moving on."

"Well, sorry for being stressed about my sister's wedding." I huff somewhat sarcastically.

"It's not just that," Carlos says softly. He reaches over and takes my hand that's resting on my thigh and squeezes it tightly. My fingers tingle from his touch, but I push the feeling away. "You're so wound up all of the time, and it's hurting you. Whenever you're in the moment, you're so happy and unconcerned."

"It's not my fault everything seems to go awry, though." I say, my voice softer now.

"Stuff is always going to go awry; it's what you do with it that counts." Carlos says as he brushes his thumb along the back of my hand. "You can't control every aspect of your life, and trying to do so is hurting you. I'm not saying that you can't plan ahead and be smart, but you're so worried about something going wrong that you can't even see the right."

"I'm sorry, are you sure this isn't the dress that was ordered?" The woman behind the counter asks. "I find it hard to believe that there would be a mix-up."

"We're certain, ma'am," I say, pulling out the photos of the receipts that Poppy sent me. "Here are the original receipts and details on the dress. This is definitely not the same dress. Even the size is different."

She glances over the information and back to the dress that Carlos is holding. "I see." She hums. "Let me make a quick call to the other bride who picked up her dress. She picked it up yesterday, so I'm not sure if she would have seen the mistake yet."

The woman walks to a back room as she places the call, and I press my lips together in worry. "What if she isn't able to confirm the mix-up and Poppy doesn't get her dress?" I ask.

"We'll figure it out even if this doesn't get fixed. We can always get another dress." Carlos says reassuringly. He reaches out to take my hand in his, and instant warmth spreads throughout my body.

"So, I just spoke with the other bride, and I showed her photos of the dress, and she confirmed that this, is in fact, her dress." The woman says slowly.

"So we're able to get them switched back?" I ask hopefully. The woman presses her lips together for a moment before speaking again.

"Well, that's the part that isn't so great. She is boarding a plane in approximately ten minutes, and the dress has already been checked." She begins. "And they're flying to Greece."

"Greece?" I echo, feeling like this must be some sort of joke.

"Yes, Greece." The woman says. "I don't know how this mix-up happened, since the dresses had the correct names on them."

"So our only option is to find a new dress?" I confirm. My knees feel weak as I say this out loud, and Carlos tightens his hand around mine.

"It appears as though that's our only option right now." She agrees. "We have quite the selection, and since you're not going to use this dress, we will happily trade in this one for whatever dress you choose."

"Thank you," I say, turning to Carlos before speaking again. "I'm going to call my sister—the bride—and ask her if she'd like us to look here for a new dress, or if she'd just like a refund."

"Go right ahead," The woman responds. She looks sorry about the incident, and I know that it wasn't her fault, but this whole situation is about to send me into a meltdown.

I call Poppy and quickly explain everything, and while Poppy's eyes lower for a moment when I mention that her dress is going to Greece, she nods when I ask about looking for a new dress here.

"Yeah, that sounds good. At least my dress will be getting a little vacation." Poppy says with a small laugh. "You're about my size, right?"

"Yeah, I am." I agree when we go over our dress sizes.

"Then you can try on all of the dresses that fit you there, since there really isn't time to do alterations, and then send me photos and videos." Poppy says easily. "I'll choose from those dresses, and you can take it home today."

"What if there's nothing you like?" I ask nervously.

"I'm going to like at least one of the dresses, Magnolia. Start sending me pictures and videos, and I'll send you my final decision once you're done."

"You're going to be such a lovely bride." The assistant who is helping me try on the first dress says as she buttons the back of the dress.

"Oh, I'm not the bride," I say quickly. "This is for my sister's wedding next week. There was a big mix-up here, so I'm trying to help her find a dress."

"My, that's quite the deadline." She gasps, bringing her hand to her chest. "I'm sorry about the mix-up, though."

"Thank you," I say softly.

This dress is absolutely beautiful, but it feels strange to be wearing it. I'm not a bride, and this isn't my wedding. This isn't my dress.

When I step out into the room where Carlos is waiting, he stands as soon as he sees me. My smile is small and maybe just a little bit shy as he glides his gaze up and down the dress. Carlos' mouth falls agape, and I feel a red blush creeping up my cheeks as his eyes return to mine.

"You're..." Carlos doesn't seem to find the right words,

but instead, he reaches to pick up my phone to take the pictures for Poppy.

"Did you get any good ones?" I ask a moment later as I take a tentative step toward him.

"No one could ever take a bad picture of you," Carlos says softly as he passes me my phone.

Carlos managed to capture my smile at his reaction, and even though I don't feel it one hundred percent, I'm glowing in these photos.

"Thank you," I say, turning to meet his eyes. "I'll send these to her and see what she says about it."

Poppy's reaction is immediate, and instead of texting back, she video chats me.

"Magnolia, you look so beautiful in that dress! Is Carlos there? Can he take the phone and step back so I can see it all again?" Poppy blurts out. I pass the phone to Carlos, who steps backwards so she can get a full view of me.

I hear her ask him a few questions, but since it's over call, I can't make out exactly what she's saying, only Carlos' *yes*.

Carlos speaks again, only his voice is lower, and now I really can't hear anything he's saying. When he steps closer, I can hear Poppy ask to show her the neckline. He meets my eyes as his fingers lift to my shoulders, and I nod my head lightly as he runs his fingers along the underside of the lace that's pressed against my shoulder. Goosebumps flood my skin, and warmth follows the path of his fingers.

"That's just so beautiful." Poppy breathes excitedly. "I think I love this more than my original dress, Magnolia."

"So this is the one you want?" I ask. "You don't want to look at any other ones before you decide? What if you don't like the way you look in this one?" I fret, taking the phone from Carlos as I speak.

"If I look even half as beautiful as you do in it, then I'll be happy." Poppy says determinedly.

She starts speaking again, but her words are lost on me as Carlos' fingers gently graze the neckline of the dress. His fingers still haven't left my collarbone, and the touch sends a trail of fire behind it. My eyes meet his as his fingers move along my shoulder and down my arm.

"Magnolia? Did you hear me?" Poppy says, her voice tearing me from whatever is happening between Carlos and I.

"Sorry, what?" I ask breathlessly. Poppy's eyes narrow for a moment, but she quickly returns to normal.

"I said that this is the dress I want you to get, and if there are any alterations that need to be made, that we can do them ourselves with safety pins or something. I don't want anything about this dress to change." Poppy says. "I really think you found the most beautiful dress ever, and it's even more special to me because you're the one who helped choose it."

"I'm glad you like it, Poppy." I say softly. "If you're sure that this is the dress you want, we're going to get checked out and drive home. It's going to be dark soon."

"That sounds perfect. Call me later tonight before bed, though. I want to talk to you about something." Poppy says hurriedly. "Thank you, Magnolia."

"You're welcome, Poppy." I say, ending the call.

I turn to Carlos, who is still watching me with so much depth that it makes my knees go weak. His fingers are still on my arm, but they're lower now. Carlos' hand is just above mine, and his fingers trail down to mine. He wraps them around my fingers and brings them to his lips.

"You're beautiful, Lia." Carlos says while his lips rest against my knuckle. I swallow at the deep huskiness of his voice, and just as I'm about to suggest that I walk back into the changing room and change out of this dress, Carlos uses his free hand to wrap around the back of my head and pull me towards him.

Carlos' lips press to my forehead, and I exhale as a sudden sense of calmness washes over me. Suddenly, all of the problems that we're facing don't seem so bad, and I feel as though I could live in this moment forever.

I could live in this moment of peace and tranquility forever, and never bore of it. Carlos' hand around mine, with his lips on my forehead, is enough to satisfy me.

"You should probably go back and tell her that we want this dress." Carlos says, his kiss still pressed to my forehead.

"I probably should." I agree, but I don't make a move to turn away from his touch.

"Probably," Carlos whispers as he pulls away from me.

"Let's try this again." Carlos teases as he hangs the dress in the spare bedroom. I press call on the video chat with Poppy, and she answers with a smile. Her hair is in a pile on her head, and it looks like Charlie is at her apartment for dinner.

"Hello to my two favorite personal shoppers." Poppy teases.

"Hey," I reply with a roll of my eyes and a laugh. "Do you want to see your dress?"

"Yes, please!" Poppy says excitedly. "Oh my gosh, I just love it so much. I can't believe that this is the first one you chose to try on. It's absolutely perfect."

"You're going to look great in it." I say with a smile. The camera pans over to Carlos standing next to the dress. He smiles once he notices it on him and gives the camera a quick wave.

"Tell Charlie I say 'hi.'" Carlos says.

"Thank you so much, Magnolia. I absolutely love it, and I can't wait to see it in person." Poppy says with a smile. "I can't wait to wear it at my wedding."

"Are you going to try it on the day before?" I ask curiously.

"I don't think so," Poppy says with a smile. "I think that we're close enough in size that it should fit, and if it doesn't, then I shouldn't marry Charlie."

"What?" I hear Charlie sputter in the background. "You're going to let a *dress* decide if you're going to marry me?"

Poppy begins giggling as she glances over at him. "Maybe."

"I don't like the sound of that." Charlie teases. "Magnolia, you're going to need to have a needle and thread on standby."

Carlos begins laughing at them, and I can't help but join in. "This is what you signed up for when you proposed to Poppy." I tease. It's true, though. Poppy is just free-spirited and has always done what feels right, not exactly what's factually right.

"I know, I know." Charlie says. "But she sure keeps me on my toes."

"That's what makes it so fun!" Poppy exclaims. "You never know what's coming next, and you're ready for whatever with me."

"That's very true," Charlie agrees. "But sometimes my toes are tired. Give a man a chance to eat dinner without worrying about his bride leaving him because of a dress."

"You'll be just fine." Poppy declares with a wave of her hand. "Anyway, I'll let you two go, but don't forget to call me later, Magnolia."

"Okay, I will. Love you."

"Love you, too," Poppy says before the screen goes dark.

"Is she always like this?" Carlos teases as he zips the dress back into the bag. "So...go with the flow?"

"She's been like this since the day she was born," I confirm. "My parents always wonder how they got two entirely different kids."

"Yeah, I'm kind of wondering with them." Carlos teases. "Hey, do you want to go take a walk?"

"Where?" I ask, surprised by his sudden change of topic.

"In the park or something, probably." Carlos says. "Maybe you know of a good place to walk around here?"

"Yeah, the park would be good. I know that there's a play happening tonight at the local theater, so we'll want to avoid going in that direction because of the parking and traffic." I comment. "Would you mind if I ran up to my room and changed first, though? I want to wear something a little bit warmer."

"Of course." Carlos says with a nod. "I'll go out to the car and get it warmed up."

Once Carlos is out of the house, I jog up the stairs and into my room, where I trade out the pants I've been wearing for fleece-lined ones. The temperature is already freezing, and who knows how long we're going to be out there.

"Ready to go," I say as I enter the car. The blast of hot air is nice on my cold cheeks, since even the walk from my front door to the car chilled them.

"Now, remind me, how do I get to the park?" Carlos asks sheepishly. "I don't have the town map memorized just yet."

"Stay on this road for about five minutes, then you can turn on the street that says *Parkway Drive*," I say easily with a smile.

"Thanks," Carlos replies. "I'll memorize all of the places, though. Don't worry about having to tell me directions for the rest of our lives."

For the rest of our lives? As in this month? Or forever? Does Carlos see forever with me? Does Carlos want forever with me? Do I want forever with Carlos?

"I wouldn't mind always giving you directions." I say, turning in my seat to face him. "You're a good driver, so I'm just doing my part."

"Yeah, but it's technically the driver's job to know where they're going." Carlos says back with a grin. "However, I don't mind listening to you talk all of the time."

"You like listening to me talk?" I ask tentatively as butterflies swirl in my stomach.

"Of course," Carlos answers. "You have a nice voice, and listening to you talk is relaxing." I smile, and I feel my cheeks redden as his words sink in.

Why am I having such a reaction to this boy that I didn't

even know or like almost three weeks ago? And why do I not even care?

"You really think so?"

"Magnolia, I really think that you have an amazing voice." Carlos teases. He reaches over to wrap his hand around mine, and tingles rush up my wrist and arm.

"Well, thank you." I say softly, squeezing his hand lightly. Why is Carlos so good at this?

Carlos steps out of the car as soon as we get to the park, and quickly jogs around the car to open my door. I grin at him, and this feeling of absolute giddiness fills me. Why am I like this with Carlos? I never act so giddy and carefree.

"So why did you want to come here?" I ask a moment later.

"I just wanted to spend more time with you." Carlos says a little bit shyly. My mittened hand is in his, and as he speaks, his fingers start to tug on the ends of the mitten.

"Spending all day at the dress shop wasn't enough for you?" I tease, glancing up at him.

"I don't think any amount of time will be enough." Carlos answers softly as the rest of my mitten comes off my hand. The contact of his fingers on mine surprises me, since he's not wearing gloves either. Carlos' hand tugs mine into his jacket pocket, and the fleece lining immediately brushes my hand.

"What are you doing?" I ask in surprise. It's not that I mind it, but now we're holding hands, only they're not swinging between us. They're warm in Carlos' pocket.

"Holding hands between gloves isn't really romantic." Carlos says with a small laugh. "Don't you think so?"

"I mean," I consider the question for a moment before

nodding my head. Does he mean romantic as in romantic with me, or just in general? "You're right, actually. I don't have an argument."

"Magnolia Larsen doesn't have an argument for me?" Carlos teases. "Who would've thought?"

"Oh, come on. It's not like I argue with you a lot." I say indignantly.

"Okay, maybe not *argue.*" Carlos agrees.

"See?" I say with a raise of my eyebrows.

"See?" Carlos teases as he glances down. My cheeks redden as I realize I completely just argued with him, proving his point.

"See what?" I reply as though I have no idea what just happened.

"Oh, nothing." He says with a small chuckle.

"Magnolia, you have to promise to tell me the truth, okay?" Poppy says over the video chat. She looks like she's doing her skincare routine, and I'm already snuggled into bed.

"Yeah, I will. What's up?" I ask. Her phrasing is a little bit concerning, but I wrap myself even tighter in my blankets. My body still isn't entirely warm from being out with Carlos, and my toes still feel frozen.

"What's going on between you and Carlos?" Poppy says, turning to the camera with the full force of an older sister stare.

"What do you mean?" I ask quickly.

"Oh, come on, Magnolia," Poppy says with a huff. "It

doesn't take a relationship expert to know that there's something between you two. Just tell me about it, please."

"Well, we've been spending a lot of time together—thanks to you—and he's kind of an amazing guy." I admit shyly. "Why? What do you think is going on between us?"

"I see, I see." Poppy says absently as she wipes her face with a cotton swatch. "Tell me more."

"No, you tell me what you think is going on between us, nosey." I say through a bout of giggles.

"I think that I saw some chemistry, and I want to know what's going on with my baby sister. It's not a crime to be interested." Poppy says with a roll of her eyes.

"Fine, there *might* be some chemistry between us." I admit. "And he might be an amazing kisser, too."

"*Magnolia!*" Poppy exclaims excitedly. "You didn't think to mention that before?"

"You didn't ask." I tease.

"Okay, I see how this is." Poppy says as she steps back from the camera so I can see most of her body and places her hands on her hips. "I want the beginning to end story with not a detail spared. I have plenty of time, so don't leave a single thing out."

I give Poppy a detailed storyline of everything that's happened between Carlos and I, and by the end of it, she's already in pajamas and in bed, but she's been nodding along the whole time with complete interest.

"Wow, Magnolia." Poppy says at the end of my little speech. "It sounds like you and Carlos really like each other."

"Well, that's-"

"Oh, don't even." Poppy huffs. "Don't even try to downplay what's going on between you two."

"I haven't known him that long, and-"

"I knew Charlie for approximately an hour before I decided that I had to marry him." Poppy begins. At my eyes widening, she quickly amends her statement. "I'm not saying that you need to know if you want to marry him or anything, but loving someone doesn't follow a list or a schedule, Mango."

I scrunch my nose at the use of the name she used to call me when I was younger. She hasn't called me Mango in a long time, and just hearing her say it brings back a time when we were younger and life was much simpler. For me, at least.

"You just need to keep getting to know him." Poppy says encouragingly. "I can promise you that he's not a bad guy or anything, because Charlie would have said something about you two spending so much time together. You can cross that off your worry list."

"It wasn't on it." I huff.

"So maybe him being a bad person wasn't on it, but what else is? I'm sure that even if you don't have it on paper, you have some mental list of reasons to not like him." Poppy says exasperatedly.

"I don't have a list at all." I admit, feeling somewhat defensive about how she's insulting my love of lists and schedules. So what if I need everything in order to properly function?

"You don't have a list?" Poppy asks incredulously. "You, Magnolia Larsen, don't have a list."

"Yes, Poppy Larsen. I don't have a list." I reply. Poppy smirks, but a blush heats on her cheeks.

"You can't use that in a week." Poppy says with an excited giggle.

"I'll just use Poppy Gonzales, then." I huff. A smile cracks through my pressed lips, and we both burst out in giggles.

"What would happen if I just started calling you Magnolia Santos?" Poppy teases. My mouth drops agape, and I start furiously shaking my head.

"Absolutely not, Poppy. You need to take ten steps backward." I say quickly. That's taking it too far.

"Oh, come on, Mango. I'm just teasing." Poppy says through giggles. "Sort of."

"No, no, no." I say, continuing to shake my head.

"You're no fun." Poppy teases exasperatedly. After a few minutes of us giggling, I'm finally able to speak again.

"How did you know Carlos' last name, by the way? I didn't really think about him and Charlie having different last names until a few minutes ago." I ask. "Sure, I've known that they're different, but right now I just kind of thought about it, I guess."

"I'm marrying, Charlie." Poppy teases. "Of course I know a little bit about his younger brother. I know his name, at least."

"Yeah, true." I agree.

"You seem to know more about him than I do," Poppy says with a smile. "A *lot* more about him than I know."

"Stop, Poppy." I groan out. "I never should have told you any of this."

"I'm just having fun," Poppy says with a roll of her eyes. "Lighten up a little. The world isn't ending just because I'm teasing you about a boy you like."

"You're the second person to tell me to lighten up recently." I say through clenched teeth.

"Who else was brave enough to tell you?" Poppy asks with surprise. She rolls over in her bed and runs her hand across her face.

"Carlos." I admit.

"*Carlos* told you that?" Poppy asks, dropping her hand and turning so her whole face is in the camera frame.

"Yeah, he did," I confirm. "Why?"

"Carlos has some guts." Poppy says through a bout of laughter.

"What's that supposed to mean?" I ask defensively.

"I mean that you act like...*that* when someone tells you to lighten up." Poppy says, motions at me through the screen.

"Like what?" I ask. My eyebrows are furrowed in both confusion and defensiveness.

"Like someone just kicked you and told you that you're the worst person in the world." Poppy says. "I don't mean this in a mean way, but you're like...*really* uptight and strict with your schedules and plans."

"Well, not all of us are willing to leave their fate up to a wedding dress that they've never tried on." I snap.

"See, Mango? You're doing it now. Just take the critique and move on." Poppy says with a roll of her eyes.

"*Magnolia*." I say. Her words sting, and while I don't like considering the possibility, maybe she's a little bit right, and I'm too uptight sometimes. Maybe that's why Carlos hasn't kissed me again recently.

"Mango, I can see your gears turning. What's going on?" Poppy asks a second later, her voice softer now.

"It's just…" Should I tell her about what I'm thinking right now? "It's just that Carlos and I kissed yesterday, but he hasn't kissed me since."

"So?" Poppy asks, as though this isn't something I should be conceding myself with. "What's wrong with that?"

"Shouldn't he want to kiss me?" I question.

"Well, he should, but maybe he does. Maybe he's nervous, or doesn't think that you want him to kiss you again." Poppy says as she offers scenarios. "Maybe he just hasn't found the perfect time to kiss you again since the first kiss was so magical?"

"Do you really think that?" I ask tentatively.

"I really think that if he didn't like you, he would've realized that when he kissed you, and he would've avoided you today. He definitely wouldn't have asked you to take a walk in the park." Poppy concludes. "Maybe he's just a little bit shy and wants the moment to be just right? Or doesn't want you to think the only thing he wants from you is physical."

"You think so?" I ask hopefully.

"I don't know anything for a fact, but I think jumping to the conclusion that he doesn't like you might be a little bit extreme," Poppy says gently. "Charlie has told me a little bit about him, and he's not someone who is just going to play you or something."

"He doesn't seem like a player." I agree with a nod of my head. "He's like, really confident, but also shy at the same time, if that makes sense?"

"That's what Charlie told me. Carlos is confident but doesn't want to seem cocky." Poppy agrees. A yawn escapes her as she's finishing speaking. "I need to get going. I have work in like six hours, and I'm tired."

"What time is it?" I ask, surprised. How much time has passed since Carlos and I walked in the park?

"It's two." Poppy says with another yawn.

"Love you, good night." I say with a smile.

"I love you, too." Poppy replies. "Thank you for being the best help with my wedding. I know you've been taking care of a lot of stuff, and I really appreciate it."

"Do you want to come over to my house for breakfast?" I ask Carlos over the phone.

I hear my parents shuffling around the kitchen as they wash out their coffee cups before leaving for work. While they have never been breakfast people besides a cup of black coffee, when I was younger, they were intentional with making me a real breakfast. Now that I'm older, I just make myself whatever I'm feeling, or occasionally, one of them will whip up a few eggs with fruit.

"Yeah, I would love that." Carlos agrees enthusiastically. "Do you need me to pick up anything from the grocery store on my way over?"

"I think I have everything." I say, thinking over my recipe before returning to the conversation. "Yeah, you can just come over."

"What time do you want me to be there?" Carlos asks.

"As soon as possible." I clamp my hand over my mouth

at the forwardness I just displayed. Who says, *'as soon as possible'* when someone asks when they'd like to see them?

"I'll be there as soon as possible." Carlos replies, and I can almost hear the smile in his voice.

"Good." I say lightly, as though I didn't just make a fool of myself. "It's never good to keep a lady waiting."

"I would never keep my lady waiting." Carlos vows as he ends the call.

My lady.

Does Carlos see me as his lady? Butterflies in my stomach flit and flutter, and a blush blossoms on my cheeks as I replay his words.

My lady.

My lady.

My lady.

A little squeal escapes me as I hurry to change into something presentable and rush to the kitchen to start on breakfast.

I quickly pull out everything I'll need to make pancakes and eggs, and rush to get everything moving. A knock sounds on the door just as I'm mixing the flour and cocoa powder, and I set everything down and brush my hands on my apron as I race to the door. Maybe I'm just a little bit excited to see Carlos, but that's to be expected, right?

I pull open the door, and Carlos' dark hair has tufts of snow on them, and as I peer closer to what's behind him, I notice that it's snowing. Even though the ground has been covered in snow for months, seeing bright clumps of whiteness falling from the sky always feels magical.

"Hi," Carlos says with a smile as I lift my eyes to his.

They're twinkling and shining as he looks down at me, and a smile lifts on my cheeks.

"Hi," I echo. A few strands of hair fall from the Dutch braids in my hair, and I reach up to brush them back from my face. Carlos chuckles, and his eyes take on a mischievous glint.

"I see you've been busy," Carlos says softly as he reaches up and trails his fingers along my cheek.

"Uh-huh," I barely make out. Carlos' touch is gentle, and it takes me a moment to realize what he's doing as his fingers move over one particular section of my cheek. "Is there something there?" I ask sheepishly.

"Just a little bit of cocoa powder," Carlos says with a smile.

"Really?" I wince. My cheeks heat in a flush, and this brings an even wider smile to Carlos' lips.

"Yeah, but it's fine." Carlos says gently. "It was cute, actually."

"Chocolate powder on my face isn't cute." I protest as a smile rises from Carlos' use of 'cute.'

Does he think I'm cute, or just the fact that there was chocolate on my face?

"Even if it weren't, you're cute, Lia." Carlos says. Just before I can respond, a gust of snow reminds me that we're standing in the open doorway, and I still have food to cook.

"Oh, you can come in," I say hurriedly as I realize just how rude I must seem. My Christmas music grows louder as I step into the kitchen, and the soft bells of one of my favorite songs twinkles over the speaker.

"Did you hear me, Lia?" Carlos asks as he follows me into the kitchen.

"What?" I ask as I reach for a measuring cup. Why did I allow myself to fall so far behind, when Carlos is literally here to eat? What's he going to eat? Raw flour and milk? "Sorry I don't have more done, I just planned on having almost everything ready and-"

"Lia," Carlos says, his voice suddenly close to me. I spin in surprise, and Carlos is right in front of me.

"Sorry, what?" I ask breathlessly. From this distance, I can see every tiny detail about his dimples and how bright his teeth are.

"Stop worrying about what you have or haven't done. It'll be okay." Carlos says gently as he steps closer. My back is now pressed to the countertops, but instead of leaning against it, I angle my body closer to Carlos.

"Yeah, but you came here for breakfast, and there's no breakfast." I protest with frustration. "It's not like-"

Suddenly, my lips aren't moving in argument and frustration. Rather, they're moving against Carlos' soft and passionate mouth.

Carlos' hand moves up my side and rests on my neck and jaw as he presses himself closer, so now I'm really against the counter, and Carlos is against me. My hands find the sides of his face as all thoughts of arguing slip away.

Carlos' mouth moves against mine slowly, and any relevance of time or the world around us disappears the longer we kiss.

The world starts to spin behind my closed eyes as I suck in less and less air. Carlos' soft lips fervently give and take with mine, and I slip my hands down the sides of his neck and onto his shoulders.

My fingers move against the hard muscle beneath his

sweater, and yes, even though I've known that Carlos has some serious muscle—he carried me across a snow-filled field—I'm pleasantly surprised by how strong his shoulders feel.

Without even thinking about it, my hands slip lower to his biceps, and if I weren't already gasping for air, the feel of them beneath my hands would leave me breathless.

I deepen the kiss even more, and just as Carlos' hands begin to slip around my waist and pull me even closer, he suddenly pulls away.

"Why did you do that?" I ask breathlessly. Carlos' eyes are dark and heated, and his breathing is erratic and unstable.

"Why did I kiss you?" Carlos asks, his voice surprised.

"Yeah, why did you kiss me?" I repeat through deep breaths.

"Because you wouldn't stop acting like you committed some crime by not having breakfast done, and you needed a distraction." Carlos says with a grin.

That's it? That's the only reason he wants to kiss me? Didn't he say something about that when he kissed me the other night? That the only reason he kissed me was to shut me up?

"Oh," I say softly, feeling slightly hurt by the fact that he doesn't have another reason to kiss me.

"What's wrong?" Carlos asks immediately, the smile vanishing from his face.

"It's nothing," I say quickly, plastering my most sincere smile on my face. "I hope you're ready for my world-famous pancakes."

"World famous?" Carlos teases lightly as he reaches out to pick up a strawberry, as though us just making out was nothing. He begins slicing it and doesn't look up as he speaks again. "Who's the judge of that?"

"Myself." I tease back, a real smile cracking on my face.

"So am I the first person to try these pancakes?" Carlos asks a moment later.

"Yeah, you are." I agree with a nod of my head. "My parents don't eat breakfast, and Poppy hasn't lived here in years." Carlos nods in understanding.

"I'm excited to try world-famous pancakes. I have to say that I don't think I've tasted anything officially rated world famous in my entire life, so this is a first." Carlos says with a grin as he turns his head to me while he speaks. I can't help the giggle that escapes me, and when our eyes meet, another bout of laughter consumes us.

Why does Carlos have this effect on me? Why do I laugh when our eyes meet?

"Consider yourself very lucky, Mr. Santos." I say solemnly. "This is a *very* secret recipe, and since only one person has ever tasted them, no one else has had a chance to steal it. You have to keep it to yourself."

"I see," Carlos teases as he slices more fruit. I never even asked him to pitch in, but here he is. Cutting fruit like he owns the place. "You can trust that your secret is *not* safe with me."

"Hey!" I blurt out. "You're supposed to say that you're going to take the recipe to the grave!"

"I just don't know if I can agree to that." Carlos says as though it's a shame. "What if I need to make them for myself when you're not around, and someone sees me? What if I become so obsessed with them that I take your recipe and shout it from the rooftops?"

"I highly doubt either of those things are going to happen." I say flatly for emphasis. "But I *can* imagine you becoming so intoxicated off them that someone will ask you about them, and then you'll share the recipe."

"That's a very real possibility." Carlos agrees with a nod of his head. "We'll just have to see, since you haven't had anyone else try them. I'm your test subject."

I roll my eyes and laugh at how Carlos is still keeping this up, but I don't mind continuing to play along.

I don't mind doing anything with Carlos, actually.

"Do you think Jacob would mind if I took that microphone from him and started reading off your pancake recipe?" Carlos leans down to whisper in my ear.

"*What?*" I blurt out.

"Yeah, I have it written down right here," Carlos says as he lifts a crumpled-up piece of paper.

"Absolutely not, Carlos." I whisper-shout back. "Under no circumstances will I be affiliated with that."

"Maybe I'm just too intoxicated with your pancakes to know the difference between right and wrong." Carlos muses as he folds and unfolds the paper over and over in his hand.

"Maybe you need to stop teasing me and listen to Jacob," I say back, glancing up with a smile.

"Maybe," Carlos muses. "Or maybe not."

"What is that, anyway?" I ask, motioning to the paper in hand.

"It's the list of things I need to pick up from the store on the way home, later." Carlos answers, offering me the paper. I'm not sure why I take it, but the part of me that longs to know everything about Carlos probably has something to do with it.

December 18th

Pick up from the store:

** Shaving cream*
** Laundry soap*
** Eye mask*
** Snacks*

There are a few other items, but I get the gist of it. Living in an inn for a month must be annoying when it comes to what you need. At least Charlie is paying for Carlos' stay, since he was initially going to stay there with him, and he didn't want his eighteen-year-old brother to be paying for a month-long vacation.

"I don't see a pancake recipe, so that's a relief." I tease as I pass him back the paper.

"Each seat will have a set of the appropriate gingerbread pieces to make a home, and there should be plenty of icing to use as 'glue.'" Jacob says. Elisa reaches out and takes the microphone from his hand before turning to him with a sly grin.

"What Jacob didn't tell you is that we're going to be judging the best groups of gingerbread houses. Our five favorites will be given a prize." Elisa says excitedly. "We're not going to tell you what the prize is, though. You'll just have to learn when we judge."

"And what Elisa didn't tell you is that the clock started a minute ago, when she started talking," Jacob says as he leans down to the microphone that Elisa still has.

Elisa glances over with a look that's supposed to look threatening, but Jacob only grins back.

"So where do you want to sit?" Carlos asks, breaking through my line of sight to Elisa and Jacob.

"Huh?" I ask with a surprised flutter of my eyelashes. Carlos' dark eyes are right in front of me, and I can't help but smile at his closeness. Around us, people are finding seats and chatting with their friends, but right now, all that I can see or hear is Carlos.

"Come on," Carlos says with a devious smirk as he takes my hand and leads me through the maze of people and tables. We're walking single file, but Carlos' hand is outstretched behind him as he leads me.

The table Carlos chose already has Anastasiya and Lennox seated at it, and I blink rapidly at the sight of them together without Maisie.

"Hey, Magnolia." Anastasiya chirps as she sees me. Her eyes drop to my hand that's wrapped around Carlos' but she doesn't say anything about it.

"Hey, Anastasiya. Hey, Lennox." I say, giving him a smile. Lennox nods and greets me back, but something is off about him. Anastasiya, too. I'm not nearly as close with her as Lennox, but I can feel it. "What have you two been up to?"

"Oh, not much." Anastasiya answers quickly. "When we

left work for the evening, we decided to come decorate some gingerbread houses."

"Yeah, but I'm the builder of both houses, and she's the decorator." Lennox grumbles. His grin betrays the annoyed voice that he tried to display, and everything makes sense now.

"He volunteered." Anastasiya fills in as she elbows Lennox.

"Hey, you just knocked over those two walls." Lennox says exasperatedly. He looks up with a smile as Anastasiya glances at the work she knocked over, and smiles grow on both of their faces when their eyes meet.

"Oops." Anastasiya says sheepishly.

I glance over to see what Carlos is doing since he isn't joining the conversation, and he's already working on his gingerbread house. I smile at his intense focus on the gingerbread and icing in his hands.

"Is Maisie here?" I ask, glancing around us for Anastasiya's best friend and Lennox's sister.

"I don't think so," Anastasiya says quickly. "We haven't been hanging out a lot recently, so I don't know what she's up to today."

"Why not?" I feel slightly bad about inquiring, but I've been left out of the loop with all of the wedding preparations. Suddenly, it's becoming more and more apparent that I'm really out of the loop. Even with my close friends like Lennox, Elisa, and Jacob.

"Oh, well," Anastasiya stutters for a word to describe it, but before she can answer, Lennox interrupts.

"She's being a jerk and won't take responsibility for how

crazy she's being right now." He says bitterly. "She's taking it out on Anastasiya and I right now."

"That's not exactly-" Anastasiya starts, but she presses her lips together before speaking again. "Things are just weird between us right now, and since I work with Lennox, that's making things worse."

"Oh, I see." I say with a nod of my head. When Anastasiya turns back to Lennox, the real reason Maisie is probably frustrated is devastatingly obvious.

"Careful, Lia. I might be finished before you if you don't start soon." Carlos says as he leans over to speak closely to my ear. Why is he doing that? Why is he intentionally making me blush and lose all track of time and everything around me?

"Maybe," I tease, turning to face him. "But mine will look better."

"Yeah, I'd like to see that." Carlos teases back.

"You'll see." I tease with a roll of my eyes.

"And our winners are Anastasiya, Carlos, Clarissa, Edward, and Rachel." Elisa calls out from the front of the room.

I turn to Carlos, who is smiling in confusion. "Did she mean me?" He asks quietly as he glances around at the other people walking to claim their prizes. Anastasiya stands, and after a moment, Elisa turns to us from across the room.

"I don't know," I whisper back. "Probably."

"Carlos, come claim your prize!" Elisa calls, looking directly at us.

"I guess she means me." Carlos says as he stands. He easily strides over to the group of winners, and I feel Lennox shift in his seat as he watches them, too.

"What's going on between you and Anastasiya?" I whisper as Elisa starts talking.

"What are you talking about?" Lennox asks quickly. He folds his arms over his chest defensively.

"I mean, the way you two are acting makes me think there might be something besides a coworker relationship between you." I say quietly, just in case someone is listening. "It doesn't have to be a secret or something. I'm your friend."

"Yeah, well, it's not like that." Lennox says dismissively.

"Okay, then." I say somewhat sharply back. "I'm just trying to be present in your life, but apparently, you're not interested in that."

"It's not that, Magnolia." Lennox says, his tone sharper now. Lennox and I have been friends since we were six. This is ridiculous. He, Jacob, Elisa, and I have always done things together, while Julia, Maisie, and Anastasiya were together.

"It's fine." I say, turning away from him.

"Wait, Magnolia." Lennox blurts out. He takes my wrist quickly, and I fight the urge to rip it away from him.

"What, Lennox?" I say, turning back to him.

"I'm sorry, Magnolia." Lennox says. "Things are just really screwed up at my house right now, and it's more than just Maisie and Anastasiya fighting. She and I are fighting, my parents aren't happy, and it's all a lot right now."

I chew my lip as I consider what he's saying. The dark circles from lack of sleep under his eyes indicate this is the truth. "I'm sorry, Lennox. I didn't mean to pry, but you know that I'm not as close with Maisie, so I have no idea about what's going on with her, Anastasiya, and you."

"I know, and I'm sorry," Lennox says, the sincerity in his eyes speaking for him. "You've been busy this month with your sister's wedding, and I've only been hanging out with Jacob and Anastasiya."

I nod, agreeing with him. "How am I supposed to be a good friend when I turn around and you're in the middle of a fight with a boy who just moved here, and then your sister?"

Lennox winces, but his face hardens slightly. "That's not related to this conversation."

"I don't even know what happened." I hiss out. "It seems like everyone else does, but just because I'm over here stressed to death about a wedding that's not even mine, no one tells me anything."

"That was something that had to be done." Lennox grits out. "Those brothers are trouble, and I don't like it."

"What do you even mean?" I ask, hearing the frustration in my voice.

"I mean that they're bad news, and I don't think they need to be hanging out with us." Lennox says with determination. "Julia and Maisie don't need to-"

"What's going on?" Carlos asks as he saunters over to the table with a red and green envelope. His eyes narrow when they land on Lennox's hand, which is still wrapped around my wrist. His grip softened a few minutes ago, and we both just forgot that it was there.

"We're talking," I say, glancing over at Lennox. He immediately removes his hand and places it on his lap.

"Yeah, Magnolia and I haven't talked in a while." Lennox

agrees with a nod of his head. He looks more than happy to move on from our previous conversation about the twins, Julia, and his sister.

"I see," Carlos says as he sits down next to me. His voice is both curious and maybe a little bit irritated. Carlos' hand finds mine, and he pulls it to his knee, where he wraps his hand fully around mine.

"What did you win?" Lennox asks, changing the topic. We both glance over to see Anastasiya speaking rapidly with Elisa, and I clench my teeth together as I imagine sitting here with Lennox and Carlos until she's back. Up until a few minutes ago, I didn't realize just how irritated I am with Lennox and most of our friend group for leaving me out of everything that's been going on.

"The bakery that made these gingerbreads—the one that your cousin and that twin work at—has a *special dessert* for me." Carlos says as he repeats the words Elisa must have told him.

"Oh, really?" I ask, glancing over at the card in his hand.

"Yep," Carlos hums as he glances one last time between Lennox and I. "Do you want to go with me tomorrow to pick whatever it is up?"

"I would love to," I begin slowly. Carlos' face drops, and I quickly rush to finish my statement. "But we're going to the parade, and the bakery will be closed."

"Parade?" Carlos asks in confusion.

"Every year, Winterberry Hollow has a Christmas parade, and it's a big deal." Lennox jumps in. Is this is way of trying to make it up to me for ignoring me? Befriending Carlos so that I'm happy with him?

"That's cool." Carlos replies with a nod. To the average

person, he would seem completely normal. To me, who's spent hours and hours with him every day for the past few weeks, he's a little bit off. "How does that work with all of the snow?"

"Huh?"

"How do you have a parade in the snow?" Carlos elaborates.

"Oh, the streets get plowed and everything before. You'll just have to see it tomorrow to get it." I say, nodding as I understand the question.

"Anastasiya and I are going to be in one of the horse-drawn carriages, so keep an eye out for us." Lennox says.

"Are you going to be driving it?" I ask, unable to conceal my curiosity.

Lennox nods a little bit proudly. "At the farm, I've been doing some of the sleigh rides, so I'm pretty trained in the driving department."

"You're still doing those, right?" I ask. "The sleigh rides, I mean. They stop January first?"

"Yeah, we are. That day that you two came was just the big day when we really pushed the rides, since the weather was most ideal and it aligned with right before most of the staff took their Christmas break off." Lennox agrees as he leans back in his chair.

"That makes sense," I say with a nod. Turning to Carlos, who is still using his thumb to rub small circles on the back of my hand, I look up at him, surprised to see that his jaw is clenched tightly and he's not wearing his usual addicting smile. "Do you want to leave?"

"If you don't want to stay any longer, I wouldn't mind getting you home a little bit early." Carlos agrees slowly.

"No, I want to come with you to the store," I say quickly. A light flush heats my cheeks as I realize just how blunt I sound, but I push past the feeling of embarrassment.

"You do?" Carlos asks, his eyes brightening.

"Yeah, of course I do." I say with a smile. "You don't know your way around here."

"Oh, so that's the only reason?" Carlos teases as he squeezes my hand lightly. "You only want to come with me so I don't get lost?"

"Thanks for helping me out, Lennox," Anastasiya says as she plops down next to Lennox. She's smiling excitedly, and she's carrying the same envelope that Carlos has in his hand.

"I just put it together, Anastasiya. You did all of the decorating, so you really deserve all of the credit." Lennox says easily, as though he did nothing.

Carlos taps my hand lightly and draws my attention away from Anastasiya and Lennox, and I blink a few times as I realize that I totally left him hanging and didn't respond.

"Sorry, Carlos," I say softly. "Yeah, let's leave now."

The walk to the car is quiet, and the only other noise besides the crunch of snow under our boots is the other cars leaving the lot. Carlos is carrying both of our gingerbread houses, and he places them safely on the floorboard of the backseat.

Once we're inside the car, Carlos turns the key and waits for his turn to back out of the spot.

"Are you okay?" I blurt out once he pulls onto the road. The streetlights are casting an orange tint on the dark night, and even though the heat is blasting, a chill still races up my arms.

"Yeah, I'm okay." Carlos answers. "Are you?"

"Why wouldn't I be?" I ask, taken aback by his question.

"You just seemed to be having an intense conversation with Lennox, and then he was holding your wrist, so I don't know." Carlos says slowly. Is that what this is about?

"I'm fine. Lennox was just being rude, and I was hurt that he's been avoiding me all month." I explain. Carlos' eyebrows flit upward at this, but he doesn't say anything and allows me to continue speaking.

"Why has he been avoiding you?" Carlos asks.

"He's just being a jerk, I think. I don't understand it all, since he's not telling me anything, and I'm not as close with Maisie as I am with him." I say frustratedly. "I have no idea what's going on with anyone now that I'm so busy with the wedding preparations, and I just feel like I'm getting left behind or something."

"It's not your fault, Lia." Carlos says softly. I suck in a deep breath at Carlos' statement, but it feels like there's not enough oxygen in my lungs to reply. "It's not your fault."

"I..." What am I even trying to say? "I didn't say it was." I finally make out.

"Yeah, but you think it is." Carlos replies, as though he can just see into the innermost corners of my mind.

"I didn't say that." I argue back as Carlos pulls into the dimly lit parking lot.

"You're thinking it, though." Carlos counters as he puts the car in park.

"How do you know that?" I ask quickly, unbuckling my seatbelt so I can slip my shoes off and pull my feet onto the chair.

"Because you think that since you've been busy this month, everyone is forgetting about you, and you should have made more of an effort to hang out with them." Carlos answers without hesitation. He reaches into the back seat and lifts his gingerbread house on the plate, and sets it on the center console.

"How do you know that?" I ask quietly, every inch of my body freezing as he says what I've been thinking for the past few weeks.

"Because you put too much pressure on yourself, and immediately blame yourself when something goes wrong." Carlos responds steadily as he starts to pull apart the house.

"That's not true," I say quickly. "It's not my fault that everyone is moving around me and forgetting that I exist."

"Yeah, but you're blaming yourself for being busy this month and not making enough time to hang out with everyone." Carlos says as he extends a piece of gingerbread that's covered in icing toward me. I glance down at his offering, and even though the idea of eating a gingerbread house in a desolate parking lot while having a deep conversation is insane, I take it.

"Okay, maybe you have a point there," I admit as I take a large bite out of the gingerbread. The candies that decorated it fill my mouth with sweetness, and I can't help the smile that escapes me. "And maybe you do deserve the award because this is really good." I say with a small giggle as I look up at Carlos.

Carlos smiles widely at this, and I can't help but smile back at him. "You need to stop blaming yourself for everything, Lia. You deserve more than that." His words stir something deep within me, but instead of responding, I take another bite of his gingerbread.

Why is Carlos so good at finding these deep parts of me

that I'm desperately trying to shove down? Why is he so good at understanding me?

"Because you're an open book," Carlos says around the bite of gingerbread he's eating.

"What?" Did I really say that last part out loud? A flush warms my neck and cheeks as I realize that I totally said that.

"You asked why I understand you, and I said it's because you're like an open book for me." Carlos repeats with a small smile.

"No one has ever told me that before." I say softly. "Everyone always tells me that I'm hard to understand, and that I'm too wound up."

"I don't think you're hard to understand," Carlos says gently as he reaches out and brushes away the tear that I didn't even realize was rolling down my cheek.

"You're the only person," I say with a small laugh as I take another bite of gingerbread and icing.

"Is that a bad thing?" Carlos asks with a chuckle. "I mean, are you upset that I understand you?"

"I guess not, but I don't know, it's just weird to me that you understand me when people I've known my whole life don't get me." I say with a small sigh. "Does that make sense?"

"Kind of." Carlos says with a nod of his head. "The day that I met you, I just felt like I knew you or something."

"Really?" I question. I don't think I felt like that, so how is it possible that Carlos does?

"Yeah, I think so." Carlos says as he bites into another piece of gingerbread. "You just seemed very...*you*. I don't know how to explain it."

"But you didn't know me before that," I say with confusion.

"Yeah, but I just knew that you were who you acted like." Carlos says as he runs his fingers through his hair. "I feel like I'm not explaining this properly, but the point is that I just felt like I knew you."

"I'm not sure I fully get it, but I believe you." I finally say.

"Thanks," Carlos replies.

"This is by far one of the strangest things I've ever done." I blurt out as I reach for another gingerbread house wall.

"What?" Carlos asks with a grin as he reaches for another piece.

"Sitting in a car while eating gingerbread houses while having a deep conversation." I say with a grin. My back is pressed to the car window, and my legs are curled under me. Surprisingly, it's extremely comfortable.

"I guess it is rather strange." Carlos agrees with a nod. "But it's not bad."

"Yeah, definitely not bad. Just strange." I agree with a nod.

"Strange is good sometimes," Carlos says softly. "Hey, if you still want to come with me to the store, then we should go in now before they close.

"Oh, that's right." I say sheepishly as Carlos turns the car off and climbs out. He comes to my door to open it, since I'm still pulling my boots on.

"Here, I can tie it." Carlos says as he gently moves my fingers out of the way as he laces up my boots.

"Thanks," I respond breathlessly. Carlos helps me out of

the car, but once he closes the door behind me, I'm standing between him and the car, and Carlos sucks in a deep breath before wrapping his hand around the back of my head and pressing me against the door, his lips crashing against mine.

Chapter Nineteen

6 DAYS 'TIL CHRISTMAS

"Why does everyone here just thrive in the cold?" Carlos asks as we walk up the sidewalk to the spot where we'll have the best vantage point of the parade.

"Because we're all elves of winter wonderland." I answer with a straight face.

"I used to think that you were joking, but now, I'm not so sure." Carlos says with a laugh as I stop in front of one of the shops.

"We can watch from here," I comment as the parade begins. Children giggle as people walking reach out and offer them candies, and the Christmas music blasting from the speakers blends with it.

"Magnolia!" Elisa calls from the float she and Jacob are on. They're dressed as elves, and Jacob has his arm poised to throw candies at Carlos and I. Before I can even register what's happening, candy is raining down around us, and Carlos is passing me a chocolate bar.

"Here," Carlos says with a smile as he extends his hand.

"Thanks," I say with a grin as I take the chocolate.

"I didn't think we would ever find you," Julia exclaims near my ear, causing me to jump as I turn to her, Maisie, and the twins.

"Gosh, you startled me." I say breathlessly. "Heads up next time."

"Give me a break, Magnolia." Julia teases as she wraps her arm through mine. "Anyway, like I was saying, we've been looking for you and Carlos."

I turn to Carlos, who is still standing a foot or two behind me, before looking back at Julia. "Why?"

"I don't know, maybe I like spending time with my cousin." Julia teases. Maisie is standing near Romero, and Leo is on the other side of Julia. "I haven't seen you all month, and I miss you."

"I miss you, too." I say, leaning my head on her shoulder for a moment. "What's up with you four? Are you all a group or something?"

Julia presses her lips together for a second as her smile falters, but just as quickly as it came, it disappears. "Something like that. Maisie is upset with Lennox and Anastasiya, and I don't know what you've gathered, but Elisa is mad that neither of us jumped to team Jacob and Lennox during that fight." Julia explains.

"Oh, I guess I didn't notice that." I admit. "I've been spending all go my time working on the wedding preparations, and I feel completely out of the loop."

"It's fine, we don't need to talk about it right now." Julia says quickly. "And I think there is some explaining that needs to be done with you and Carlos."

I roll my eyes, but instead of denying anything, a small giggle escapes me. "Hey, let's not deflect from the elephant in the room. What caused that whole fight?" I ask quickly.

"Well, that's the thing. I'm not really sure how the rumors all started, but apparently Lennox heard that-" A few horses whinny so loudly as they start to pass by that I can't even hear the end of what Julia's saying, and I glance up to see that it's the sleigh in front of the one Lennox and Anastasiya are on.

"This isn't good," Leo says as he leans into Julia's ear. He's close enough that I can hear, too, and when both of their eyes move to Romero and Maisie, I quickly understand what they're getting at. We all turn back to Lennox, who has completely dropped the smile that he was just wearing.

"He's totally not looking at all of us, right?" Julia asks with a smile as she tries to appear oblivious to Lennox's angry scowl.

"I mean, judging by his face, probably not. He's just angry that people are enjoying the parade and cheering for him." I say lightly.

"Yeah, let's go with that." Julia says as she squeezes my arm.

"So what were you saying before all of that?" I ask a moment later, just as Julia turns at the sound of Maisie's raised voice.

"I'm not going to do this anymore. It's all so stupid, and it's not fair to me." Maisie says before taking off down the street. Romero is standing in shock, but before he can do anything, Julia drops my arm and races after her.

"Sorry, Magnolia!" She calls as she runs after Maisie.

"Just let them figure it out," Leo says to Romero as he starts to follow them.

"They wouldn't need to figure it out if you didn't-" Romero starts before he clamps his mouth shut. "Forget it, *Leo*." Leo winces at the harsh emphasis on his name and doesn't protest when Romero brushes past him to walk down the street.

"What's going on?" Carlos asks, leaning down to whisper in my ear as Leo shoves his hands in his pockets, seemingly deciding whether or not to follow his brother, or Julia and Maisie.

"I have no idea." I answer, feeling just as bewildered as he does. "Julia was trying to explain it all to me, but that's when Lennox went by, and then Maisie was arguing with Romero, so she wasn't able to tell me."

"So we're back to square one?" Carlos asks as his lips lift in a small smile.

"Basically." I agree with a nod of my head. I turn to Leo, who still looks flustered, and only glance back at Carlos for a second before stepping towards him.

"Hey, I say politely as I step towards him. "I know we met at the park a few weeks ago, but I don't think we've ever really introduced ourselves. I'm Magnolia, Julia's cousin."

"I'm Leo," He says curiously as he shakes my hand. "I work with Julia at the bakery."

"How's that going?" I ask, a small laugh escaping me at Leo's face.

"Well, has anyone ever told you that your cousin is rather stubborn?" Leo asks with a laugh.

"Just a few times." I tease.

"Besides the fact that we have differing opinions

sometimes, and that Julia is very committed to her job, it's been amazing." Leo says with a nod. "We get along really well, and..." He trails off as a different look takes over his eyes.

"You think she's pretty?" I fill in. Leo immediately swallows loudly at this, and a small smile creeps up my cheeks.

"No! Well, yes, of course, but that's not why I like her." Leo says quickly. "She's really pretty, obviously, but she's also just so amazing otherwise."

"Yeah, she is pretty amazing," I agree.

"Hey, Lia, what's going on?" Carlos asks from a few feet away. While I've been talking to Leo, he's been watching the rest of the parade, but now he's pointing to the small group of people near the end of Main Street.

"I don't know," I say hurriedly as we begin jogging towards the people surrounding what looks like a...fight? As I push closer, the figures become clearer. The first boy I recognize is Lennox, and the second is Jacob? What?

"Hey! Break this up!" I man in a police uniform calls out as he shoves through the people. My eyes focus, and I realize that it's Lennox's dad, and he does *not* look happy.

Lennox either doesn't hear him or is ignoring him as he and Jacob continue to tussle in the snow.

"Does he have a track record of fighting or something?" Carlos asks near my ear. "This is getting ridiculous, right?"

"Yeah, I'm beginning to think he doesn't hate my brother and I. He just likes fighting." Leo chimes in.

"Well, I know he seems bad right now," I start, unsure of what else to say.

"You're defending him?" Leo blurts out incredulously.

"Hey," Carlos says somewhat sharply. Butterflies dance in my stomach at his defensive voice.

"It's not that I'm defending him, necessarily," I begin as Lennox's dad and another police officer rip the boys apart. "But I know his heart, and he's probably just really out of sorts or something right now. I don't know, but really, he's not like this all of the time."

"So fighting every other week is new?" Carlos asks, not like he doesn't believe me, but like he's not understanding why we seem to know two different versions of Lennox.

"He's always fought here and there, but this is entirely new. He's never fought Jacob before." I say, realizing how weak my defense is. "I'm not trying to say he's in the right, but before this month, he wasn't like this."

"He's just deciding to give us new guys a scare, then?" Leo asks under his breath as Lennox's dad instructs both of the boys to enter the nearby SUV.

"I guess," I say. "He's not going to arrest either of them, I'm sure."

"I didn't think he was going to," Leo replies. "Having a dad as the police chief probably has a few perks."

"How did you know that?" I ask, turning to him in surprise. "Who told you that their dad is the police chief?"

"Julia, I think." Leo says nervously. "Why?"

"It just seemed weird that you knew who his dad is when you haven't been here for very long." I answer, feeling slightly embarrassed.

"Oh, well, sorry for surprising you." Leo says. "Julia has told me a little bit about their family, since Romero works with Maisie. I don't want him working with a bad influence or something." He says with a laugh.

"Are you the older twin?" I ask curiously.

"I don't know," Leo says. "We turned eighteen a few months ago, but since we're going to be living with them until we graduate, they're not telling us until next summer."

"I can't imagine not knowing who is older," Carlos comments. "For me, it's always been very obvious."

"You have a brother?" Leo asks, turning to Carlos.

"Yeah, he's marrying Magnolia's older sister on Christmas Day." Carlos says easily. "He's ten years older than me."

"Ten years? That's crazy." Leo says in surprise. "I bet Romero and I weren't even ten minutes apart."

"My older sister is ten years older than me, too." I chime in.

"What's with these crazy age gaps?" Leo asks with a chuckle. "Here my brother and I are, the weirdos for being twins, when there are people with ten-year age gaps."

"Leo, we should get out of here." Romero says as he pushes through the crowds behind us. I turn to face him, surprised by his sudden appearance, but he doesn't even seem to notice Carlos and I.

"What's wrong?" Leo asks in confusion until he turns to Romero. Something dawns on his face, and he nods quickly. "Okay. Hey, Magnolia, Carlos, thanks for hanging out with me when everyone else left."

Romero just clenches his jaw at this, but doesn't say anything to him. "It's nice to see you again, Magnolia and Carlos. Sorry that we have to leave right now."

Once they've left and most of the crowd has dispersed, Carlos reaches down and takes my hand in his, and we begin walking down the street, completely aimlessly.

"Hey, Magnolia. Tell Poppy congratulations!" One of my teachers says as she passes me on the street with her husband and child.

"Thank you, Mrs. Paige." I call back with a wave.

"You know, it's so strange to me that you know everyone here." Carlos says absently as we walk.

"What do you mean?"

"Well, in New York, sure, you know people there, but it's not like you're just likely to pass them on the street and exchange a greeting. Everyone has somewhere to be and something to be doing. Just strolling like this is completely unheard of. Much less making conversation as you go." Carlos answers.

New York.

Carlos is from New York.

Carlos lives in New York.

My breath quickens as the realization finally hits me. Carlos doesn't live here. Of course, I've known this. I haven't thought about it in a long time, though. In my mind, he lives here now. He's so much a part of my day-to-day life that he's never leaving. He's never going back across the country to a giant city where he's going to forget about me the moment he steps off his plane.

"Lia?" Carlos asks a second later. "Are you okay?" Concern fills his eyes, and if at all possible, my heart beats even faster now that he's looking into my eyes. How did I allow myself to like someone so much when he's going to pack up in leave in just two weeks?

The world around me starts to grow hazy, and Carlos' face begins to blur as these past two weeks flood my mind.

"Lia, you're really freaking me out." Carlos says as he

reaches out to place his hands on either of my shoulders. "Are you okay? What's wrong?"

"I-" I suck in a deep breath before continuing. "I just lost my balance there for a minute."

"Are you sure? That didn't seem normal to me." Carlos questions. "Is something wrong?"

"Nothing's wrong." I say with a quick shake of my head. "I just want to go home, actually." Carlos' face twists in confusion.

"If this is what I said about knowing everyone, I didn't mean it in a bad way at all." Carlos says, as though this is the only thing that he can think of that's a problem.

"No, it's not that at all." I insist, starting to walk back to where we parked the car. "I'm just really tired and need to lie down when I get home."

Carlos immediately follows and opens the door for me. "Are you sick? If you need to go to the doctor, I can take you."

"Carlos, I'm fine. I just got dizzy for a moment, and I just need to go home." I say sharply. I wince immediately at the hurt on Carlos' face. "Sorry, I didn't mean to snap at you, Carlos. You didn't deserve that."

"It's fine, Lia." Carlos says gently as he begins driving. "You don't owe me any kind of explanation."

The gentle stillness of my house usually comforts me, since I'm here alone most of the time. However, it feels anything but nice. After I got home, I ran a hot bath and curled up in my robe under all of my blankets.

How did I ever allow myself to feel like this for Carlos? How did I think that allowing him to nestle himself so deeply in my life was the smart thing to do?

Carlos is *leaving* in a few weeks. He's going back to the big city where he can have anyone he likes, and forget about me in the blink of an eye. There's no way Carlos is going to remember me when he leaves. How could he? I'm just the girl who pulled him around town to plan a wedding that means nothing to him.

By the end of next month, he'll have forgotten I exist. He'll forget all of the times we laughed together, figured out problem after problem, and felt the rush of sparks around us when our eyes met.

If he even felt that for me. What if he just sees me as the girl who's available for the month, and I'm just his Christmas fling?

Regardless of any of that, the fact of the matter is that this will never work out between us. Carlos lives in New York City, and I live in Winterberry Hollow. Those names alone are enough to make another sob escape me. Why in the world would Carlos even *want* to be in a relationship with a girl from some tiny town in the mountains called Winterberry Hollow?

I freeze when my phone starts ringing from the nightstand, and suck in a few deep breaths before reaching for it.

Carlos.

His name is lighting up the screen, and for a second, I

debate whether or not to ignore it. No, I'm not that mean. Whatever this is, it must be important.

"Hello?" I answer, stabilizing my voice as much as possible.

"Lia? Are you okay?" Carlos asks quickly, too soon to have been the reason he actually called me.

"Yeah, I'm fine." I lie, rolling a little bit on the bed, so now I'm sitting up. "What's up?"

"So, there's like, a tiny problem with my tuxedo, and I'm hoping that it's just mine, but there's a good chance it's Charlie's, too. Can you go to it and tell me something?" Carlos says hesitantly.

"How big is this problem?" I ask, jumping out of bed faster than someone who's been sobbing for the last hour should.

"Well, it's kind of just that this is a white tie tuxedo, when it's supposed to be a black tie." Carlos says slowly, as though this is earth-shattering information. Which, as someone who knows nothing about tuxedos, makes no sense.

"What's that supposed to mean?" I ask as I take the stairs two at a time.

"They're completely different. The fitting, styling, everything." Carlos explains. "You'd have to see them next to each other to tell the difference, but you'd be able to tell which one is more desirable for a Christmas wedding."

"I'll send you a picture of this one," I say as I flick on the lights and open the closet.

"You can turn it to video chat," Carlos responds, since in a situation like this, it would make more sense.

"No!" I blurt out before internally face-palming myself.

"Why?" Carlos asks, confused. He's not trying to be pushy about it, but I can tell that he's curious.

"Because I'm in my pajamas." Seriously? I couldn't have come up with anything better than that?

"Oh, well, okay." Carlos stammers. "You can send me the photo and I'll tell you if it's right or wrong."

"Sent," I say after snapping the pictures. I'm not too sure what I'm supposed to be taking photos of, but hopefully they're enough for Carlos to tell if it's also messed up.

"Yeah, this one is a white tie tuxedo, too." Carlos says with a huff. "I'm going to call my brother and see what he wants to do, because these aren't what he and Poppy said they wanted."

"So we have to drive *five hours* away to get the tuxedos they want?" I ask incredulously. Carlos is on my doorstep, ready for travel, while I'm wearing a pair of leggings and a sweater.

"Yeah, Charlie called around and found somewhere that's willing to extend business hours as long as we pick them up today." Carlos explains sheepishly. I hate that he can tell I'm not feeling like myself right now.

"Fine, let me just grab my purse and jacket." I say, reaching over to the entryway closet to grab my stuff. My feet slip into my boots, but I don't even bother to lace them, since I'm going to be sitting in the car for three hours.

"I'm sorry, Lia." Carlos says as he walks next to me. He opens the door, and I close my eyes for a second, trying to remove myself from here mentally.

"My name is *Magnolia*," I say quietly as he closes the door behind me. Once Carlos is inside and driving, he reaches out to take my hand in his, but I quickly reach up to brush my hair away from my face. When Carlos tries again a few minutes later, I reach down to fix my shoes that totally don't need fixing.

"Are you going to tell me why you're upset with me?" Carlos asks as he merges onto the main road that will lead us around the mountain and onto the highway. I turn in his direction at his blunt question, and swallow as I try to come up with a response that doesn't make me seem as hurt as I am.

"I'm not really-" I begin before he cuts me off.

"Lia, don't. You're upset about something, and at first I tried to believe that it was something not related to me, but now I have no choice but to believe that you're upset with me. What is it?" Carlos interrupts. With anyone else, I would've snapped at them for interrupting me, but I don't have the heart to do that to Carlos.

"My name is *Magnolia.*" I say quickly, trying to regain control over something as simple as my name. "I'm just upset right now about something you can't fix."

"*Lia,*" Carlos begins with a small smile.

"*Magnolia.*" I say sharper than necessary. Carlos' smile drops, and while he tries not to seem obvious about it, I can tell that I've now hurt his feelings.

Why does Carlos keep trying to draw me back into this little bubble where we joke and he makes everything better with a simple smile? "I'm sorry." I say softer now.

"It's fine, Magnolia." Carlos says, his words clipped and cool. "I'm sorry for butting into your internal battle."

"Internal battle?" I ask quickly. "What's that supposed to mean?"

"It means that you're fighting something in your head right now and you don't want me involved." Carlos replies.

"What if it's not internal?" I demand, as blood rushes through my veins and my heart starts to beat even louder.

"Then what is it?" Carlos counters, his voice slightly irritated now. I don't think he's ever really sounded irritated with me, but now that he is, it makes me even more hurt and frustrated.

"Why do you care?" I question, my voice higher now. Why can't I just get control over my emotions and stop caring about Carlos?

"I mean, I don't know. Let's think about it." Carlos replies sarcastically. "I care about you and want to know what's bugging you? Let's start there."

"You care about me?" I ask, softer now. Carlos' face shifts into one of deep confusion and hurt, and now, I'm the one wondering why he's upset.

"Do you really not think I care about you?" Carlos asks, his voice cracking just a little bit. His eyes never leave the road, but they look dimmer now.

"I don't know," I answer truthfully. Carlos doesn't respond for a moment, but his hands tighten on the wheel.

"What are you upset about?" Carlos asks, his voice defeated.

I'm not sure why, but my mouth starts working on its own accord, and everything starts spilling out. "You're going to be leaving here in a few weeks, and you're going to forget about me." Carlos' jaw clenches, but he doesn't say anything as I continue. "I'm just really hurt that I won't be seeing you after this, and you've basically made it impossible not to fall for you, so now what am I supposed to do other than cut you off now?" The silence around us is deafening, and for a few minutes, I wonder if Carlos is even going to respond.

"Why are you so ready to see the worst in me?" Carlos asks, his voice barely audible.

"What are you talking about?" I ask, feeling slightly defensive about the question.

"I mean that you're basically accusing me of using then leaving you, and that I'm some heartless person who wants to see you suffer." Carlos answers, his face twisting in hurt.

"I never said that." I snap.

"But you're essentially thinking it." Carlos argues back.

"No I'm not." I argue.

"You keep doing everything in your power to twist or misunderstand my intentions." Carlos says, his voice full of what must be hurt.

"I'm not doing that."

"Then how do you explain not knowing that I care for you?" Carlos asks softly. "After all of this, I don't care about you?"

"I don't know." I say, pressing my lips together instead of continuing to argue back.

"How do you not know that I care about you? When have I done anything to indicate that I don't care about you? I keep trying to prove to you that I'm not the person you immediately jumped to conclusions about when we met, but you're so determined to find something to keep that theory alive." Carlos says, his tone more and more hurt the longer he speaks. "When did I ever indicate that I'm going to forget about you when I leave? Do you know if I even want to leave? Or did you jump to conclusions about that, too?"

"That's not fair," I say sharply.

"It's not fair for me to jump to conclusions about that, but it's totally fair for you to do the same and think the worst of me at the same time?" Carlos asks, his voice cracking just as he finishes speaking. "I'm not a bad person, and I never want to hurt you, but you're so determined to find something that doesn't exist in me, and convince yourself that it's a fact."

"I didn't do that." I snap, knowing full well that's what I did.

"Then how do you explain all of this?" Carlos asks incredulously. "It's hurtful that you believe that I'm just here to use you and then leave town and forget about you. I would think that you know me better than that, but I don't even know if that would be enough for you. You analyze every single move I make, and you study it for some indication that I don't care for you."

"Maybe I just like having all of the data and want to know what kind of person you are before I fall in even deeper to whatever *this* is." I defend, gesturing between us.

"What is *this* to you?" Carlos asks, his eyes still never leaving the road. "What do you think is between us?"

"I don't know, Carlos." I admit. "I don't know what your intentions are, or what you think of me. I don't know what to think of our future, or if we even have one. I don't know why you keep digging down into the deepest corners of my mind like it's nothing, and I don't know why you confront me about them."

"I just understand you or something, Magnolia. I don't know why, but you're like an open book for me." Carlos answers. "Also, I feel like you just assuming that I don't want anything from the future with you is hurtful in so many ways. You've questioned my character and how I feel for you. You've admitted that you don't know if I feel for you, which is kind of crazy, since I've done nothing this month besides try to prove to you that I'm not some idiot from the city who is wildly uncomfortable with most of the things we do."

"I was just supposed to know that you don't want to up and leave me as soon as you're able to go back home?" I question, throwing my hands up in exasperation.

"Did I ever do anything that would indicate it? I've tried to show you how I feel so many times, and every time I tried to tell you how I felt, you brushed it off. I'm failing at everything for you, Magnolia. I'm not enough for you, and you've made that very apparent." Carlos admits, his voice echoing with hurt.

"That's not true, Carlos." I say quickly.

"I don't really believe you, because how do you explain just thinking that I'm going to leave and never think about you again?" Carlos asks, his tone coming out even more hurt. I press my lips together in not quite defeat, but in self-preservation. How do I even explain what I'm feeling? How do I explain that in my brain, I'm always going to jump to the worst-case scenario, no matter the situation?

"Magnolia, I'm sorry," Carlos says after he loads the new tuxedos in the back of the car.

"For what?" I ask, glancing over as Carlos merges onto

the highway. Earlier, the rest of our drive had been silent, neither of us speaking the entire time.

"I'm sorry for ever making you doubt that I care for you, and I'm sorry for being upset with how you felt." Carlos answers, his voice calm and controlled, but full of emotion.

"You don't need to apologize, Carlos." I say, another round of emotions cycling through my body. Why is Carlos apologizing for me attacking him? Why does he have to be so good at disproving the narrative I've created in my head?

"I do." Carlos says, not even considering what I've said. "I made you feel unsafe emotionally, and I need to take responsibility for that."

"Carlos, it's also that you're going to be leaving. That's not your fault, and I just want to move past this." I say quickly, hating that we're having this conversation again.

"What's *this* mean?" Carlos asks as he begins to chew on his lower lip.

"Us. I want to move past us. I want to move past whatever fling this is, and I want to not feel for you anymore." I say, harsher than intended. "I want to move past whatever has been between us, and I want to go on as maid of honor and best man. Nothing more."

Carlos is silent as he listens to everything I'm saying, and after a few seconds, he nods. "If that's what you want, then I'm sorry for ever making you feel anything for me."

Chapter Twenty-One

"*You did what?*" Poppy gasps over the phone.

"Poppy, you don't get it. He's going to leave here and forget all about me, and it will have been stupid to think that we had something." I respond defensively.

"And you know that because why?" Poppy asks incredulously. "Did Carlos ever communicate that he plans on breaking up with you as soon as possible?"

"He didn't have to." I say sharply. "Why in the world would he be interested in staying with someone who lives across the country?"

"Why would he be interested in being with someone he's only going to have four weeks with?" Poppy counters.

"I don't know." I admit, flopping back against my pillows.

"Because he likes you, Mango." Poppy hisses.

"Why are you being so mean to me? Shouldn't you be

taking my side since I'm your sister?" I demand, the sting of Poppy's words cutting deep.

"I'm not being mean to you, Magnolia. This isn't about taking sides." Poppy retorts. "That boy went way out of his way to try and show you how he felt, and you told him it meant nothing."

"What are you even talking about?" I ask, inhaling sharply.

"Carlos has been telling Charlie about what he's been doing with you, and in turn, Charlie has been telling me. Carlos really cares for you, and you just blew up on him because the moment you felt insecure, you took it out on him and tried to find a way to blame him for it." Poppy says matter-of-factly.

"I didn't do that!" I say sharply. "I simply looked at the facts and statistics of what is most likely going to happen, and decided to save myself from heartbreak sooner rather than later."

"That's the problem, Mango. You're coming at this like your relationship is some statistic that you can calculate just right to potentially save yourself." Poppy says. "Remember when I asked if you made a list? This is what I'm talking about. You're trying to hold onto every inch of control, and your knuckles are white at this point."

"So what if I'm relying on facts to keep me safe? That's not a crime." I retort, hating just how right Poppy is.

"Because you're hurting other people in the process, and it's not good for you." Poppy says simply. "Carlos tried so hard with you. Did you know that?"

"What are you even talking about?" I question, intrigue filling me even though it shouldn't be.

"I mean, I told him that you were going to be hard on him, and that he didn't have to help you with any of the wedding stuff if he didn't want to." Poppy blurts out.

"You told him that?" I ask, now hurt with Poppy, too.

"Magnolia, it wouldn't have been fair of me to plead for him to help you. When he told Charlie about this girl he met at the ice rink and how she's obsessed with candy canes, I immediately knew it was you. I told him that I just got off the phone with you, and that I'd asked you to include him, but that he didn't have to if he didn't feel like he'd be able to make you happy."

"And he still chose to help?" I ask, even though I know the answer.

"Yes, he still chose to help, even when he asked Charlie to pass me the phone on the very first day you spent together because he hurt your feelings and he wanted to know how to not do that in the future." Poppy says. "You've convinced yourself that Carlos is someone who doesn't care about you, when that couldn't be further from the truth."

"How am I supposed to know that, when it makes sense that he's going to leave town and never look back?" I ask.

"Maybe you could ask him. Or, you know, you could've asked him *before* you blew up on him. Just a suggestion." Poppy says. At my hurt expression, she softens a little bit. "Mango, I'm not trying to be mean to you, but I'm just frustrated that you hurt Carlos when he didn't deserve that, and it wasn't even necessary. He *really* likes you."

"You don't get it, Poppy. You just live this whimsical life where you say you're going to leave your wedding up to a dress, and you aren't even going to get here a full day before your wedding." I say as tears start to form at the corners of my eyes.

"We're just different, Magnolia." Poppy says, her voice even softer. "You can be all about your lists and order, but you also expect perfection from everyone and yourself. It's not good for you."

"Or Carlos." I finally say, her point finally sinking in.

"Or Carlos." Poppy agrees. "Most people would flee at the idea of planning a wedding with you, but he did it with excitement and willingness."

"And now I've ruined it all by freaking out on him when my emotions went to war." I fill in. "I've really screwed everything up with him, haven't I?"

"I would say that he's probably—understandably—upset, but I don't think you've ruined everything for good." Poppy says slowly. "I would also say that you're going to have to put in a lot of effort, because that was what Carlos did. Now you need to prove to him that you feel for him, because he probably thinks that everything between you meant nothing to you."

"You're probably right." I agree with a nod. "But I can't just come out and say all of this, right?"

"Why not?" Poppy asks, and it sounds as though she's slapping her forehead in frustration.

"Well, I can't just come out of the gate with, *hey, I'm really sorry for assuming the worst about you, will you give me another chance? Right?*" I ask, leaning back into my pillows.

"Magnolia, I think this is where my advice ends. You need to do whatever feels true to you, and while you're at it, don't hurt Carlos again." Poppy says abruptly.

"You're not worried about me getting hurt?" I ask, slightly offended again.

"It's not that, Magnolia. I just know that you're able to inflict a lot more pain on him than you think, and I want you to be careful." Poppy says slowly.

"Okay, I understand. I'll be careful." I agree.

"I love you, Magnolia."

"Love you, Poppy."

"Now, tell me the whole story, beginning to end." Julia says as I sit down across from her in the living room. She's the only person I could think of to call, since I need a ride to the inn if I'm even going to try to reconcile with Carlos.

I begin with the whole story, and even though I can tell Julia is extremely disapproving of everything I did, she listens and doesn't interrupt. Her eyebrows shoot up when I get to the part about blowing up on Carlos, but again, she doesn't speak until I'm done.

"So, this is quite the situation." Julia begins, her voice hesitant.

"I know, I really messed up." I blurt out before she can continue. "I was stupid for just jumping to conclusions and looking for the worst in him. I know."

"Well, at least you're being self-aware." Julia says, her face squeezed into frustration. "I'd like to say that I'm surprised that you did that, but I can't say that I am."

"Thanks, I guess." I say defensively. "At least I'm admitting my mistakes and trying to fix them."

"You're right, you are admitting to them." Julia agrees as she nods her head. Her jet black hair swings in her ponytail, and I admire the stark difference between our hair. Hers is box-dyed, and mine has never been touched.

"So now we need to move to the next phase of the plan." I say, suddenly feeling self-conscious. "Or maybe not. Maybe I should just avoid Carlos until he leaves."

"No, no, no. We're not doing that." Julia interjects. "You're going to at least apologize to Carlos for treating him so poorly."

"Well—"

"No, he deserves an apology." Julia cuts in, her words harsh, but her tone soft. "Carlos deserves to know that you don't think of him as some terrible person, and you owe it to yourself to know that even if he never talks to you again, that you at least tried."

"So you think he's never going to talk to me again?" I blurt out.

"I think that I have no idea what he's going to say. Hopefully not, but there's still always a chance." Julia answers, reaching out to place her hands on my shoulder. "The main thing is that you do as much as possible on your end to fix this. Everything after that is just a bonus. Maybe you'll get back together and be happier than ever."

"Okay, okay." I agree, breathing in and out. "Just tell me what to do."

"Oh, Magnolia, I can't tell you what to do." Julia says quickly. "You have to do this from the heart. From you."

"Wait, I thought you were over here to help me." I plead.

"I am helping you. I'm being your emotional support

right now, and then you're going to come up with something to tell Carlos."

"So I have to come up with the perfect speech all by myself?"

"No!" Julia exclaims. "No coming up with the *perfect speech*. Nothing you do is going to be perfect, and some grand speech that you go over and over is not going to land the same as something real and raw from your heart."

"When did you become all good with love advice?" I huff, leaning back into the cushion.

"I'm not good with love advice, Magnolia. This isn't love advice at all." Julia says. "This is life advice. This is Better Magnolia's Life Advice."

"So this is really more about me than it is about Carlos?" I ask, looking up to meet her eyes.

"Yes, this is really more about you."

"Then why haven't you told me any of this before?" I ask.

"Because up until now, nothing has ever shaken you this much. If anyone even broached the topic about you being too intense and type A, you would lash out." Julia answers with a straight face.

"No I-"

"Magnolia, don't even. This isn't an attack on you. This is about bettering yourself and apologizing to Carlos for assuming the worst of him and telling him to his face for no reason." Julia interrupts.

"Okay, fine. Just tell me at least what I need to do." I finally give in.

"All I'm going to tell you to do is that you need to apologize without explaining away everything and trying to defend yourself. Listen to what Carlos says, and go from there." Julia says. "Oh, and whatever you do, don't break down on him and accidentally guilt him into agreeing with you."

"Is that something I need to be worried about?" I ask hesitantly.

"Well, it's just something girls tend to do sometimes." Julia says gently. "I just want you and Carlos to have a fair chance at this."

"See, love advice." I cut in.

"No, life advice."

After hours of pondering, the perfect idea comes to mind. My big apology gesture will be perfect.

Tomorrow morning, I'm going to call Maisie and ask her if she can pick me up and take me to the inn, since she'll be working. Then, I'm going to ask her to tell Carlos that there's a visitor for him, and once he comes down and sees me, we'll go into one of the recreational rooms, in which I'll apologize for treating him terribly. At the end, I'll offer for him to come with me to the ice rink, where we can just hang out away from the wedding preparations.

I've dwelled on the possibility that he's going to say that he would rather sleep in the snow than spend time with me, which is why it's taken me all day to form this plan. Maybe the self-doubt took over more planning time than I'd like to admit, but the important thing is that I at least have the perfect plan.

Chapter Twenty-Two

"Sorry, can you repeat yourself?" I say over the phone.

"Is this Magnolia Larsen?" The man's voice asks again.

"Um, yes, it is." I answer, completely off-guard. "Sorry, who did you say you are?"

"I'm Kane, a representative for the flower shop that you ordered fifty amaryllis from." He says slowly.

"Oh, yes, those are supposed to be delivered today, right?" I ask, glancing over at the calendar that's hanging from the fridge.

"Yes, they were."

"Were?" I ask quickly.

"Yes, they were supposed to be delivered today, but I'm sorry to say that the delivery has been canceled." Kane says.

"Why was it canceled?" I ask, already feeling my pulse pounding in my throat.

"Well, our delivery driver got stuck in the snow just

shortly after leaving here. As of now, he's still waiting on the tow truck, and then per company regulations, the delivery has to be canceled and then rescheduled." Kane explains calmly.

"But we can't reschedule. The wedding they're going to be used in is in three days." I plead, hating how desperate I sound.

"I'm sorry, ma'am, but the safety of our drivers and upholding company policy is our top priority." Kane says gently.

"What if I pick them up from the delivery driver?" I blurt out, not even fully considering what that will entail.

"You want to pick them up from the driver who is stuck in the snow?" Kane asks, as though he misheard me.

"Yes, is that possible?" I answer, swallowing the nausea that threatens to take over.

"I mean, I guess it is?" Kane says, as though he's never dealt with this particular situation. "You'd need identification to pick them up. By then, hopefully the driver will be able to pull into a rest stop or something."

"By then? Won't he be between Winterberry Hollow and May?" I ask, his statement strange.

"No, the driver is coming up from Garland, and when he called in, he said that he had only been on the road for about thirty minutes before he came upon the snowdrift." Kane says smoothly.

"So he's about four hours away from Winterberry Hollow?" I gasp.

"Yes, I'm afraid so." Kane says. "Again, we always have the option to reschedule, if you're interested in that."

"No, we need those flowers either today or tomorrow, so

another delivery won't work." I say, shaking my head as though he can see me. "I will be there to pick up the flowers as soon as possible. Is there a way to communicate with the driver?"

"Unfortunately, I cannot provide that information, but I can be your *middleman,* for lack of a better word. As of now, you need to start driving down to Garland, and once you're about an hour out, we can coordinate a little bit more." Kane says. "I look forward to communicating with you before you pick up the flowers."

"Okay, thank you." I say before Kane hangs up.

Now what? Am I going to call Carlos and tell him that we need to drive four hours away to pick up flowers from the side of the road? This is going to completely foil my perfect plan to reconcile with him, because now he's forced to be with me. Do I even say anything at all?

There's no way I can do this alone. I mean, Carlos still has my car. I can't drive four hours in the snow.

My only option is Carlos.

Before I can chicken out, I scroll through my contact list and press *call* next to Carlos' name.

"Hello?" Carlos' voice is confused, and I wince before speaking.

"So, there's like, kind of a large situation with the flowers." I blurt out.

"What's wrong?" Carlos' tone goes from confused to concerned within seconds.

"Well, the driver got stuck in the snow four hours away, and the only way to get them is to go pick them up from him ourselves. Otherwise, they would have to reschedule everything, and we won't get them on time." I explain, leaning against the doorframe for support while I speak.

"I see." Carlos says calmly. "We need to go get them now, right?"

"Yes."

"I'll be at your house in twenty minutes."

So, maybe I redid my hair three different times and changed my outfit no less than five times, but can you really blame a girl in this predicament?

The knock on my front door sends a tremor of nervousness down my body.

Can I really face Carlos?

Maybe he can go by himself?

No. That's not an option. I need to grow up and fix the problem I created.

As I tug the door open, the first thing I land on is Carlos' face, and it steals the breath right out of my lungs. Has he become even more beautiful in just two days?

"Hi," Carlos says politely. His hands stay at his sides, and even though it would be totally wrong since I haven't done my perfect apology yet, I want to reach out and take his hand in mine.

"Hi, Carlos." I breathe out.

"Are you ready to go?" His voice hasn't left the even, polite tone that he used a moment ago, and it physically hurts to know that just a week ago, he was laughing and talking to me like we'd known each other for years.

I hurt Carlos, and now he's completely withdrawn from me.

"Yeah, I am." I say softly, closing the door behind me.

"So, explain to me how all of this came about." Carlos says once we're on the road. "Why are the flowers so far away, when we ordered them from a shop an hour away?"

"Apparently, the shop had to order them in, and that truck is the one that's stuck in the snow." I explain, noticing just how nervous my voice sounds. "And the only way to get them on time is to pick them up from the driver, because once the delivery is cancelled, they have to redo it all, and by then the wedding will already be over."

"Interesting." Carlos comments as he taps his fingers along the steering wheel.

"Yeah," I agree with a nod. "At least we can still get them, and not be in a scramble for new ones." I'm rambling at this point, but I don't think I can handle silence with Carlos after our last conversation.

"That's a bright outlook." Carlos says, his voice slightly surprised. What? Why is my outlook so interesting to Carlos?

"I guess so." I say, thinking for a minute before continuing. "There's really nothing else we can do, so at least this is the best option."

"You're right, it's the best option." Carlos replies, but the way he says it leads me to believe that he wants to say something more.

For three agonizing hours, we drive in almost complete silence. Occasionally, one of us will say something like, *Are you okay if I change the heat?* Or, *Can I switch the radio station?* But other than that, we keep to ourselves.

Maybe I should just wait until tomorrow and talk to him then. I'll have had more time to rehearse my lines, and everything will be perfect.

"I'm going to call the shop and let them know that we're about thirty minutes from Garland, and that he can give us more directions." I say, turning to Carlos for the first time in two hours.

"Okay," Carlos says, not missing a beat.

"Hello?" Kane says, answering the phone.

"Hi, this is Magnolia Larsen. We spoke earlier about the flowers."

"Ah, yes, Ms. Larsen." Kane replies. "I assume you're near Garland?"

"Yes, we're about thirty minutes away."

"Okay, there's a rest stop called Drew's Yard, and once you're there, you should be able to spot the delivery truck. The logo on the side reads something along the lines of, *Flowers for You.*" Kane responds, and there's a scratching noise on the other end of the line as he presumably writes something down on a piece of paper. "I'll call the driver and give him your information. Since you've already paid, there's nothing else for you to do besides show him your identification and sign off on the order."

"Thank you."

"My pleasure. Have a nice day, Ms. Larsen." Kane replies before ending the call.

"There's a rest stop ahead where the delivery truck is parked. It's called Drew's Yard or something." I say, relaying the conversation to Carlos. My eyes can't help but focus on his concentrated face as he drives.

"I saw a sign saying that it's off the next exit, so we're not too far off." Carlos responds, his fingers tightening around the wheel as we hit a small patch of ice on the road. We slide ever so slightly, and immediately I suck in a deep breath and flatten myself against the back of my chair. "Did he say what the truck would look like?"

"Oh, yeah, he said that it has a flower logo on it. I can't remember exactly-" I suck in another breath as we pass a car that's slipped on the ice onto the shoulder.

"Did he say anything about what we need to do to get the flowers?" Carlos asks as I suck in deep breaths. I shouldn't be so terrified of snow and driving on ice, but after the one time when I slid into a snow drift two years ago, it always makes my heart race.

"He said that I need my identification, and I'll need to sign that I picked up the flowers." I recite, reaching into my purse to pull out my wallet. "I have my identification here, and then I'm sure he'll have a pen to sign with, right?"

"I'm sure he'll have a pen, Magnolia." Magnolia. Not Lia.

"Right, he probably will." I agree, releasing the breath that I've been holding.

"Hopefully, all of the flowers will fit," Carlos comments as we pull into the parking lot.

"You don't think they will?" I ask, turning in my seat to glance into the back row and trunk.

"They probably will." Carlos amends as he parks next to what has to be the delivery truck.

"Hello," The driver calls as he steps out of the truck. "May I see your identification before we get to unloading?"

"Sure," I say, passing him my driver's license. He nods and hands it back after glancing down at it.

"Alright, we can get them out and into your car." He says. "They're here in the back." The eighteen-wheeler has a large shipment container in the back, and the man climbs into it and starts passing the bouquets to Carlos.

"I'll take them from him, and then pass them to you." Carlos offers. "I can reorganize them if you just put them in the trunk."

"Okay," I agree, taking the first set from Carlos. We work quickly, and within ten minutes, we have all fifty of them.

"I'll just need you to sign here, and then you're good to go." The driver says, reaching into his truck to pull out a paper with a dotted line to sign. "Perfect." He says after I pen my name.

"Thank you," I call as he climbs into the truck. "I think we should secure them a little bit before we drive." I say, turning to Carlos.

"I'll do it, and you can warm up in the car." Carlos offers as he walks to the trunk. Should I? Or should I help?

"No, I'll help." I blurt out as I follow him to the back of the car. "I'll hold some of them so you can organize the other ones."

"Really?" Carlos asks in surprise as he turns around with a few sets in his hands. My breath catches when our eyes meet, and I feel as though at a gentle gust of cold wind I could fall over. The deep intensity in them dries my throat, and for a second, I forget that he's even said anything.

Maybe it's just me being hopeful, but the look in Carlos' eyes leads me to believe he's forgotten about that, too.

"What?" I finally make out, stepping closer to take the flowers from him.

"Nothing." Carlos says with a quick shake of his head.

He quickly organizes the other flowers and extends his hand for the few that I'm holding.

I inhale quickly when his fingers brush against mine, and for the briefest of seconds, Carlos freezes. Goosebumps flood my arm, and it feels as though there's heat coming straight from his touch that's strong enough to burn my skin. His eyes lower to gaze down at the fingers that are still ever so slightly on mine. My eyes follow his, and Carlos' fingers twitch for just a moment as if he's considering what to do next.

"Here, I'll take this from you." Carlos says quickly, gently tugging it from my hand. Just like that, the moment is gone. The feeling, however, isn't. My fingers still burn, and my breath still hasn't caught up.

Carlos climbs into the car next to me, and neither of us speak for a little bit. In fact, I'm beginning to wonder if even if I tried to speak, anything would come out, since I haven't spoken for so long.

When I start to notice the familiar landmarks that indicate we're about thirty minutes from Winterberry Hollow, I take in a few deep breaths before words start pouring from my mouth without consent.

"Carlos, I'm really, really sorry. I had a whole apology planned, but then this came up, and I've been scared to talk to you." I begin. If Carlos responds, the pounding of my heartbeat is too loud in my ears to hear. "I was so wrong to accuse you of those things, and I feel terrible about it."

Carlos blinks in surprise before nodding his head. "It's okay, Magnolia. You don't need to try and smooth things over so they're not awkward when Charlie and Poppy are here."

"No! That's not why I'm doing this!" I exclaim, frustrated that my apology is already coming across all wrong. Maybe I should have just waited until the chance to do my perfect apology. "It was wrong, and I need to own up to it. You didn't deserve that, and I was wrong for taking out my fears on you."

"What are you so scared of?" Carlos blurts out, as though this question has been plaguing him for too long. "Sorry, I shouldn't have asked that."

"I'm scared of falling for you too much and then being left behind. I'm scared that you're going to leave and forget that there's a girl in a tiny town who cares for you so much it hurts." I admit, my voice rising a few octaves. "You've made me step out of my comfort zone so many times this month, and I'm not going to ever be the same if you just leave."

Carlos just nods, but doesn't speak, since there's obviously more to what I have to say.

"Maybe it's just the protective part of my brain that's trying to stop me from falling for you, so that if you leave, I won't be as hurt. I don't know." I say, a few tears prickling in my eyes. "It's wrong, and talking about it right now is making me realize just how messed up it is, and I'm sorry for ever dragging you down this and hurting you in the process. You don't deserve that. I don't deserve you."

Carlos pulls the car into my driveway, and it takes a moment for him to turn to face me. His face is full of emotion, but I can't decipher any of it.

"Lia, you don't need to keep apologizing. We're just different people, and I was wrong to think that we would work out in such a short amount of time. It's my fault that we're in this position." Carlos says softly.

Carlos doesn't want me. Carlos has realized just how hard I am to love, and he's checking out before he falls in even deeper. I should have known this would be the outcome.

"Carlos, I'm sorry." I say again as more tears flow down my cheeks. My hands find the car door, and just as I'm rounding the front of the car in the darkness, my vision blurry from tears, I run right into something. Or, someone.

"Lia, stop." Carlos says as he wraps his arms around me. My arms find their way around him, and we're wrapped in an embrace so tight that if I weren't already crying, I would have trouble breathing.

"I'm sorry," I whisper into his chest.

"Stop being sorry," Carlos says into my hair. "This is more my fault than it is yours."

"You're not the one who always messes things up, Carlos." I say as another sob escapes me. If I were just a little bit more coherent, I would be horrified by how deranged I appear. "I'm sorry for hurting you."

"It's okay, Lia." Carlos whispers into my ear as he leans his head down to rest it on my shoulder. "We're just different people who didn't know everything."

"No-"

"You should go inside, Lia. I'll unload these into your garage." Carlos interrupts, pulling back from me. "I'll see you around."

More tears stream down my face, but I just nod and walk into my house. What am I even going to do now? I've royally messed everything up and hurt the one person who effortlessly pulled me out of my comfort zone and made me feel more this month than I have in my entire life.

When I enter my room, I walk to the window and curl up on the window seat. Carlos is dutifully unloading the flowers into the garage, and even though I can't see his face, I hope that he's not near as sad as me.

He doesn't deserve to be treated the way I treated him. He doesn't deserve to feel like nothing he ever does is enough.

Chapter Twenty-Three

"You did the best you could in this situation, and now you can just move on with life." Poppy says over the phone. It looks to be propped on the edge of her suitcase as she packs to leave tomorrow. There is nothing more Poppy than waiting two days before her wedding, and one day before she leaves, to pack.

"I know," I agree. "I just wish I hadn't been such an idiot. Why was I so careless with Carlos?"

"Sometimes you just don't know what you have until it's gone." Poppy says as she presses her lips together. "Look at Charlie and I. We broke up for a few weeks right after we started dating."

"Really?" I ask, turning to face the camera. "Why?"

"We just were so different. Charlie wasn't used to spur-of-the-moment, and I wasn't used to having everything so planned out." Poppy says with a shrug of her shoulders. "After a few weeks, Charlie called me and said that no matter how spur-of-the-moment life became, he would deal with it."

"And that's it?"

"Well, I was planning on calling him that day, too, because I decided that I didn't care if he planned our lives out down to the last second; it would be worth it." Poppy continues. "We've met in the middle now on a lot of things. It's not the exact middle all of the time, and sometimes we still have conflicts because of how different we are, but in the end, we know that we can't do life without each other."

"I should have come to that conclusion." I mutter as I pull the threads on my blanket. "I should've just never allowed myself to like him."

"Everything happens when it does for a reason. Either Carlos was a lesson, or you still have a chance together. You can't regret any of it, Mango. That's the worst possible thing to do." Poppy says firmly. "Regretting that you loved someone is the worst thing you can do. Be glad you at least had the chance to love him."

"I can't wait to see you." I say softly. "I miss you a lot, Poppy."

"I miss you, too. We're going to have an amazing time there, and you're going to be the best maid of honor ever." Poppy says as she folds a pair of pants and drops them into the suitcase.

"Hopefully I don't let you down."

"You could never let me down, Mango." Poppy says encouragingly. "You being there is enough, and I don't expect anything else from you."

"Yeah, but what if I don't do something right?" I push, wallowing deeper and deeper into my misery.

"What could you do wrong?" Poppy asks, throwing mismatched and unpaired socks into the suitcase.

"I don't know. What if I forget to fluff your train? Or don't take your bouquet at the right moment?" I ramble, trying to picture every terrible scenario.

"You won't forget, and even if you did, those wouldn't be the worst things. The worst thing you can do is look anxious in every photo." Poppy says with a quick laugh.

"You're right! What if I look terrible in all of the photos and draw attention away from your special day?" I question, Poppy's statement sending a new wave of panic over me.

"Mango, this isn't even your wedding. You can chill out just a little bit. Nothing will be so terrible that you ruin it." Poppy says reassuringly. "The only thing you can do that will ruin it is not be there. Take a deep breath. You're going to do great."

"Okay," I say, taking a few exaggerated breaths in and out to show Poppy that I'm willing to do whatever she needs. Even if it's taking a few deep breaths in and out."

"Perfect. You're ready to be the best maid of honor ever, now."

"You should totally come in and make a candle or two." Elisa says through the phone. "Maybe Carlos wants to, as well?"

"I don't think I'm really up for it. Carlos is...busy, too." I say, hesitating to talk about him.

"Oh my gosh, are you two together right now?" Elisa squeals. "If so, don't worry about it."

"No, we're not. We just had to do a bunch of stuff yesterday with the flowers." I say quickly, trying to shut down anything Elisa is thinking.

"Oh, okay. You should still come by, anyway. Maybe you'll have some fun." Elisa says, less enthusiastic now.

"I don't know," I sigh.

"Well, I *do* know. I'll be over at your house in about three minutes. Be ready." Elisa says in a singsong voice.

"Wait-" The line clicks off, and I'm left to scramble for a pair of socks and my jacket. If there's one thing that Elisa is, it's stubborn. She's not going to leave without me, and I might as well be ready. There's no sense in arguing with her.

Elisa's rapid knock on the door is almost exactly three minutes from when she said she'd be here, and I have to admire her promptness.

"Where is your jacket? We need to get moving because we need to make just about ten thousand candles." Elisa fires off as soon as the door is open.

"It's right here." I say, reaching out to pull it off the hook. "I'm ready."

"Perfect! Let's go," She says, already stepping off the porch and down the steps. "Jacob has been texting me for the last half hour about needing help, but I was a little bit late, since I had to help Mom prepare some of the pies for Christmas Eve dinner."

"That sounds fun," I comment as I slide into the passenger side of her car. "I bet they'll taste good, too."

"I hope they do." Elisa agrees with a nod. "At least I won't have to be there if they don't." She says with a giggle.

"What do you mean?" I ask, turning to face her.

"Tomorrow is the ball, so I won't be there when

everyone eats them." Elisa says, her voice somewhat confused. "You're going to the ball, right? It's not like you to forget about it."

The ball.

The ball that Carlos and I were supposed to go to together. The ball that I will now be attending alone, because I lashed out at Carlos.

"Oh, yeah, of course I am." I say quickly. "I just forgot about it right now, because I've been thinking about the wedding so much. Earlier today, the cake was delivered, and I've been busy with everything else, too."

"Right, I bet that's pretty busy." Elisa agrees empathetically as she pulls into The North Pole. "Jacob should already have most everyone else working on the candles, so we should just be able to get to work pretty quickly."

"Is there a certain number of them that we should be making?" I ask when we stride through the doors. I take in the meticulous task of making the candles, and I can only think one thing.

Carlos would love this.

How is my mind so focused on him? How come I can't do a simple activity and not think of Carlos?

"Magnolia?" Elisa's voice breaks through my train of thought, and she waves a hand in front of my face. "Earth to Magnolia."

"Oh, sorry." I say sheepishly. "I just got lost in thought. What did you say?"

"As long as you make two candles, we should be good." Elisa says, placing her hands on my shoulders to turn me towards the tables with people working intently on their candles. "Now get to work, love."

"Thanks," I say, pulling her into a quick hug before sitting down at the nearest table.

"Hey, Magnolia." Anastasiya says as I sit down across from her. Lennox is to her left, and while I shouldn't be, I'm surprised to see them together.

"Hey, Anastasiya, Lennox," I reply, glancing down at the instruction note taped to the table. "How are you doing?"

"We're good," Lennox says coolly as he pours the hot wax into the jar. "Busy with work, but good. What about you?"

"I've been..." Terrible. That's the first thought that jumps to mind, and I inwardly wince. "I've been okay."

"What's wrong?" Lennox asks.

"I didn't say anything is," I reply, beginning to align the wick in my jar.

"Yeah, but your face said it." Lennox says with a chuckle. I roll my eyes, but there's no effort in it.

"I'm just struggling right now, and I needed a distraction, which is why I'm here." I say, mixing the wax in the pot.

"Why?" Lennox asks, finally setting down his candle.

"Because I'm just struggling." I huff, not removing my eyes from the wax I'm beginning to pour.

"Because of Carlos?" Lennox guesses. At my pause, he nods as though he's already cracked the case. "I knew it."

"No, that's not-"

"These guys just came into town and screwed everything up." Lennox bites out.

"What are you talking about?" I ask sharply, jerking my head up now. "Carlos didn't screw anything up."

"Yeah, right." Lennox mutters.

"Why are you so against him and the twins?" I demand, feeling ultra defensive over Carlos, and somewhat of the twins. Maybe I don't know them very well, but it's not like they've ever done anything to prove themselves guilty of something.

"I have a thing against people coming in and messing everything up. Do you know what their being here has done to my sister and Julia?" Lennox asks, his tone sharp.

"No? What has them being here done?" I question, hesitant to believe anything he says. Sure, Lennox has never lied to me in the past, but Lennox is also super protective, and his judgment gets clouded sometimes.

"Maisie is completely out of her mind, and apparently Julia is, too. The twins aren't a good influence on either of them." Lennox says, as though this is common knowledge.

"What does Julia have to do with you?" I ask. For some reason, that's the only thing that caught my attention.

"Besides the fact that she's my friend, she's also being a terrible influence on my sister by hanging out as a group together with the twins." Lennox replies.

"Hey, she's not a terrible influence." I bite out, setting down my wax. Lennox's eyes soften for a moment as he realizes that I'm going to be protective of Julia, just as he is of Maisie.

"Sorry," Lennox finally says, pressing his lips together before he talks again. "Now there's whatever's wrong with you and Carlos, and it's just frustrating me all over again with the whole Maisie situation."

"Carlos hasn't done anything wrong." I say quickly. "This is my fault."

"What did you do?" Anastasiya asks. I turn, surprised by her voice. Throughout our conversation, she hasn't spoken a word.

"I was a jerk." I admit, not even trying to sugarcoat it. "Carlos didn't deserve that."

"You're not a jerk." Lennox says quickly.

"No, I was." I say before he can try and smooth over what I've said. Maybe it's because we've spent so much time together, but Lennox has always tried to be extra kind to me, even when I don't really deserve it. "I treated him really unfairly and misjudged him."

"I'm sorry," Lennox says gently. "Maybe he'll come back around."

"I wouldn't be surprised if he never does." I say, wallowing in my own misery as I begin on my second candle. "I said some really hurtful stuff."

"You never know," Lennox laments as he toys with the stuff to make another candle. "Carlos seems okay."

"Five seconds ago, you were ready to blame him for everything." I say with a small laugh. "Now he seems okay?"

"Hey, I was going to take your side on the issue, no matter what it was. Don't blame me for trying to be supportive." Lennox says with a chuckle. "Isn't that what friends are for?" I look up with a smile, happy to have my friend back.

"Yeah, something like that."

Chapter Twenty-Four

1 DAY 'TIL CHRISTMAS

"Do you have everything you're going to need for the ball tonight?" Mamma asks as I pour her a cup of coffee.

"Yep, I do." I say with a nod. "What are you two going to do this evening?"

"We're going to pick up Poppy and Charlie from the airport and drive them in, since most drivers will refuse to drive them out here in the dark. There's supposed to be quite the snowstorm tonight." Mamma answers as she sips her black coffee. I'm not much of a coffee person, but anytime I drink it, there must be more cream than coffee.

"You'll be safe, right?" I say, already worried about my whole family being out on the roads at night in the snow.

"Of course we will be, honey," Mamma says, opening her arms in a hug. "You have nothing to worry about besides looking beautiful and having an amazing time at the ball tonight."

"Just be safe in the snow," I say, sitting down at the table with my breakfast.

"We always are." Pappa says from behind me as he reaches out to ruffle my hair.

"Will any of your friends be over to get ready for the ball with you?" Mamma asks as she finishes her cup of coffee. "I feel terrible about leaving you here all alone, but it's not like we can leave your sister and Charlie without a mode of transportation."

"I don't know yet. Maybe." I reply, only now realizing just how alone I'm going to be tonight. I'll be putting on a false smile while everyone around me dances with their partners and hangs out with their friends. This month, I've been so busy with everything to do with Poppy's wedding, and the world around me kept spinning. My friends all hung out without me, no one included me in anything, and I have no idea what's going on in any of their relationships.

"Just remember to have fun." Pappa says as he reaches for his coat near the doorway. "If you're going to be out late, make sure you're prepared to be awake early."

"I will be." I agree with a nod. "Have a good day." With that, they're both out the door. This morning, they let me know that they were going to spend the day in May and that they'll be doing all of their last-minute Christmas gift shopping.

My bowl of yogurt and fruit suddenly feels unappealing, and the thought of taking another bite feels sickening. Will Carlos even come tonight? Will he just stay home? Has he forgotten about it altogether?

The ringing of my phone from the living room couch

catches my attention, and I abandon breakfast. Maisie's face illuminates the screen, and I press accept to the video chat.

"Hey, Magnolia, I know this is going to sound kind of crazy, but can I ask you for a favor?" Maisie asks over the phone.

"Yeah, of course. What's up?" I ask, already knowing that I'm going to agree.

"So, I'm not really sure what you've heard, but my brother and I are fighting. Same with Anastasiya." Maisie says sheepishly. "I really want to hang out with someone while I get ready for the ball, but I don't want to be at home or with Anastasiya. Elisa and Anastasiya have already made plans, and I'm not sure about Julia. Maybe she wants to be invited, too?"

"Yes, for sure." I agree with a nod. "I was just wallowing in the fact that I thought I would have to get ready by myself."

"Thank you so much." Maisie says earnestly. "When do you want me to come over?"

"As soon as possible would be good." I start. "After we hang up, I'll call Julia and invite her over. We can spend the day together."

"That sounds so perfect." Maisie says excitedly. "I'll be over in about fifteen minutes."

"I'll see you then."

"Guys, let me in! I can't knock, and it's *so* cold out here."

Maisie calls through the door. Julia and I turn to each other before racing to the door.

"What..." I start. Maisie's hands are holding a drink carrier and a large bakery bag.

"What's a get-ready-together party without hot chocolate and sweets?" Maisie asks as she pushes past us into the living room. Julia and I giggle, but follow her in nonetheless. "Just give me a minute to grab my dress and makeup, because the liquids will freeze out there."

"Okay, let's talk about our dates for tonight," Julia says as we curl up on the couch, our hot cocoa in hand, a few minutes later. "You're going with Romero, right?"

"Yeah, I am." Maisie agrees with an excited nod. "You're going with Leo?"

"Yep." Julia clarifies. "Did things between you and Carlos get worked out?"

"Um, kind of?" I don't want to go into all of this right now, but Maisie and Julia both appear curious.

"Kind of?" Julia presses, her eyes searching mine.

"Can we not talk about this right now?" I plead. "Maybe we can talk about Romero and Leo or something?"

"Definitely." Maisie chimes in.

There's silence for a few minutes before Maisie starts talking again. "So, I'm not sure how much you all know, but my best friend is dating my brother, and she completely went behind my back about it, and my brother is mad that I'm mad at her, but also is mad that I didn't tell him that I'm dating Romero." She says brightly, as though this is all a normal topic. "Did I mention he's also mad at me, because I'm mad at him, and that he hates Romero?"

Julia and I turn to each other and back to Maisie, neither of us quite sure what to say.

"That's a lot." I comment. "I saw Anastasiya and Lennox yesterday, and they're definitely together."

"She told me as much." Maisie says cheerily. "*After* I saw them kissing, though."

"Wow." Julia says as she covers her mouth.

"Just laugh already," Maisie says with a giggle. "I can admit that while it's bad, it's also just funny at this point."

"I feel like every big thing that could possibly happen has happened this month." I lament as Julia giggles with Maisie.

"I guess so." Julia agrees. "I think there's been a lot of change, and we all kind of went our own ways."

"Maybe there's been some Christmas magic, too." Maisie says with a twinkle in her eyes. "Think about it. In one way or another, everyone has fallen in love, and while there's some...discourse between us right now, we're all happy."

"Ouch," I say lightly.

"Sorry, sorry." Maisie says apologetically. "I forgot."

"Okay, we're moving past all conversation and watching a movie." Julia says abruptly as she stands and walks towards the movie player. "We'll start getting ready at two, but until then, we're relaxing without talking."

"Magnolia, your dress is so beautiful!" Maisie exclaims as I step out of the bedroom.

"Maisie is right. This looks *so* good on you," Julia says, her eyes taking in my body.

"Thank you," I reply to both of them. "Hurry up and change into your dresses! We need to leave in thirty minutes." Julia takes the bathroom, and Maisie takes the spare bedroom as they change. We've already done hair and makeup, and once they have their dresses on, we'll be ready. Julia coordinated with Leo, and he agreed to drive her, Maisie, Romero, and I to the ball.

When they both emerge, my jaw falls slack. Julia took her hair out of the bun it was in, and for once, it's falling dark and shiny down her back. It looks amazing with her light green dress. Maisie's red dress is stunning on her, and with her light red hair in loose curls, she's adorable.

"You are so beautiful. Both of you!" I exclaim. "Your dresses fit you both perfectly." They both reply and start chattering about their dresses, and I feel my smile start to crack at the edges.

Why can't I be this excited about the ball? Sure, maybe I really screwed things up with Carlos, but shouldn't I be able to move past that for one day?

"Romero just texted me and said that they're going to be here in two minutes." Maisie says with a squeal as she bounces on her feet.

A knock on the door a few minutes later alerts us to the twins' arrival, and I step back as Julia opens the door and invites them in. Both of the twins smile widely as their eyes land on their dates, and a small smile finds my lips as I take in the excitement around me. Maisie is excitedly chattering to Romero while holding his arm, and Leo is whispering something in Julia's ear. They're all adorable together.

"Magnolia, are you ready to go?" Julia asks, turning to me. Her smile is soft as she takes my hand in hers.

"Yep," I agree with a nod. No matter how I feel tonight, I'm going to make the best out of it and show up one hundred percent for Julia and Maisie. There's no reason to drag down the mood just because my date didn't work out.

Once we're in the truck, with Leo and Julia up front, Maisie in the middle of the back seat, and Romero and I on either of her sides, do we leave. Julia reaches for the radio and switches it to the Christmas channel. Pretty soon, we're all singing the familiar tunes, and my smile and laughter are real.

Maisie reaches over and wraps her hand around mine and squeezes it lightly. "Thank you for letting me come over. This would've never been nearly as fun at my house."

"Hey, you cheered me up, too." I reply, squeezing her hand back. "I'm glad you came over."

"I'm glad, too." Maisie says brightly. Romero is glancing over at us with a questioning look, but he doesn't say anything. Suddenly, the fight between him and Lennox a few weeks ago makes more sense. It was over the fact that Lennox doesn't want him with Maisie.

Of course.

I'm not sure why Leo and Jacob were a part of it, but that part suddenly falls into place. When Maisie ran between them, she was telling him to drop his issue with Romero. Not with Maisie.

Leo pulls into the venue where the ball is being held, and I gasp at the decorations on the outside. The building is already gorgeous, but the Christmas trees, lights, and decorations are stunning. Just as we step out of the truck, small tufts of snow start falling from the sky, and Julia squeals.

"It's snowing!" Julia exclaims as she twirls. "How magical is this?" Leo laughs and reaches out to catch her hand and pull her closer.

"It's pretty magical," He says softly as she moves closer to him.

"Let's get going!" Maisie says excitedly as she tugs Romero's hand towards the main entrance. There are men positioned on each side of the doors, dressed in nutcracker costumes, and they open the large doors for Maisie and Romero, then close them before turning to Julia and Leo, and opening them again, so everyone gets their entrance moment.

"Lia! Wait!"

Carlos is here.

I whirl, and Carlos is running towards me through the falling snow. His black tuxedo stands out in the white, and he's as devastatingly handsome as ever. My heart swells, and when he stops in front of me, his breath coming out in white clouds, his dark hair littered with snowflakes, I almost lose my balance.

Carlos is here.

"Carlos?" I breathe out, as though there's another person who could make my heart and body react this way. As though there's another person I feel weak from looking at. As though there's another set of dark eyes I've found myself in.

"Lia, I'm so sorry." Carlos begins, reaching out to wrap my hands in his. "I was a terrible person for not talking to you yesterday, and I was a terrible person for taking it personally when you said those things. I told you that I knew you, and then when you did your most natural reaction when scared, I was upset by it. That was wrong."

"Carlos, it's not your fault," I say softly, squeezing his hands lightly. "I attacked you and made it seem as though it would be easy for me to forget about you. *That* is what was wrong. I told you that I wished I had never felt anything for you, and that I never wanted to feel for you again."

"No, Lia, I'm in the wrong. I'm really, really sorry. I thought I could respect your wishes and stop making you feel anything for me, but today I realized that no matter how much I wanted to respect that, I couldn't stop feeling for you. I've felt for you since the moment we fell on the ice, and nothing is ever going to change how I feel about you." Carlos says breathlessly. "If you'll give me a chance to prove to you that I mean that, I promise to never make you feel as though your only option is to leave before it gets hard."

"Carlos, this really wasn't your fault. I should be asking you for another chance. You tried so hard to prove to me that I would be happy, but I decided to push past that and only see the negative. I refused to admit that anything you did for me was you putting yourself out there." I insist. "It's like you said the other night. We're two different people, and we just didn't see eye to eye hardly at all, and I used that to drive a wedge between us."

Carlos begins to open his mouth to protest, but I reach up and press my finger to his lips. Carlos grins at this and doesn't speak again.

"Will you give me another chance, Carlos?" I whisper. More snow is falling now, and under any other circumstances, I would be cold. Instead, I can't even feel the cold flakes landing on my bare arms.

"Yes." Carlos says earnestly. "As many chances as you need."

"Thank you, Carlos." I say softly. I stand on my tiptoes and lift my lips to his. "I love you, Carlos."

"I love you, Lia." Carlos whispers back as he wraps his hand around the back of my neck and pulls me closer.

Our lips brush against each other, and I feel as though my feet aren't even on the ground. The world around me fades into the distance as I reach up and tangle my fingers through Carlos' hair, drawing him closer. My breath is coming in and out in unsteady rasps, and Carlos' is doing the same.

"Go Magnolia!" A voice a few feet away calls out, and Carlos pulls away to turn towards the people walking in. Elisa is the one who called out, but Jacob is with her. My cheeks heat into a deep flush, but she just claps before continuing to walk towards the doors.

"Oh my gosh," I mutter embarrassedly into Carlos' chest. "I can't believe her."

"It was actually kind of funny." Carlos says with a chuckle as he wraps his arms around my shoulders. "Well, as funny as being cheered on while kissing can be."

"Stop!" I barely make out through giggles. "You can't side with her over me."

"I can't believe her." Carlos echoes into my hair. "How dare she?"

"Right? How dare she?" I giggle, pulling away from his chest. "Let's go inside before we get frostbite."

"Frostbite doesn't sound too bad with you," Carlos comments as he wraps his hand around mine.

"Good evening." One of the nutcrackers says as we step up to the doors. "May I have your names?"

"Carlos Santos and Magnolia Larsen." Carlos says with a smile.

"Thank you," He says as he and the other nutcracker pull open the large wooden doors. The wreaths rustle and the bells jingle as they open widely. "Have a nice evening."

"Thank you, sir." Carlos replies, giving the man a nod before turning to me and smiling. As we walk down the hallway lit by candles, Carlos leans down to whisper in my ear. "This is really cool."

"I know," I whisper back. "It's so whimsical."

Just as we step into the light at the end of the hallway do I realize that we're on a large balcony that overlooks the ballroom, with staircases on either side. A man catches my attention to the left of Carlos, but before I have time to ponder what he's doing, he taps the tiny hands-free microphone near his mouth.

"Carlos Santos and Magnolia Larsen." I squeeze Carlos' hand in excitement as the man taps off the mic. "Please use the staircase to the left, and be careful. With the fresh snow, shoes are still a little bit wet, and we don't want a spill."

"Thank you," I say, turning to him before Carlos leads me to the stairs.

The decorated garland is wrapped around the marbled staircase, and the tiny bells hanging from it catch my attention.

As soon as we begin walking down the stairs, my eyes are laser-focused ahead of me, and quick flashes of light alert me to the fact that we're being photographed. I'm sure we were when we were being announced, but now that the cameras are closer, I feel a slight tremble of nerves.

"You look amazing, Lia." Carlos says softly through his smile. I turn my face to his, surprised by his voice. I smile at this, and it feels as though I could go all night just looking at him instead of anything around us. I could spend the rest of my life without looking at anyone or anything else, as long as I have Carlos.

"You made it!" Julia squeals as she rushes up to us once we've stepped away from the stairs. "I knew Carlos would come."

"Thanks for the confidence," Carlos replies with an easy chuckle. Everyone is standing in a group together, and I'm surprised to see Lennox's arm around Maisie's shoulder, as though they were just hugging. Did they get everything resolved?

"Ladies and gentlemen, please file to the end of the room, where you will be ushered to your seats for dinner." The man says from the balcony as his microphone sounds over the speaker.

Elisa looks back at me with a smile as she takes hold of Jacob's hand and leads the rest of us to the end of the room as the ushers begin guiding us to the tables at the edges of the room. Carlos and I are the last in our group to be seated, and I'm between Leo and Carlos.

Carlos glances over with a smile that's both amused and curious, and I can't help but mirror it. Every year, the ball is completely different. Down from the theme, to where it's held. It's almost as though this is my first time here, too.

"Julia wants you to know that she wants us four to do

the Photo Booth together later." Leo says, leaning down to my ear to be heard over the chatter and clinking of silverware as the appetizers are delivered.

"Okay, tell her to remind me when we're done with dinner." I agree, leaning over to meet Julia's eyes as I talk to Leo.

Turning to Carlos, I tap his arm so he lowers his head. "We're going to do the Photo Booth with Leo and Julia tonight. I'm sure we'll do it with most everyone else, but I just wanted to let you know." I say into his ear. As I speak, my hand snakes up to wrap around the hair at the base of his neck, and I feel the goosebumps under my fingers on his skin. Carlos nods in agreement, and when I pull away from him, I can almost see a pink flush under his dark skin, as though I've flustered him. At this thought, I feel heat rushing up my neck and to my cheeks.

Dinner passes by rather quickly, and after dessert has been served, we all make our way to the dance floor when a slow song starts playing. Everyone around us begins to slowly sway with their dance partners, and Carlos reaches down to pull my hand to his shoulder.

"Keep your hand resting here," Carlos says softly, his voice deep. "Mine goes here." He says, dropping his hand to my hip, which I can just barely feel through the fabric of my dress. Carlos' fingers wrap around mine, and he steps impossibly closer to me.

"Am I doing this right?" I whisper as I begin moving with Carlos. He's an amazing leader, but I've never danced as professionally as this before.

"You're doing amazing." Carlos answers with a smile.

"Step back, and then come back to me two beats later." He says gently as I miss the step for the third time in a row.

"I can't keep track of the beats," I admit sheepishly. Then, without saying anything, Carlos begins lightly tapping my hip with his index finger, tracking the beats for me.

"Try it now, Lia." Carlos says softly. This time, I'm back in his arms at the right moment, and when I glance up to meet his eyes, they seem even darker than usual.

"Thank you, Carlos." I say, leaning into his touch even more.

A few more songs go by, and now a few people are milling about near the edges of the room. Julia lifts her arm to catch my attention, and I notice that she and Leo are next in line for the Photo Booth.

"It looks like it's photo time," Carlos comments with a chuckle as he begins leading me to the Photo Booth.

"We're going to need to squeeze in." Julia says excitedly as she follows Leo into the booth. Julia and I squish between Carlos and Leo, and we meet each other's eyes with a smile before turning to the screen in front of us.

Three, two, one.

We all smile widely, and the flash of light snaps the photo.

Three, two, one.

Carlos reaches out and turns my face to his, and the flash of light photographs me looking through my lashes up at Carlos' eyes.

Three, two, one.

I lift my hand to Carlos' cheek and tilt my head slightly

as a shy smile finds its way onto my cheeks just as the flash alerts me to another photo.

Three, two, one.

I tug Carlos closer, and our lips press together just as the last flash of light goes off.

"Oh my gosh, this has to be the best Photo Booth collage to exist." Julia exclaims as she picks up the four photo collages. She passes them out to us, and while it's hard to tear my eyes from Carlos and I, Julia is right. She and Leo matched the vibe, and their poses were pretty similar to ours. Just before we can walk away, Romero calls out to Leo from the line.

"Hey, you two need to be in ours." He says to Leo and Julia. Maisie's hand is wrapped around his, and as the couple in front of them exits the booth, Romero reaches out to grab Leo's shoulder, who, in turn, tugs Julia's hand.

"I guess it's time for the twin session." Julia calls out with a giggle as she disappears into the booth.

Over the course of the next two hours, Carlos and I have been in the booth with all of the couples in our group, I've been in some with just the girls, and even Carlos gets pulled into the booth with some of the boys. By the end of the night, we've all laughed and danced enough for a year, but I'm not even tired.

"Hey, Lia, we should probably be getting home." Carlos whispers into my ear as Maisie and Julia tug the twins onto the dance floor.

"Why?" I ask, turning to him. Carlos' arms are wrapped around my middle, and with the way I'm twisted to face his lowered head, the overwhelming urge to kiss him right here and now is irresistible.

"It's already midnight, and we'll need to be up in a few hours for the wedding," Carlos replies. His mouth is so close to mine that when he speaks, I can almost feel his breath.

"Oh my gosh, you're right." I say, blinking rapidly. "How did I even forget that?"

"We've just been having fun," Carlos answers with a shrug. At his casual reply, I feel my shoulders sag in relief a little bit. Everything is still under control, and even though I lost track of time, nothing bad came of it. Nothing bad came of my loosening up and having fun.

"Yeah," I agree, pressing my head into his shoulder. "Let's get going, then." After saying our goodbyes to everyone, we walk out to the car.

"Were you still going to come to the ball?" I ask once Carlos has pulled onto the road.

"What do you mean?" Carlos asks, confusion in his voice.

"You came here without me, not knowing if I was here." I reply, suddenly starting to feel self-conscious.

"I knew you were here." Carlos admits sheepishly. "I went to your house at seven like we agreed a few weeks ago, but when you weren't there, I texted Romero, and he said that you were in the car with him and the rest of them."

"Really?" My heart swells at this, and I feel a giddy smile rise on my face.

"I decided this morning that spending a whole day without talking to you was agony, and living a life without you would be torture. My plan had been to show up like a knight in shining armor, but that plan was foiled."

"Hey, it worked out for the best, and you showing up walking through the snow was way more romantic than you at my door." I respond, reaching over to take Carlos' hand in mine.

"I'm glad it worked out." Carlos says decidedly. "This will be my favorite Christmas for the rest of my life, Lia."

Tears begin to form in my eyes, but for once, they're tears of joy, and not pain. "Me too."

Carlos kisses me as he opens the passenger door when we arrive at my house, and even though I could go on kissing him forever, we also have company.

"Let's go inside." I whisper against his lips.

"Magnolia! Carlos!" Poppy squeals as we walk through the door. She wraps me in the largest big sister hug ever before turning and giving Carlos the same. Charlie gives me a hug and turns to Carlos to clap him on the back.

"Well, aren't you two quite the couple." Poppy says as she steps back from us. "I feel severely underdressed in comparison."

While Poppy's baggy shirt and leggings are quite the stark contrast to my ball gown and Carlos' suit, I just shake my head. "You look fine."

"Mamma and Pappa have already gone to bed, but why don't you go get changed and then we can hang out together in the living room?" Poppy says a moment later. "Charlie, you have something Carlos can change into, right?"

I leave for my bedroom and change into a large sweater, leggings, and fuzzy socks. I'm walking into the living room just as Carlos is emerging from the downstairs spare bedroom in a large shirt and sweatpants, and a giggle escapes me as I take in our new outfits.

"We look different now," I tease through laughter as we flop down on the couch across from Poppy and Charlie. His arm is wrapped around her shoulder and is finger-combing her hair while she talks. I can't hear exactly what she's saying, but Charlie is nodding along, completely immersed in whatever she's telling him.

"They're kind of cute," I whisper to Carlos as I lean into him on the couch.

"I don't think I've ever called my brother *cute* before, but yeah, they are." Carlos agrees as he wraps his arm around my shoulder.

"So, tell us all about the ball," Poppy says a minute later when she realizes that we're sitting across from her. "Leave no details out."

Carlos and I launch into an explanation of the whole night, and both Charlie and Poppy nod along as they listen.

"So you two are officially back together, and I'm not going to have to worry about any arguments tomorrow?" Poppy teases as we finish the story. My cheeks heat in a blush, and just as Carlos is responding, Charlie points out the flush on my face.

"I think the blush on Magnolia's face says it all." He says with a chuckle.

"Hey!" I yelp, hurrying my face into Carlos' chest.

"You and Poppy are really similar," Charlie comments a moment later as he begins to work small braids into Poppy's hair.

"Us?" Poppy asks, motioning between her and I. "We're more different than night and day."

"Your mannerisms are the same." Carlos agrees. "I noticed that earlier, but I really see it now that Charlie has pointed it out."

"We're completely different." I protest with a shake of my head.

"Yeah, you two are totally wrong." Poppy agrees as she pushes away from Charlie's chest. "There have never been two sisters as polar opposites as us before."

"Is this a hill you're willing to die on?" Charlie teases.

"Absolutely." We say at the exact same time.

Chapter Twenty-Five

CHRISTMAS DAY

"Just put that last pin here," Poppy instructs as I pin her hair into the bun she's been directing me on. "Perfect."

"You look so beautiful." I breathe as I step back. Her dress fits her perfectly, and even though I was skeptical, it proved me wrong.

"Thank you, Mango." Poppy says, turning to pull me into a hug. "I couldn't have done any of this without you."

"I'm sure you would've figured it out." I protest. "Everything went right to plan."

"You and Carlos really pulled through, and I can't thank you enough for that." Poppy insists as she steps back. "Which, speaking of, you need to smile the whole time you walk down the aisle together, because I've instructed the photographer to take a billion photos of you together. Who knows, we might need them for the future."

"Are you ready?" Carlos asks softly. My hand is nestled in the crook of his elbow, and our cue to walk down the aisle is nearing.

"Yes."

Our cue plays, and we begin walking down the aisle. True to Poppy's word, the photographer snaps what feels like a million photos, but I push the thought to the back of my mind.

"Lia," Carlos says softly about halfway down the aisle. He stops completely and turns to me, and instead of panicking and urging him to keep walking, I turn and look up at him with a smile.

"Yes?"

"You're beautiful." Carlos whispers before we begin walking again.

A stupid smile is plastered on my face, and I don't even care to ask why he stopped, because we split at the end of the aisle and within what feels like seconds, Charlie and Poppy are in front of the pastor, and he's pronouncing them husband and wife.

Poppy squeals as Charlie pulls her towards him and dips her. He's even bigger than Carlos, so his body almost fully covers hers. When she straightens, she giggles before turning to give me a smile. It's wide and so *Poppy*. She turns back and wraps her hands on either side of Charlie's face before pulling him in for another kiss.

After about thirty minutes, Poppy, Carlos, Charlie, and

I are getting ready to leave back to the house, since we're going to be there for a little bit before the reception, which will be dinner. Mamma and Pappa are going to hang behind and mingle with their friends before coming back with us.

"Magnolia! Carlos! You're riding with us!" Poppy exclaims as she rushes over to me, Charlie in tow. "Come on!" She tugs my hand, and in turn, Carlos is tugged at the end of my hand, and we're like a line of children as we run through the snow and into the car. Charlie slides behind the wheel, laughing as he starts the car.

Beside me, Carlos shakes snow from his hair as he buckles his seat belt, and I laugh, leaning into him.

"You're married!" I exclaim a few seconds later. I don't think it's fully sunk in yet that she's married, and it sounds crazy to say.

"I know! I can't believe it!" Poppy replies, her eyes sparkling with excitement. "Charlie? Can you believe it?"

"I can definitely believe it." Charlie teases. "I didn't wait months of being engaged to the most wonderful woman in the world to not believe that we're married."

"Fine, you're right about that." Poppy agrees with a nod. "It felt like the wedding was never going to come, and then *poof*. Here we are! Married!"

Charlie pulls into the driveway, and we all hurry inside to escape the freezing temperatures. Poppy and I rush to my room to change into dinner dresses, and when we remerge, Carlos and Charlie are wearing nice slacks and matching sweaters.

"Look at you, all handsome." Poppy says with a giggle as she wraps her arms around Charlie's middle and presses her head into his chest. Charlie welcomes her embrace, and

Carlos reaches out for my hand before pulling me into the living room.

"I saw something last night right before we left, and I wanted to ask you about it." Carlos says as we walk to the large Christmas tree in the corner.

"What is it?" I ask, following in step beside him.

"This," Carlos says, reaching up to brush his fingers against the ornament that doesn't quite fit the matching ones already hanging.

"Oh," I say sheepishly. "Do you like it?"

"I didn't think you'd hang it," Carlos says, as though seeing it is a real shock.

"You made an ornament, gave it to me, and didn't expect me to hang it?" I blurt out. "Do you hear how ridiculous that is?"

"What's ridiculous?" Charlie asks as he and Poppy appear behind us.

"Carlos made me an ornament and didn't expect me to put it on the tree," I say, as though we should all be ridiculing Carlos.

"You made her an ornament? That's *so* sweet." Poppy exclaims. "Mango, you can never break his heart again."

"Hey-" I begin, cringing inside.

"It's fine." Carlos says lightly. "We needed to come to our senses sooner or later, so it was for the best. I'd like to say that my apology was quite the gesture, though, and it was almost worth it."

"You never gave me an apology candy cane, though." I tease. "I would've thought you'd know me well enough for that."

Carlos' eyes dart to Charlie for a split second, and then Charlie starts speaking. "He gave you apology candy canes?"

"Yeah, all of the time." I say with a nod and a smile. "He figured out early on that they're my favorite candy, so whenever we were driving somewhere or arguing, he would open a candy cane and pass it to me."

"Is she being for real?" Charlie asks, turning to Carlos in surprise.

"Yeah, she is." Carlos admits sheepishly.

"Does she know?" Charlie asks curiously.

"Does she know what?" Poppy and I ask at the same time. I glance between Carlos and Charlie in suspicion.

"Carlos is allergic to peppermint." Charlie says bluntly. "If he gets it on his skin, he breaks out, and if he comes in contact with it orally, his throat will close up."

"*What?*" I practically scream.

"It's not a big deal." Carlos says bashfully. "I was careful with my contact with it."

"You put your life in danger to give me a piece of candy?" I exclaim, feeling more and more horrified. "You could've died."

"Yeah, you really could've." Charlie agrees.

"I had my EpiPen with me at all times," Carlos says with a bashful roll of his eyes. "And like I said, I was careful to never touch it or do anything that would put me in danger."

"You were around me all of the time, though." I say, still feeling shocked.

"And I never kissed you after you had any." Carlos says unashamedly. "I was careful."

"So that's why you wanted me to drink water that one time!" I blurt out, realizing just how hard this must've been for him. "All of those times you were dealing with peppermints for me, you were being careful because you didn't want to die. Not because you're some sanitary freak."

"Yeah, you're right." Carlos agrees with a nod. "I just didn't want to ruin your love for candy canes, because it was so apparent you liked them, and you're the type of person to give something like that up in a heartbeat."

"You're right." I agree. I can feel Poppy and Charlie's eyes on us while we talk, but I can't bring myself to care. "I'm never having a candy cane again."

"No, you can't do that." Carlos says with a shake of his head. "You love them."

"And I love you more." I say confidently. "What would I have done if I accidentally killed you with a candy cane?"

"It would've been impossible." Carlos says with a shrug. "Things could've gotten hairy, but it wouldn't have come to that."

"You don't know that." I refute.

"Lia, it's going to be okay. You don't need to give up candy canes for me." Carlos says before turning to Charlie. "Really, man?"

"Hey, don't look at me. I was just worried about my little brother." Charlie says as he raises his hands in a back-off gesture.

"Well, let's discuss candy canes later." Poppy interjects. "Because I have a question."

"What is it?" I ask, turning to her.

"Why does Carlos have your car?" She blurts out, as though she's been dying to ask for hours.

"Oh, I told him he can use it until he leaves, since the

person who was supposed to get a rental car wasn't here." I say with a pointed look at Charlie.

"So he was just your personal chauffeur?" Poppy asks with a giggle.

"Well, I couldn't drive it through the snow, and-"

"I valued my life." Carlos deadpans. I turn to him with my mouth agape before trying to stifle my giggle.

"Ah, there it is. I knew it had to do with how terrible a driver my sister is." Poppy says with a grin.

"Well, that's not exactly true," I begin, trying to think up a reasonable defense that isn't me hitting a curb every time I drive.

"Oh, it's absolutely true." Poppy teases. "Did Mango ever tell you about the time she was so excited to show me her driving abilities and she hit the mailbox backing out of the driveway?"

"Poppy!" I gasp indignantly. "That was supposed to stay between us!"

"Do you think it magically fixed itself before we got home?" Poppy teases. "Pappa saw it happen."

"Ugh," I say, burying my face in my hands. "Why don't we talk about the time you snuck out and I had to unlock the door when I was seven?"

"Let's not, actually." Poppy says with a giggle.

"I want to hear this story," Charlie says with a chuckle. "Do you have anything to add?"

"I'll just say that my friends and I were having fun at a bonfire, and I might have lost track of time," Poppy says slowly. "And the spare key."

"You lost your house key?" Carlos asks in surprise.

"Well, when you're out for a few hours, it's bound to slip

out of your pocket at some point." Poppy says as though this is a normal occurrence. "Right?"

"I've never lost my house keys before." Charlie teases.

"Well then, you're just going to be responsible for our keys for the rest of our lives," Poppy says with a smile.

"Let's go back to you needing Magnolia's help getting back in." Carlos asks, wrapping his arm around my waist. "You're on the upper floor, right?"

"Not this part." Poppy groans exaggeratedly.

"She stood on her car and threw rocks at my window until I woke up." I explain.

"Enough, enough," Poppy says through giggles. "Seventeen-year-old Poppy was a different person."

We begin talking about other things, and soon enough, catering and guests start arriving. Just as Carlos and I are about to sit down for dinner, Poppy rushes over to us.

"I know this is a big ask, but could you two run to the grocery store for more punch?" Poppy asks. "I know that the market is still open."

"Yeah, we can." Carlos agrees with a nod before turning to me. "Ready for one last wedding adventure?"

"I can't believe this is our last wedding adventure." I say quietly as we near my house. The punch is securely placed in the trunk, and we're almost back to the party.

"I know," Carlos agrees. "But we'll have a lot of other adventures in life, though."

"Like what?" I ask, turning in my seat to face him.

"Whatever we want to do," Carlos answers with a shrug. "We can make our own adventures."

"So you think we're going to have more adventures together?" I ask as he pulls into the driveway and stops the car.

"I know we will."

Carlos exits the car and walks around to open the door for me, and through all of the darkness and flurrying snow, I can't see anything but him. He takes my hand, and as we begin walking to the door, I stop in my tracks and turn to Carlos.

"What's wrong?" Carlos asks, turning to me.

"I love you, Carlos Santos." I say softly, reaching up to brush my fingers along his cheek. Carlos' smile is immediate, and even though his skin is cool from the freezing temperatures, my fingers feel as though they're on fire as they intertwine with his hair.

"I love you, Magnolia Larsen." Carlos says, lowering his lips dangerously close to mine.

"My name is *Lia*." I say just before my lips brush against his. "To you, it's Lia."

"I love you, Lia."

$\mathcal{S}$*even years later*

CHRISTMAS EVE

"Can you believe that seven years ago we were at the Christmas ball?" I ask Carlos as we stride through the town square to the giant Christmas tree.

"I was quite the knight in shining armor, wasn't I?" Carlos teases as he squeezes my hand.

"You definitely were." I agree with a nod. The illuminated tree shines brightly enough for us to walk without any other source of light, and when we stop in front of it and glance up at the tree that seems to go miles into the air, there's nothing but silence around us.

"There's a different title that I want, though." Carlos says softly, and my body shifts to face him.

"Really? What is it?" I ask, smiling curiously.

Carlos drops to one knee, and I gasp, covering my mouth with my hand.

"Lia, from the day I met you, I was drawn to you. Spending a month with only you solidified my feelings, and these last seven years, even as we've graduated high school, college, and been pulled in so many different directions, have proven that no matter what we're doing or where we are, we will make it work." Carlos says, his voice the epitome of calm. "After all of that, we're never going to be apart again, because I'm moving and starting my law firm here. None of this would've been possible without you, and I never want to spend another day thousands of miles apart."

I'm already nodding, but Carlos continues to speak. "Will you do me the greatest honor and marry me? I promise to always support and honor you, and never take a single day for granted."

"Yes, Carlos, I will marry you."

Stay Connected!

Hey!! You made it this far!
Thank you so much for reading Carlos and Magnolia's
story! If you loved it, I would love to see your review on
social media or any book retailers!

If you'd like to keep up with me and stay in the loop, I'm on
social media *and* I have a newsletter! Feel free to check all of
those out! I'm always happy to have you.

Acknowledgments

Wow, where do I even start? This is my fifth book, and it doesn't even seem real that I'm here again. I like to say that the acknowledgments take longer to write than the actual book, because there's always so much I want to say, but surprisingly, I can never find the words for them.

I guess we can start with THANK YOU for reading Kisses and Candy Canes. Without readers like you, authors like me wouldn't be here. I'm eternally grateful for you!

Thank you so much to my family. I'm sure everyone has seen them pop up in the acknowledgments and dedications of my books a few times now, but it's because this book wouldn't be in your hands without them.
From the endless talks where I discuss plots, covers, blurbs, and everything else, none of this would be possible without the constant encouragement and excitement.

Thank you, Heavenly Father, for this gift you've instilled within me, and thank you for your son, who is the reason for the season.

About the Author

Jenevieve Hernandez is the author of sweet and swoony romances, filled to the brim with the feeling of falling in love. She loves portraying character growth, unique plots, and, of course, romance in her books. Her books will never contain any explicit content, and are always guaranteed happily ever afters.

She enjoys spending her time in the pages of books, traveling from one story to the next, or outdoors, exploring the world around her.

www.ingramcontent.com/pod-product-compliance
Lightning Source LLC
Chambersburg PA
CBHW061233310726
48971CB00007B/2045